EXTINCTION RED LINE

THE OFFICIAL PREQUEL TO
THE EXTINCTION CYCLE SERIES

NICHOLAS SANSBURY SMITH
TOM ABRAHAMS

GREAT WAVE INK
PUBLISHING

Extinction Red Line

GREAT WAVE INK
PUBLISHING

Cover Art by Hristo Kovatliev
Proofreading by Pauline Nolet
Interior design by Stef McDaid at Write Into Print

GREAT WAVE INK
PUBLISHING

For Courtney, Samantha, and Luke
My personal Team Ghost

—Tom

For the Extinction Cycle readers, the best fans in the world!
Team Ghost is proud to have you on board for future
Extinction Cycle stories.

—Nicholas

Whoever fights monsters should see to it that
in the process he does not become a monster.
—Friedrich Nietzsche

Foreword
by
Nicholas Sansbury Smith

Thank you for picking up a copy of *Extinction Red Line*, the official prequel to the Extinction Cycle. This is the origin story of Lieutenant Trevor Brett, the tortured Marine that was first given a dose of the early version of VX-99. It's a story that I always wanted to tell, but never had the opportunity. Until now.

Working with author Tom Abrahams, best known for his bestselling Traveler series, we set out to tell the backstory of Lieutenant Brett and the Red Line of carnage he left behind during and after the Vietnam War. This origin story plays a vital role in the VX-99 program designed to create supersoldiers, a program that also sparked the Extinction Cycle.

Please note, *Red Line* was previously published in Amazon's Extinction Cycle Kindle World. As you may know, Amazon ended the Kindle Worlds program in July of 2018. Authors were given a chance to republish or retire their stories, and I jumped at the chance to work with Tom. Writing as a team, we added new chapters, expanded the story line, and brought Lieutenant Brett's story to life in a way never before published. We're very excited to bring *Red Line* to paperback, audio, and to readers outside the United States for the first time.

For those of you that are new to the Extinction Cycle story line, the series is the award-winning, Amazon top-rated, and half-a-million-copy best-selling seven-book saga. There are over six *thousand* five-star reviews on Amazon alone. Critics have called it "*World War Z* and *The Walking Dead* meets *The Hot Zone*." *Publishers Weekly* added, "Smith has realized that the way to rekindle interest in zombie apocalypse fiction is to make it louder, longer, and bloodier... Smith intensifies the disaster efficiently as the pages flip by, and readers who enjoy juicy blood-and-guts action will find a lot of it here."

In creating the Extinction Cycle, my goal was to use authentic military action and real science to take the zombie and post-apocalyptic genres in an exciting new direction. Forget everything you know about zombies. In the Extinction Cycle, they aren't created by black magic or other supernatural means. The ones found in the Extinction Cycle are created by a military bioweapon called VX-99, first used in Vietnam on Lieutenant Brett and his men. The chemicals reactivate the proteins encoded by the genes that separate humans from wild animals—in other words, the experiment turned men into monsters. For the first time, zombies are explained using real science—science so real there is every possibility of something like the Extinction Cycle actually happening. But these creatures aren't the unthinking, slow-minded, shuffling monsters we've all come to know in other shows, books, and movies. These "variants" are more monster than human. Through the series, the variants become the hunters as they evolve from the epigenetic changes. Scrambling to find a cure and defeat the monsters, humanity is brought to the brink of extinction.

We hope you enjoy *Extinction Red Line* and have included the prologue of book 1, *Extinction Horizon*, at the beginning of *Extinction Red Line*, and the first chapter of *Extinction Horizon* in the back of this book for you to sample if you do wish to continue the adventure of the Extinction Cycle.

Thank you for reading!
Best wishes,
Nicholas Sansbury Smith,
USA Today Bestselling Author of the Extinction Cycle

Prologue

Operation Burn Bright, Northwest Vietnam
July 10, 1968

Operation Burn Bright started off with a smooth insertion. Lieutenant Trevor Brett and thirty-one other Marines jumped into the fray from the crew compartment of multiple UH-1 "Huey" choppers.

The stink of the jungle filled Brett's lungs as soon as his boots hit the ground. They'd been dropped on the outskirts of a swamp, and the rot lingered in the sultry air.

Brett gagged at the smell and promptly clenched his jaw shut. He moved with his lips sealed and was careful not to swallow any bugs when he was forced to open his mouth and bark orders. Vietnam was the worst place for someone who suffered from a borderline case of obsessive-compulsive disorder. There was simply no way to maintain good hygiene in the jungle.

Breathing through his nostrils, Brett led his men slowly into the knee-deep water in a wedge formation. Every few steps he would pause, scan the area, and then flash a hand signal to advance. The men were experienced enough to know they should maintain combat intervals. Enough of them had seen buddies die from clustering together, forming double targets for the enemy.

If he didn't have his lips closed, Brett might have even smiled at the sight of his well-organized platoon. But smiling was reserved for peacetime, not war. In Brett's eyes, Vietnam was just a place for Marines to go and die.

The farther they moved into the muck, the deeper the swamp became. Stagnant water crawled up his legs, sending a cold chill through his body.

Goddamn, he hated the fucking jungle and everything inside it—the snakes, the bugs, and, worst of all, the leeches. He stifled a curse when he saw a foot-long leech swimming in his direction. The last thing he wanted to do was notify Charlie they were coming. The sloshing water was already loud enough to tell every Vietcong in the area that a platoon full of fresh meat was on its way.

As he slopped through the water, Brett wondered how he had gotten so unlucky. The war had ruined everything. After graduating college, he had looked forward to a career in banking, with a nice little cookie-cutter house, a gorgeous wife, and a warm dinner waiting at home for him every night. Instead, his girlfriend had left him, and he was wading through water toward one of the most ruthless enemies the American military had ever faced. To make things worse, he and his men carried an experimental drug that they were supposed to take right before reaching their target. Command had said it would negate the effects of any chemicals lingering in the area, such as Agent Orange, but Brett had his doubts. It sounded more as if they were being used as guinea pigs.

"Shit," he muttered as a fly the size of a peanut buzzed by his helmet. He swept the muzzle of his M16 over a clearing at the far end of the swamp. They weren't far from their target, a remote village that brass claimed was secretly supporting the local VC.

Brett wasn't so sure. He'd been down this road many times before. Most of the time, they didn't find shit.

When they reached the edge of the swamp, Brett balled his hand into a fist. He jerked his chin toward the platoon sergeant, a stocky Texan named Fern. The man was built like a football player, with wide shoulders and tree trunks for legs. He approached with a toothy grin, revealing a wad of chew that bled a brown trail of juice down his chin strap.

The two men were exact opposites. Fern cared nothing for hygiene and seemed to thrive in the disgusting jungle. The thicker the muck, the more he enjoyed himself.

"Lieutenant," Fern said, squinting, with a hand shielding his eyes.

"The village should be just beyond that ridgeline," Brett said, pointing toward an embankment across the field. "Tell everyone not holding security to pair up and take their doses of VX-99, and make sure they actually do it."

"Roger that, sir," Fern replied. He spat a chunk of tobacco into the soupy water, and Brett watched it vanish into the mouths of some small fish. His stomach churned at the sight. Brett followed Fern onto solid ground. They stepped over rotting vegetation and slapped away sharp branches. When they got to the edge of the clearing, Brett dropped to his right knee and reached for his bag. He removed the small syringe of VX-99 and eyed it suspiciously. There was nothing he hated more than needles except the jungle and everything inside it. If sticking the needle in his arm meant he would get out of here quicker, well, then, fuck it.

He bit off the plastic tip and spat it out, found a bulging vein in his wrist, and jammed the point of the needle into his arm. Slowly, he pushed the mysterious cocktail into his bloodstream. A sharp pain instantly raced down his arm. Brett tossed the syringe into the brush and placed a finger over the spot. The other men were taking turns: one man on guard with weapon at the ready, the other with his weapon cradled while jabbing the chemicals into a vein.

Brett waited there, listening to the hum of oversized insects and the chirps of exotic birds, for several seconds, wondering if the platoon would notice any side effects.

After a minute, the tingling sensation in his veins passed. He stood, shouldering his rifle and leveling the muzzle over the field. So far there was no sign of the enemy, but that didn't mean they weren't out there. Charlie was always out there, waiting to strike like the drugs in his veins.

"Move out," Brett said.

Fern nodded and flashed a blur of hand movements to the men on their right. The Marines fanned out over the field at a brisk pace, their boots slurping through the mud.

Before they'd made it halfway, Brett felt a burning. At first he wondered if the wind had carried Agent Orange into the area, but this burning wasn't the same. It wasn't coming from outside his skin—it was coming from inside his chest, as if he'd swallowed an entire bottle of Vietnamese hot sauce.

Small jolts of pain raced through his body with every heartbeat. The agonizing burn spread to his head and lingered there. He blinked, tears welling in his eyes. He felt as if he was being burned alive, only from within.

Out of the corner of his eye, he watched a PFC named Junko collapse to both knees, clawing madly at his skull. Then came the screaming. Wails of pain broke out as other Marines fell.

What the fuck is happening to us?

The pain was so intense Brett could hardly think. Shimmering arcs of bright light broke across his vision. The oranges, reds, and yellows swam before his eyes. The jungle faded behind the colors.

Dropping his rifle on the ground, he cupped his hands over his ears to drown out the pained shrieks.

Whatever was happening to the platoon wasn't the effect of some chemical lingering over the field. Brett could hardly form a cohesive thought, but he knew the pain was a result of the VX-99.

A sudden surge of fire blasted through Brett's body. It was followed by a sharp tingling sensation, as if hundreds of bees were stinging him all at once.

He fell to his back, itching the bare parts of his skin violently. There was no relief, only more pain.

His mind responded by taking him away from the jungle, to a place where there were no massive bugs, rotting vegetation, or men trying to kill him.

A brick house, with a stone path leading up to it, emerged. At the front door, an attractive woman held a glass of ice water. She smiled. "Come in, honey. Dinner is almost ready." Brett felt the pain diminish as he slipped deeper into this fantasy. He knew that the house and the woman weren't real, but he didn't care. He wanted to escape the godforsaken jungle.

He needed to escape.

When he got to the door, the woman was gone. The door was closed. He tried the knob. It was locked. Then the house was gone too. The bright colors returned. He could feel his body again. Fear replaced the pain.

When his eyes popped open, he saw the cloudless sky and the brilliant white sun above.

Where was he?

He heard muffled voices, the rustling of gear, and the shriek of some exotic animal.

There were other noises—distant noises.

The world became exceptionally vivid. Brett could hear the bugs crawling through the underbrush; he could smell the stink of sweat on his uniform. He could taste coffee he didn't remember drinking. His senses were heightened to a level he'd never experienced before.

It was terrifying, but at the same time it was oddly liberating. He clenched his fists, feeling his muscles contract.

He stared at his hands with grim fascination. He felt stronger than ever before, as if he could take on an entire army. He felt…

Invincible.

Dazed but alert, Brett leaped to his feet. Tilting the front of his helmet upward, he ran his sleeve across his face to clear the sweat dripping into his eyes.

When his vision cleared, he instantly stumbled backward, nearly tripping over his own feet as he sloshed through the mud. Brett spun to see two dozen men staggering across the moist dirt. They wore the same fatigues he wore and carried the same gear he did. They were Marines, like him. Several of the men walked off aimlessly in different directions, cupping their heads in their hands. He felt there was something almost familiar in their faces, but he couldn't place it. Did he know these men?

He heard a woman's voice. *Kill them*, she croaked. *Kill them all.*

Brett spun again, his boots sinking in the mud as he searched for the woman. It was then he realized the voice was coming from inside his head.

You must kill them, said the voice again. She snarled, *Do it before they kill you!*

Brett smacked the side of his helmet.

Who was this woman, and why did she want him to kill these men?

Brett focused on the Marine in front of him. He was a short, stocky fella with a wad of chew jammed inside his lip. Brett could smell the tobacco juice dripping off the man's chin.

When he saw Brett, he held up his hands and balled them into fists. The Marine growled, "Get away from me, y-you"—he stuttered, swallowing a chunk of the tobacco—"you fuck!"

Brett experienced an abrupt wave of adrenaline. He reached for something to protect himself. His fingers found the warm metal handle of a blade on his belt. He pulled the knife from its sheath in one swift motion, as if he'd done this many times before.

The woman's voice returned, booming inside his mind. *Stab him. Stab him right in his fat little gut.* It was an awful voice, the kind that scraped at the inside of his brain with its jagged claws. But it was somehow familiar. In some distant world, he knew this voice.

"Get away from me!" the man yelled, a vein bulging in his neck as spit flew from his mouth. Brett narrowed in on the vein. He could see it pulsating. He imagined the blood flowing through the thin passage.

The image sent a thrill through Brett's body. His own

blood tingled inside him. In one move, he jumped to the side with impressive speed. The stocky man moved quickly too, throwing a jab that whooshed through the air.

Brett ducked and plunged forward, sinking the blade deep into the man's stomach, just as the woman had told him to. The Marine let out a scream of agony, blood gurgling from his mouth. Brett wasted no time. He withdrew the knife, took a step back, and then jammed the blade into the man's neck.

The stout man clutched both wounds and dropped to his knees before collapsing face first into the mud.

Taking a short, satisfying breath, Brett picked up a new scent. He could almost taste it.

It was the scent of death.

The sudden crack of automatic gunfire pulled Brett back to the rice field as if a switch had been flicked. His gaze roved across the embankment beyond the field, noting each flash.

An explosion went off a few hundred yards away. The deafening blast sent a red geyser of dirt and body parts into the sky. When the mist cleared, a bloody crater was all that remained of the Marine who had been standing there seconds before.

Run! cried the woman's voice.

Shocked into motion, Brett gripped the knife tightly and took off at a dead sprint. The sound of his boots stomping through the muck faded against the sounds of war.

More explosions rocked the dirt around him. Mud, water, and vegetation rained down. He ignored the burning sediment that landed on his bare skin and ran faster.

The other Marines ran too. Some of them dropped as bullets tore into them. He saw a man to his right disappear as a grenade detonated under his feet.

Brett felt nothing for the man. Nothing fazed him. There was only one thing that mattered…

Killing.

Something nicked him as he ran. He looked down, expecting to see a fly on his skin, but instead saw a quarter-sized hole where a bullet had torn into his bicep. A second round pierced his side. The impact slowed him momentarily. The coppery taste of blood filled his mouth. Licking his lips, he continued running.

He could see the faces of the men trying to kill him as he approached the embankment. They hid under straw hats and helmets, screaming in a language that he did not understand.

He could smell the sharp scent of gunpowder and the salty sweat on their uniforms.

When he was ten yards away from the bottom of the hill, he dropped to all fours, gripping his knife between his teeth, and galloped, using his back legs to spring forward. He leaped up in three rapid movements and landed on the chest of one of the Vietnamese soldiers. Pulling his knife from his teeth, he speared the unsuspecting man through the chest, penetrating his heart. The man's eyes rolled back in his head, and Brett moved on to the next soldier.

Every thrust sent a thrill through his body. A wide grin spread across his face. He felt insanely powerful.

Minutes later, the ridgeline was littered with the mangled corpses of the enemy soldiers. A growing river of red seeped down the hill.

Brett pulled his gaze away to scan his own body.

Blood oozed from his wounds, but there was little pain. He ignored the injuries and stepped over one of the bodies.

The woman's voice boomed inside his mind. *You're not done!*

Glancing up from a nearby corpse, he saw a slender African American Marine glaring at him with crazed eyes from the bottom of the embankment. The man licked his lips and tossed a knife from his left hand to his right. His green uniform was soaked with blood from a bullet that had clipped his neck. Behind him, Brett could see the field. Pockmarks littered the ground where grenades had exploded. Dozens of bodies lay in the shallow water around the craters.

Brett looked back and met the man's dark gaze. Gripping his own knife tightly, he swung the blade toward the skinny Marine. The tip whooshed through the air, but it didn't deter the man. He dropped to all fours and climbed the hill quickly, his joints clicking with every motion.

Before Brett could move, the Marine lunged toward him. They collided, tumbling across the bloodstained dirt. The air burst from Brett's lungs as he finally landed with a thud on the hard earth.

Brett sucked in a deep breath and then pushed himself to his feet with his knife still in his hand. He caught the other man off guard with an uppercut that lodged the blade inside his skull.

A strangled sound escaped the Marine's mouth. He grabbed the knife's handle as he dropped to his knees. Brett kicked him in the chest and watched with grim fascination as the man hit the dirt on his back and choked on his own blood. He kicked against the ground violently, struggling for several minutes before finally going limp.

Gasping for air, Brett stumbled away. He dropped to both knees and squinted as a gust of wind swirled dust around him. Stars broke before his eyes. Dizziness set in. He was finally starting to feel the effects of blood loss, but there was still no pain.

As he looked over the field, a distant memory of a brick house and woman entered his thoughts. He quickly pushed them away. There was only one thing that he wanted now. Only one thing he desired.

To kill.

***

A bird's caw startled Brett awake. He peeled a muddy leaf off his face like a scab and glanced up through the canopy of trees at a brilliant moon. The sun had long since gone down, darkness swallowing the jungle.

Brett pushed himself out of his makeshift bed, flexing his muscles and cracking his neck from side to side.

It was time to hunt.

Setting off into the dense vegetation, he used his enhanced vision to search for prey. His eyes roved back and forth, penetrating the darkness. And they continued to improve, giving him borderline night vision.

A deep growl came from the pit of his stomach. Not the type of pain when you're hungry, but the type when you're starving. *Odd*, he thought, considering he had eaten just a few hours earlier.

I need more! he thought.

Brett hadn't eaten anything *substantial* for over a day. Mostly just bugs, worms, lizards, and the snake he'd killed with his bare hands.

He needed something bigger.

Something *human.*

Memories of humans from his recent and distant past surfaced in his mind as he moved through the jungle. Images of his mom, brother, sister, friends, and his ex-girlfriend. Even his dad, who had abandoned him at the age of ten.

But they all felt disconnected like they didn't belong to him anymore.

They came and went like puffs of smoke from a cigarette, vanishing into the night and replaced by a memory so vivid and clear it was like he was there now, back at the forward operating base Condor with the rest of his platoon, preparing to load their choppers for Operation Burn Bright.

Brett put his filthy hands on his head and bent down behind a tree, closing his eyes as it replayed. In his mind's eye, he saw Sergeant Fern chewing a wad of tobacco near the tarmac. He spat in the respite of barking at the thirty-plus-man platoon.

"Today the Marine Corps transcends above what we were put on God's green Earth for!" Fern shouted. "Today, ladies and gentlemen, you become the most *elite* warriors ever to set forth on this planet and will do battle under our Lord's merciful eyes."

Fern spat a stream of juice onto the dirt, directing his gaze at a private named McDonald. "Even you, shit-for-brains McD. You might even become a warrior worth a damn."

The other men laughed, including Brett, who watched with his arms folded across his chest. He already knew what was coming. They were all about to get the speech about a unique and important opportunity. All of them would get prophylactic injections. All of them would get to go home early. All of them would be better for this. That was what he'd been told. But none of it was true. He wouldn't learn that, none of them would learn that, until it was far too late. And then the clear memory dissolved into chaos.

He was back in the jungle, fighting men in uniforms that looked like his, and men wearing rice-farmer hats. A voice commanded him to kill, and kill he did. By the time it was over, he was the last man standing in the gore-filled battlefield, surrounded by a mountain of corpses. He looked down at one of them, a man who looked familiar.

A man who had been his friend.

Not only had the true nature of the VX-99 been a lie, its side effects hadn't ceased after he ran from the blood-soaked hill.

They had gotten stronger…

Brett had gotten stronger.

He snapped out of the memories, his hands outstretched, fingers like claws. A guttural scream erupted from his mouth, scaring off the birds perching in the canopy above. The call of a monkey replied to his scream.

Brett took off running and jumping over fallen logs. He tore through foliage that stung his skin. His boots slopped through swamps, and branches broke against his muscular body.

Lancing pain finally stopped him, and he looked down at his bicep in the drip of moonlight. The tattered remains of his camouflage uniform hung off his filthy flesh. A brown scab covered the wound from the battle several days earlier, already healed.

But how was that possible? Humans weren't supposed to heal like this. Yet here he was, standing in the Vietnam jungle, looking at a bullet hole almost completely healed.

It wasn't just the rapid healing that had changed his body—it was almost like he had become an animal. He was now hearing things that he had never heard before: the whipping of wings in the air, the crunching of bugs scuttling over the dirt and leaves.

And he could smell like never before.

Not just his own sweat, but the scent of animals, birds, and decaying carcasses. His nostrils flared, taking in the fetid jungle air, and led him right toward the intoxicating smell of rot and death. He could almost taste the flesh.

You must feed.

The voice in his mind made him flinch, and he crouched down, glaring in all directions. He hadn't heard her since he woke from his slumber.

You must eat and regain your strength.

The female voice growled.

Brett stopped at the edge of another swamp, the musical sound of insects filling the night. He slowly made his way along the sloped bank, his legs tingling and muscles throbbing.

Then he saw it.

A frog the size of an apple.

Capture and consume, came the raggedy old voice.

Brett froze and held a breath in his chest. Ever so slowly, he carefully walked through the mud, making sure his boots didn't slurp. When he was five feet away, he bent down and then leapt. The frog jumped too, but not fast enough. Brett snatched the back leg in his fingers and stuffed the creature in his mouth, biting off the upper half in a sickening crunch.

He sat in the mud as he enjoyed the treat. For now, the meal satisfied his urge to kill and consume flesh.

But he knew the hunger would return.

Every day that passed, he lost more and more of himself to the violent urges in his mind. He wasn't even sure how much time had passed since he was dropped off in the jungle, but he knew he was losing snippets of his past life. Eventually it would be gone. He would forget everything that made him who he'd been before the VX-99 had forged a new creature.

The moon climbed higher into the sky, and Brett continued deeper into the jungle. He hunted until the predawn glow brightened the trees, and the nocturnal creatures returned to their lairs.

But Brett wasn't done hunting. His stomach wasn't full, and the voice urged him onward. He sniffed the air, picking up on something…different.

Smoke.

He sniffed the air again, identifying another scent. His eyes widened and his stomach growled at the new odor. It was sickeningly tempting and was all he needed to take off running at a sprint, ducking under branches, navigating a floor of tangled roots, and jumping over puddles of standing water.

Lieutenant Brett ran until he saw the source of the smoke—a village in a clearing beyond the dense canopy. Using trees for cover, he kept to the shadows that clung to the edges of the dim early morning light. People were talking quietly so as not to disturb those still sleeping. Several groups headed out to feed the livestock and work the land.

He jumped onto the base of a tree and climbed the branches to the top, looking out over the village. Several men holding weapons patrolled the outskirts, and more stalked the muddy roads carving up the camp.

At the far end, a group of shacks with barred windows caught his attention. Inside, half-naked men sat in the dirt, bone thin and bearded. A guard tossed a bucket of slop through the bars, covering one of the men in brown sludge.

Laughter followed.

And so did the voice in his mind.

Her words sparked a jolt of adrenaline through his warm veins.

Kill them. Kill them all.

Brett climbed back down to the dirt, where he rubbed mud over his exposed flesh for camouflage. Then he set off for the village, heading for a pen of livestock. Farmers stood around the outside, tossing in food. They were older, wrinkled, and hunched. They wore the difficulties of their lives in their shoulders and in the creases that marked their faces.

He already knew the older people didn't taste as good, but he didn't come here to kill them. He came here for the cleaver jammed in a log of wood. Carmine stains covered the blade from chickens that had lost their heads here.

Hatchet in hand, Brett moved around the farms and into the heart of the village. A guard wearing black fatigues and a tan rice-farmer hat stood with his back to Brett, holding an AK-47.

Rip his throat out, the female voice barked. *Take his eyes!*

Brett hugged the shadows, most of the villagers still sleeping in the shacks and huts. The soldier turned right when Brett got within striking distance. He planted the cleaver in his skull, the crunch echoing. The man dropped to his knees, and Brett yanked it out.

Take your trophy, the voice said.

Using the sharp blade, Brett hacked off the man's right ear and then tucked it in his vest pocket. The body slumped to the ground as he took off. For the next fifteen minutes he killed his way through the village, taking down five soldiers and two villagers that had spotted him murdering. He slit their throats, hacked off their limbs, and took more trophies.

By the time the sun shone over the village, a dozen people were dead, and he had two fresh limbs in a bag over his muscular back.

It was then an alarm finally sounded.

Voices called out in all directions. No more laughter, only frightened and panicked voices that brought him a grim sense of joy.

Brett had made his way to the far edge of the village, where the half-naked men were being kept in barred-up huts. He crawled in the mud toward the prison, wiggling across the dirt like a worm. A voice sounded as he approached and this wasn't the one in his mind.

"Someone has come to rescue us."

"Where?" came another voice. "I don't see anyone."

To Brett's ears the words meant nothing, but he still turned to look at the group of four men who had made their way to the bars, clutching them with blistered fingers and peering down. One of them spotted him.

"Hey…hey, you," he said.

"He's an American…" another guy said, pointing.

Their bearded, gaunt faces all looked down at him, blue and brown eyes pleading. Ribs showed under filthy tattered clothes, and yellow bandages covered infected wounds.

He followed the man's finger to his shoulder and the red, white and blue flag sewn onto the camo. A brief moment of pride flashed over him, but it passed just as suddenly as it emerged. The symbol meant something to these men, and perhaps it had once meant something to him, but Brett was no longer the man he was days earlier.

He had changed.

Transcended into something even more powerful than he ever thought possible.

More voices yelled across the village, and a gunshot sounded.

Brett crawled away from the hut, deciding these men would not be good killing, too easy. And they probably wouldn't taste all that good either.

"Don't leave us!" one of them shouted. It was a cry for help. It was a call for sympathy. A cry for humanity. But to Lieutenant Trevor Brett, the pleas meant nothing. He was no longer a Marine—he was a beast.

On all fours, Brett scampered away like the animal he had transformed into. When he got far enough away, he stood to run with the bag of limbs slapping his shoulder and a breast pocket full of ears and noses. They would make good trophies for his necklace.

— 1 —

London, England
April 17, 1980

Jimmy Linh read the words again. They resonated.

Ma Trang. *White Ghost.*

He leaned back in his seat, dropped the newsprint, and bobbed the Earl Grey tea bag up and down in the steaming cup near the edge of the table. *White Ghost.*

He was at his regular breakfast spot in Lewisham, a borough in southeastern London, and had a few minutes to spare before he'd need to catch the tube to work. He picked up the cup and blew across the steeping tea, preferring the English Earl Grey over the traditional Vietnamese *trà mạn* tea with hints of jasmine or lotus. He looked again at the Vietnamese community paper he read to keep his native language fresh in his head. The headline was the grabber. He wondered if he was translating it correctly.

White Ghost Kills Again, Terrorizes Villages along Da River

Linh read the short article for the fourth time, lingering on the details about a half-human beast that ate its victims alive. For nearly a decade, the Ma Trang, as villagers called it, would appear from nowhere. It had unearthly speed and large claws it used to attack its victims. It always left behind the remains and disappeared into the jungle.

Some even claimed it was the ghost of an American Marine killed by the Vietcong. Ma Trang was exacting its revenge, they said.

Linh checked his watch and cursed, drawing the offended glare of an older, proper woman at the table adjacent to his. He took his first and last sip of tea and winced when it burned the tip of his tongue. He puckered his lips and pushed himself from the table, tucked the paper under his arm, and grabbed his brown leather satchel from the floor to head for the Lewisham station.

He rushed through the morning crowds, plucking and weaving his way amongst the other commuters to find his seat on the train bound for London's central station. It was a forty-five-minute ride and he'd need every second of it to perfect his pitch.

Linh found an empty spot at a window near the front of a car, thanked Buddha for his good fortune, and plopped into the seat. He put his satchel at his feet, opened it, and drew out a reporter's notebook and a pen.

He placed the notebook on one leg, the newspaper on the other, and held the pen between his teeth as he thought about the best way to convince his boss that Ma Trang was a story he had to tell.

Linh was a cub reporter for the *London Morning Reflector,* a widely read daily newspaper known as much for its flash as its substance. Linh was cutting his teeth and needed a good pitch, not only to impress his editor, but to ease the pressure from his parents.

They believed him too smart to waste his life as a reporter, as the teller of other people living their lives.

Linh had resisted their pull to the family business so far, but if he didn't do something big and soon, he knew he'd be forced into servitude.

The train eased from the station with a whine and sudden jerk before reaching its rhythm on the tracks. Linh was so deep in thought, he didn't notice they'd left Lewisham or that a young woman in a brown trench coat was trying to get his attention.

Finally, she tapped his shoulder. "Pardon me," she said with a demure smile. "Is this seat occupied?"

Linh flinched at her touch and blinked her into focus. "No," he said. "You're free to sit."

"You were deep in thought," she said, sitting next to him, her purse in her lap.

He flashed a polite smile. "Work," he said and turned his attention back to the notepad until she put her hand on his leg.

"What do you do?" she asked.

Linh suppressed a sigh and looked to the woman. "I'm a reporter," he said. The words leaked from his mouth before he'd noticed her wide, icy blue eyes. Her thick blonde hair was pulled into a bun atop her head. She was dressed in a dark blue suit. He'd noticed her before. At least, he'd noticed those blue eyes. It was hard not to take notice.

"That's fascinating." Her accent was more Liverpool than London. "I've never met a reporter."

"What do you do?" he asked, suddenly interested in his originally unwelcome seatmate.

"I'm a receptionist and telephonist for the Home Office," she said brightly. "Nothing exciting like being a reporter."

Linh's cheeks flushed. He looked down at his notepad

and back at the woman. She was smiling, her eyes focused on his. Her body was turned toward his.

"I've seen you before," she said. "On the tube. I just…"

"Just what?"

"I just couldn't grasp the nettle," she said, her face turning red.

Linh laughed. "A woman as beautiful as you?"

She slapped his thigh. "Oh, go on, then."

Linh allowed an awkward silence to build between them before he looked back at his notepad. He bit the inside of his cheek to keep a toothy grin from exploding. When he'd bit down hard enough for his eyes to well, he turned to her with as serious a face as he could muster.

"How's this," he finally said. "I have a lot of work to do today. I'm making a big pitch. I'd like to talk more, though. Could I have your telephone?"

She pursed her lips. "This is a blow-off."

Linh shook his head. "No," he said. "Better yet, let's exchange telephone numbers. Then we have no excuse. Plus, we take the same ride every day."

The smile returned. "That we do," she said. "My name is Molly."

"I'm Jimmy."

They shook hands, their grip lasting a beat past formal, and exchanged numbers before Molly stood.

"I'll let you finish your work," she said. "I do expect a ring."

"I promise."

Jimmy looked back at the notepad and then over his shoulder at Molly as she walked toward the back of the car. She was beautiful and seemed sweet. She wasn't Vietnamese though. His parents would kill him; a job as a reporter and a date with a Caucasian woman?

He shook his head and refocused on his pitch.

He'd lived in England his entire life. Well, all of his life since evacuating Vietnam in 1969. He'd escaped the war, but a ghost from that war seemingly was still alive. He wanted to find out exactly who it was.

— 2 —

Near Son La, Vietnam
April 1, 1980

Lieutenant Trevor Brett nibbled on the woman's ear, paying special attention to the lobe. He'd first seen her weeks ago and there was an instantaneous, animal attraction. Her musk was intoxicating and narrowed his fractured mind to a single focused thought.

He had to have her.

His memory flashed to that moment. Her smooth skin looked delicious. Her silky black hair framed her features in a way that made her all the more inviting. She was thin, which wasn't necessarily good. Lieutenant Brett had long ago given up being picky about those upon whom he'd set his sights.

The woman had had no choice but to succumb to his advances. She was like the others before her. The initial fear and pulse pounding gave way to resignation and acceptance.

So Brett nibbled. It wasn't flirtation.

No.

He was *chewing* on the ear, rolling the chunks of cartilage around his tongue and between his jagged yellow teeth. He held it between his gnarled, claw-like fingers for leverage. It was the newest addition to the necklace he wore around his neck. Like a piece of sugary sweet candy on an elastic string, he couldn't keep it out of his mouth. He couldn't resist the urge to gnaw. His thickly rounded sucker lips popped and slurped.

There was little satisfaction from the gristled piece of skin, but it kept his mind from fixating on the relentless hunger that ate at his gut. The woman, as he'd suspected despite his attraction, wasn't enough to satiate the hunger for long.

Women often weren't enough. Men, thick and greasy men, were the prize. He needed another man.

Brett was perched fifteen feet off the ground on the gnarled limb of a tamarind tree. His clawed feet gripped the knotty wood with calloused, elongated toes that had the appearance of vulture's talons.

He suddenly stopped chewing and held the snack against the roof of his mouth. He tilted back his head and closed his eyes. He inhaled through his nostrils, first with a long pull of air and then with short quick bursts. A slow, rounded grin crept across his face. The odor was unmistakable. It was thick and greasy.

Filtered through the scent of rotting vegetation and mildew was the sweet smell of Brett's favorite prey. He took another quick suck of air in his nose. The odor was intensifying. The prey was moving toward him.

Brett was hunting a narrow stretch of land between the Da River and the mountains that stretched most of the distance from Lao Cai to Hanoi. It was a good spot that offered unsuspecting farmers and preoccupied fishermen.

The prey came from the river. Brett opened his eyes

and narrowed his gaze, scanning the green landscape for visual confirmation. He shifted on his feet, the callouses scraping against the wood and his knees clicking as he moved.

He gripped the thick tree branch with his clawed hands to steady himself. Nine of his ten fingers, or what resembled fingers, were adorned with long hooked claws. One of the fingers was missing a claw. Brett had lost the weapon fighting a woman in the river. It didn't diminish his abilities to pounce, slash, and feed. It had been more than ten hours since he'd fed. Warm saliva pooled in his mouth and oozed from his lips, mixing with the omnipresent stain of blood that painted his face.

Then he saw it. The prey. Brett leaned forward. He was ready to pounce.

Wait for it, growled the woman's voice that occupied his head. She was always in control. *It will come closer.*

The hunger in Brett's gut screamed at him to jump, to use his speed and agility to overtake the prey and feed. The ache emanated from his stomach to his chest and into his throat. He longed for the warmth of raw meat and the delicious satisfaction of blood.

The prey moved closer, carrying a net of silver and coral basa fish over one shoulder. Even from a distance of fifty yards, Brett's bloodshot eyes could see the basa's tiny heads, their eel-like eyes, and the thick underbelly that distinguished them from others in the catfish family.

He wasn't interested in the fish, though, and his glare darted to the chunky man carrying the net. He was walking with the low energy of a man who'd spent his day fighting for his food. Brett inhaled the sweet odor of the man's sweat. His eyes narrowed on the beautifully full artery running along the man's strained neck.

Another flood of saliva poured into his mouth. His sinewy muscles tensed, twitching almost, as Brett awaited the command. He was so hungry. So. Hungry.

Now, snarled the voice.

Brett pushed with his thighs and jumped from the branch to the muddy ground below. He landed solidly on both feet, his shoulders rolled forward, as he caught the fisherman's full attention.

The man froze. His eyes grew wide. He dropped the net.

Brett sniffed the distinctly acidic smell of urine. His lips pursed and popped. His joints clicked and snapped when he dropped to all fours.

In the time it took the man to open his mouth, but before he could force a scream, Brett was on top of him. Brett's razor teeth ripped at the man's throat. His lips found that juicy arterial flow and he fed. Oh, he fed.

Brett grunted and snarled and slurped as he worked the prey to a pulp. He scratched and clawed the meat free of the bone when his teeth and lips were otherwise occupied.

When he was finished, when he'd put the hunger at bay for the moment, he squatted on the jungle floor, admiring his work.

He was delicious, said the voice. *Mmmmmm.*

Brett snatched a thin bone from the ground next to him. It was a finger. Maybe a toe. Brett picked it up with his own clawed hand and slid the bone between his lips. He bit down and raked his teeth across it until the last remnants of flesh were stripped away.

Brett then tore what was left of the man's nose from his mangled face and held it tight in his hand. It would make a wonderful addition to the cord around his neck.

He stood and then crouched on his knuckles like an ape. He inhaled deeply through his nose, threw back his head, and howled. Even after a decade, it was a sound that chilled what little humanity remained in Lieutenant Trevor Brett. That speck of his former life couldn't reconcile the monster he'd become. That speck, that spot of reason and love and compassion, was buried so deeply within his core, it might as well not have existed at all.

Time to move, growled the voice. *I'm hungry.*

Brett charged toward the mountains, away from the river. He left the fisherman behind. A few of the basa still flopped and twitched in the netting as Brett disappeared.

— 3 —

Philadelphia, Pennsylvania
April 17, 1980

Nick Womack took a swig of Old Dutch and swished it around in his cheeks like mouthwash. He was leaning forward in a worn leather easy chair dinged with cigarette burns and stained with the sweat from countless cans of beer.

On the old tabletop television in front of him, familiar images of American hostages flickered under the drone of the network news correspondent explaining the latest lack of developments half a world away.

Womack swallowed the corn-infused, bitter, body-temperature beer and grumbled at the screen. "Send me in," he said. "I'd have all fifty-two back and eating bacon within ninety-six hours."

It wasn't hyperbole.

Womack was a man of unique abilities and rare gut. He was a living, breathing, drinking and smoking superhero. His skills were prized and expensive to employ.

He tightened his grip on the near empty can and drew it to his mouth to finish it. He winced at the bitter draw of the beer. It wasn't his favorite. It was cheap.

Womack liked cheap things, which explained his proclivity for easy women whose last names he'd never learn, and his large cache of free ammunition taken from the corpses of the men he was paid to eliminate.

He crumpled the can and set it on the table next to his easy chair. The black rotary phone caught his eye. It had been two weeks since it rang. Womack was surprised his friends at the agency hadn't called him about Iran.

The whole thing was a big cluster as best he could tell. They needed some extractors to ply their trade and end the drama. He half thought there was some deal in the works to keep the men and women held until after the election, but he discounted it as a figment of his conspiratorial imagination.

"One chopper, five men," he said, leaning back into the comfort of the leather. The tufted chair back hissed and deflated as his cartoonish, muscular frame sank into it. "Quick, silent, violent."

QSV. That was Nick's mantra. It was what he told his team every time they saved a friendly or raided the enemy. Their job was as simple as those three commands.

Nick would outwardly tell his men they needn't kill without cause. They knew. There was always cause. It was better they have trouble sleeping at night for what they'd done, Nick reasoned, than take a permanent dirt nap absent regret.

"Not gonna lie," he said to the news anchor, who'd shifted to the ridiculous price of oil, "this is all a bunch of crap. Everything you liberal commies say is propaganda. It's all rigged. It's all fixed. And the little people like me, the grunts, we're always going to take it in the hindquarters. That's just a fact."

Nick had reason for his skepticism. He'd seen the worst in man. Three long tours in Vietnam had assured him a life of dependency and nightmares.

A half decade after he'd been among the last to leave that forsaken, blood-soaked jungle, he could still smell the rot. He could still feel the leeches stuck to his neck and forearms, the stockade bruises on his wrists. He could taste the warm droplets of rain that mixed with the salt and dirt on his face before finding their way between his lips and onto his tongue.

He couldn't shake the horror of that place. That was part of the reason he'd gone freelance. It got him out from under Uncle Sam's thumb and allowed him to exorcise demons one trigger pull at a time. More than anything on the planet, he hated the jungle.

Nick belched and smacked his lips against the bitter taste of the Old Dutch. He pushed himself to his feet, wobbled before steadying himself against the arm of the chair, and walked across the room to turn off the television.

On the table, next to the TV, was an eight-track player. He ran his fingers along the minimal selection of tapes stacked on top of the machine and drew a cartridge from the middle.

He pushed the tape into the slot, hit the play button, and selected program two. He cranked up the volume on the amplifier and closed his eyes to soak in the sounds of the trumpets and drums playing the intro to Stevie Wonder's "Sir Duke". He involuntarily started swinging his head back and forth, his foot tapping on the floor. He mouthed the words as Stevie paid tribute to jazz greats in his inimitable way.

Nick walked over to the doorway that led into his

bedroom. At the doorway, he reached up and grabbed an aluminum pull-up bar lodged into the frame.

He grabbed the bar with one thick mitt and then with the other. He dropped down, his feet still on the floor, and hung from the bar to stretch his arms and back.

"Time to sweat out the Dutch," he said and pulled his feet up behind him, crossing them at his ankles.

He tightened his grip and pulled upward until his lips were even with the top of the painted wood frame. He kissed the frame.

"One," he said and lowered himself until his arms were almost, but not quite, fully extended. He inhaled and then pulled his weight upward again. Another kiss.

"Two."

Nick repeated the routine until he'd reached fifty, sweat stung his eyes, and his arms burned with lactic acid. He dropped his feet to the floor and let go of the bar. He shook his arms loose and took deep, slow breaths until his pulse evened.

Then he dropped to the floor and spread his arms shoulder-width apart. Push-ups. Five sets of twenty.

When he was finished, he rolled onto his back for two hundred sit-ups. Each time he pulled his chin even with his knees, he glanced across the room at the black rotary phone.

He'd be ready when it rang. It would ring. He knew it.

— 4 —

Frederick, Maryland
April 17, 1980

Major Rick Gibson pinched the bridge of his nose. His eyes were squeezed shut. His jaw was clenched.

"I'm sorry," said Dr. Justin Starling, a civilian researcher on Gibson's team. "It won't synthesize. I've tried everything."

Gibson sighed. "Clearly," he said, "you haven't tried everything. Otherwise it would work."

Starling protested. "We keep reaching the critical moment in the life cycle and then it breaks down. We can't get it to hold and replicate. I've tried different proteins. I've tried—"

Gibson held up his hand. "Justin," he said, "I brought you here from Stanford because I believed you were the best. If you're not capable of the job, I'll find someone who is. I need to know now, son. Have you really tried everything?"

Starling lowered his head and shook it back and forth. "No," he said. "I'll get back to work."

"Good," said Gibson. He turned on his heel and marched away from the young scientist. He reached a secured door, slid a magnetic card, waited for the metallic click, and moved from one corridor to the next.

Gibson navigated the maze of hallways that connected the various sections of the United States Army Medical Research Institute of Infectious Diseases. USAMRIID was comprised of more than seven hundred civilian, military, and contract workers whose publicly stated goal was "to protect the warfighter from biological threats and investigate disease outbreaks and threats to public health."

In reality, they did much more than that. Gibson was among the men charged with leading their unstated goal, which was to biologically enhance warfighters in ways that made them unstoppable, amoral killing machines.

Gibson turned down another long sterile corridor, his boots clacking and echoing against the tile flooring. He found another secure door, slid his card, and strode into his office.

He shut the door behind himself, leaving the overhead light off, and dropped into the large chair behind his desk. He bellied up to the desk and pulled a computer keyboard closer. He turned on the attached computer, an IBM Model 5150. It was state of the art, with a 4.77 MHz Intel 8088 microprocessor that wouldn't be available to the general public for another year.

The desktop hummed to life and the black screen flickered until the white dot-matrix lettering glowing on the display told Gibson the system was booting properly. The home screen populated and Gibson typed in his credentials.

He was logged in to a local web of computers that allowed him to communicate secret, top secret, or confidential information without putting anything in writing. It was a secure system that allowed for moderately sized text document transmittal. The files were stored magnetically and only accessible to a handful of people with the proper clearance and knowledge of the system's existence.

Gibson rolled his chair closer, sat board straight, and planted his fingers on the home keys. He began typing his note.

EYES ONLY, CLASSIFIED
PROJECT BESERKR USAMRIID TRIALS
Latest testing yielded negative results.
Molecular structure is unstable even when combined with new renditions of VX-99.
Hypothesize the need for active VX-99 culture for synthesis to occur.
Request live test subject.

Gibson hit the enter button and sent his message. He spun in his chair and looked at the framed photograph of his infant son. Even in the dark he could see the snapshot. The major couldn't help but smile looking at the boy nestled in his mother's arms. He had her eyes.

He picked up the frame and ran his thumb across the glass. Gibson's worldview had changed when the boy came into the world. It amplified his belief that modern science would end war, even if it meant making it bloodier in the meantime.

They'd failed miserably with VX-99 the first time. They'd mistakenly deployed it in Vietnam before it was ready. They'd ordered Marines to inject VX-99 into their bloodstreams before engaging the enemy. The thought was the engineered virus would create superpowered

Marines who would quickly, and without remorse, annihilate the Vietcong with minimal American casualties.

Instead, the American Marines tasked with Operation Burn Bright had turned on one another. The experimental drug had made monsters of them in a way command never intended.

Of course, the Marines hadn't known what they were doing. They'd been told the drug would protect them from the effects of Agent Orange. They'd followed orders. They'd injected VX-99. They'd gone crazy. They'd ripped each other to shreds.

Since that failed experiment, Gibson, his superiors, and his team had worked to refine the process. They knew VX-99 was the building block upon which all of their work must be based.

Blended in the right way, the concoction would work as intended. The hitch was that they'd not been able to mix the concoction. Trial after trial failed. They were getting close to losing their funding. Command was on the verge of shutting them down if they didn't make a major breakthrough soon. Gibson believed the only way to breach the next level of research was with a live subject.

He wanted to inject a healthy Marine or soldier with VX-99, observe the transformation, and then add a newer, experimental cocktail to the mix. Then, he believed the molecular issues they experienced in test tubes and petri dishes wouldn't exist. In a live, breathing human, the metabolic changes he hypothesized would happen would be more likely.

Command wasn't so sure. Repeatedly, they'd rejected the notion of subjecting any more healthy humans to VX-99. It was too risky, they'd said.

The computer beeped and Gibson spun around, the photograph still in his hand. He looked at the screen. He'd already received a response to his most recent request.

EYES ONLY, CLASSIFIED
PROJECT BESERKR USAMRIID TRIALS
Request denied.
Project Berserkr is terminated effective 20 April pending new, actionable information.

Gibson read the words on the screen over and over, hoping he'd find something different with each subsequent pass. He didn't.

Request denied. Project Berserkr terminated.

Gibson gently placed the picture frame on the desk next to the computer. He took a deep breath and slammed both fists onto the oak.

"Twelve years," he grumbled through his teeth. "Twelve years of work terminated."

He pushed himself back from his desk and stood. Major Gibson pinched the bridge of his nose and squeezed his eyes shut. He needed to tell his team they were almost out of time.

If they couldn't synthesize the right chemical cocktail in two weeks, they were done. He wouldn't let that happen.

— 5 —

Near Son La, Vietnam
April 17, 1980

Lieutenant Brett was drenched. He'd trudged along the banks of the Da River for more than two miles in search of food. He ran the clawless finger along the edge of his protruding tongue, relishing the friction of the thick callouses on the tip.

The voice in his head was relentless. *I'm hungry.*

For a dozen years, she'd guided his movements. She'd dictated his actions.

Her first words, in the minutes after Brett had injected the VX-99 with a syringe, had been laced with her venom. *Kill them all,* she'd croaked. *Kill them all.*

He'd flinched the first time she'd spoken to him. He'd not realized the voice was coming from inside his head.

You must kill them, she'd repeated. She was growling. *Do it before they kill you.*

Brett had resisted her command at first, unsure of who she was or why she wanted him to kill. Now, with more than a decade together roaming the jungle, river, and farms for fresh, tasty meat, her voice was indistinguishable from his own.

You must find another one, she said as Brett's taloned feet sucked and smacked through the mud at the edge of the river. The morning-long rain had given way to a fine mist that rolled along the bright green fields on either side of the snaking waterway.

I'm hungry. I must feed.

Brett didn't need the voice to remind him of the hollow ache in his gut that lived there every moment of every day, except during those moments he was feeding. That was his lone respite from the pain, from the voice, from the hunger. His joints clicked and popped as he moved.

Do you smell that? said the woman. *It must be close. It's so strong.*

Brett stopped in the muck, his feet sinking to his scabbed, swollen ankles. He tilted his head back and flared his nostrils. He inhaled deeply and exhaled before a series of rapid machine-gun-like sniffs confirmed the scent.

You smell it now. It's close.

Brett pivoted to look over his shoulder. He narrowed his eyes to focus through the mist. His ears pricked, listening for a sound to accompany the odor of his next prey. There was nothing at first, but then he heard it. She heard it.

Straight ahead, she said. *On the bank in front of you. Maybe twenty yards. He's there. He's thin but muscular. Oh, he smells delicious.* Her voice was guttural. *Kill him now.*

Brett resisted the urge to howl, to scream his excitement into the damp, fetid air. Instead he crouched low onto all fours, wrestled his feet from the mud, and leapt. In a single pounce he was within striking distance.

Hurry, cried the voice. *He sees you.*

The fisherman did see him. Brett locked eyes with him, freezing him at his perch along the bank. He held a net in his hands, his knuckles white from the grip and his face pallid with fear, his jaw dropped open.

"Ma Trang," he gasped in his native tongue. "You are real. You are—"

Brett pounced on the fisherman, knocking the man into the shallow coffee-colored water. Together they splashed and thrashed. Claws and teeth and flesh and blood mixed together in the hellacious flurry of a ravenous assault.

The man screamed and gargled the Da River until he couldn't breathe, until what was left of him didn't look human anymore. He was in pieces, some floating and bobbing in the water, some sinking to the bottom, some filling the emptiness in Brett's gut.

Brett was waist deep in the river, his balance shaky against the silt bottom and the current. He held an arm in his hands and tore at the flesh as the voice coaxed him.

Eat it all. Fill yourself. Nourish yourself.

The lieutenant responded with a visceral grunt and obeyed the order. He tore and chewed and swallowed. The watery blood of his victim trailed from the corners of his puckered sucker lips. He'd eaten just an hour earlier. He'd fed four times already that day.

It was never enough.

Every. Last. Bit, she spat. *Don't leave any of it for the fish. They don't need to feed like you do. They don't need the charity.*

Brett finished his meal, gnawing on the bones until he caught splinters in his cheeks. He was full. For the moment.

He crawled from the water, through the mud, and into the high grass that separated the water from the jungle. In the grass, he knuckled himself upright. He threw his head back and howled with delight.

That was good, the voice confirmed. *He was delectable.*

Brett dropped down onto all fours and shook his head back and forth before translating the movement to his shoulders, back, and hips. As he shook, the water sprayed from his body in all directions.

He stood again, much drier than he'd been moments earlier. He opened his lips and flicked his tongue across the swollen puckers, lapping up what was left of the fisherman's blood.

It's time to feed, came the voice. *You need to eat.*

Brett sniffed the air and began his march through the grass. His joints clicked as he moved away from the water and toward the jungle. He was tired. He would eat after he slept.

— 6 —

Hòa Bình, Vietnam
April 17, 1980

A chill ran down Chi Dinh's spine. "Did you hear that?" he asked his sister, Lan. "It was the howl."

Lan's eyes were wide; her lower lip quivered. "Yes," she whispered and ducked behind the high grass next to their home in the riverside village of Hòa Bình.

"It sounds close," he said. "Closer than it has been in a long time."

"Several months," said Lan. "Maybe more."

Chi Dinh knelt down and crab walked to his sister. The thirteen-year-old put his arms around her and held her. He felt the shallow, jagged rise and fall of her lungs as she whimpered.

The twins were orphans. Both of their parents had disappeared within weeks of each other two years earlier. They lived in their modest one-room house with their paternal grandmother. They took care of her as much as she took care of them.

Many of the other villagers, all of whom had missing family, refused to believe the legend of the White Ghost.

At least they wouldn't give it credence aloud. Privately, Chi Dinh believed, they all whispered about the creature that snatched their loved ones and devoured them whole.

"Do you think it is coming here again?" Lan asked. "Do you think he'll find us?"

Chi Dinh didn't lie to his sister. In part, he was truthful because he believed honesty was best. He also knew that if he lied to his twin, she would know.

He exhaled, his mouth close to her ear as he held her, hiding in the grass. "I hope not."

Chi Dinh couldn't remember a time when there wasn't the specter of Ma Trang hanging over their village like the mist that clung to the clusters of mangroves along the river. His entire life he'd lived with the uneasy feeling in the back of his mind that nothing was ever settled.

His parents had warned him, as soon as he was old enough to fish, that he should never leave the village alone. They'd urged him to work only in the middle of the day and only when the sun was shining on his back.

The night, the mist, the distance from others were all the White Ghost needed to find him and take him. Chi Dinh's friends had received the same lessons from their parents.

It didn't matter.

Every month, it seemed, somebody disappeared. Somebody left the village to fish or farm or trade an ox, and he or she never returned. Nobody could ever be certain the White Ghost was to blame. His people believed it to be true.

Chi Dinh's father had worked on one of the collective rice farms not far from the village. The government assigned him the work. Once a month, the collective would take half of its haul to Hanoi. It was a two-day trek each way across difficult terrain. Chi Dinh had always implored his father to stay home. His father, of course, never did.

His father had tried explaining to Chi Dinh the importance of his work. It wasn't only a government directive, it was a holy mission.

"In ancient days," he'd told his son, "we did not grow the rice. We prayed for it. We asked the heavens to give us gold. If our people prayed with enough love, the rice would come from heaven to every house. The rice would appear in large balls."

Chi Dinh had interrupted. "Rice doesn't come in large balls."

His father had raised a finger, a smile creeping across his wise face. "Correct. One day a ball appeared in a woman's house. Her husband ordered her to sweep the house clean to welcome the ball. As she swept, she hit the ball and broke it into countless pieces of rice. Since that day, the heavens have made the people work hard for the rice. I work hard. I cannot abandon my duty."

He'd kissed his twins and his wife goodbye. It had been the last time they'd seen him. A week later, a search party had found human remains and a rice cart belonging to Chi Dinh's father.

Village elders had tried to blame a leftover land mine from the war and scavenging animals. Nobody had believed them. They'd known the White Ghost was responsible.

Weeks later, Chi Dinh's mother had been washing clothes in the river. Chi Dinh and Lan had been playing hide-and-seek in the grass. They'd heard a howl. A scream. Their mother was gone. The elders couldn't blame a land mine, but they refused to publicly agree the

White Ghost had taken her.

Now Chi Dinh and Lan hid in the grass again, but not from each other. They were wary of Ma Trang. Chi Dinh whispered again in his sister's ear.

"We should go into the house," he said. "We will stay low until the grass ends. Then we will run as fast as we can to the door."

He pulled away from his sister and held her face in his hands. He held her frightened gaze. "Do you understand?"

Her eyes searched his for reassurance. "Yes," she said. "Hold my hand."

Chi Dinh nodded and took his sister's hand, the sweat on her palm making it difficult to maintain a tight grip. He laced his fingers between hers and squeezed. He raised his head up above the grass to see their path to the house. It was clear. He turned back to Lan.

"Let's go," he said and tugged her arm. He pulled her with him and they darted toward the house. The blades whipped against their legs and arms as they hustled to the dirt clearing behind their home.

They reached the clearing and Chi Dinh accelerated, almost dragging his sister across the dirt to the cloth door in the long side of the rectangular house. Despite the relatively short distance, he was winded when he pulled back the curtain and shoved his sister inside.

Their grandmother was sitting cross-legged on the dirt floor, praying before the family's ancestral altar. She opened her eyes and stopped her prayer when the children tumbled inside.

"I was praying for your parents," she said. "I heard the howl and I thought of them."

She waved the twins closer to her and they joined her

on the floor. Together, the three of them prayed for the heavens to watch over them.

— 7 —

London, England
April 17, 1980

Jimmy Linh's editor, Gertrude Wombley, peered over the top of her rimless reading glasses. Her deep-set, heavily lidded eyes perpetually cast judgment on whatever it was she set them upon. Gertrude was leaning on her desk. Her lips were pursed like a disapproving librarian.

Gertrude had worked at the *London Morning Reflector* for the better part of three decades. Starting in the early 1950s as a secretary, she'd worked her way into a reporter's position, a copy editor's slot, and then news editor. Under her guidance the *Reflector* had become the city's second most circulated daily newspaper. She was the brains and the heart of the operation, wielding more power than the editor in chief. She'd turned down *that* job several times, telling her bosses she wanted to stay in the trenches.

She'd overseen award-winning coverage of the spate of IRA London bombings between 1974 and 1976. She'd masterminded the Queen's silver jubilee celebration, which Buckingham Palace had commended as "breathtakingly magnificent". And she'd insisted on a six-page spread profiling Barbara Hulanicki's London boutique Biba that put the designer on the map and changed bell-bottom fashion across the globe. She was an ink-stained newspaper ingénue who'd earned unparalleled respect in a profession run by men. Even the paper's publisher, a crusty old duke, would ask, "What does Gertrude think?" before making any critical decisions.

When Linh joined the staff, other reporters had warned him she was always tough and mostly fair. They'd told him she admired hard work and rewarded genius. He sat opposite her, rubbing his sweaty palms on his pants, hoping Gertrude saw him as a combination of both attributes.

She tugged at the collar of her thin, tartan-pattern cardigan. "White Ghost?" They were the first words she'd uttered in the fifteen minutes he'd sat across from her, making his pitch.

Linh loosened the constrictive Windsor knot of his tie and swallowed hard. "Yes. It's the—"

Gertrude raised her hand, her creased palm inches from Linh's face. "I know what it is," she said. "I'm merely considering the cost benefit of a story that affects virtually nobody I know."

"We have a Vietnamese community that—"

"Your community is small," Gertrude said before clasping her hands. Her long, thin fingers intertwined as she leaned toward Linh to emphasize her point. "We have a wide audience. I'm trying to picture our readers' interest in a third-world legend half a world away."

"They won't care that it's half a world away," argued Linh. "It's sensational. You ran a weeklong series on the Loch Ness Monster," said Linh. "I remember you telling the staff the circulation was brilliant."

Gertrude's meticulously drawn eyebrows twitched. "I did say that, didn't I?"

Jimmy Linh sensed an opening. "And if I get a photograph of this White Ghost, could you—"

Gertrude pounced. "A photograph?"

"Of course. What's a story about a ghost if there's no photographic evidence?"

Her right brow arched. "If it's a legend, how would you get a photograph? For all we know, this is nothing more than a Vietnamese version of the Mexican chupacabra."

Linh shrugged. "The photograph will be of something in the jungle," he said. "It'll be blurry. It'll lead readers to speculate. They'll talk about it over tea and biscuits. It could be fantastic."

Gertrude's eyes lifted. She was looking above Jimmy Linh's head into the newsprint ether. She slowly nodded her head. "Okay," she said. "You've got your story. Talk to travel about a flight and a room. Get petty cash from my assistant. Find yourself a fixer. I want you leaving tonight."

"Tonight? I—"

Gertrude narrowed her focused glare on Linh. "Is that a problem?"

Jimmy shook his head. "No."

"You know a fixer?" she asked. "Someone who can guide you to where you need to be, keep you out of trouble, grease palms that need greasing?"

"I know someone."

"Good, then. You have four days to have something in writing. You can overnight the film and your draft. I want something ready for Tuesday's morning paper."

Gertrude shooed Linh from her office. "Close the door behind you," she ordered and spun in her chair to light a cigarette. Linh nodded, almost genuflecting as he shuffled backward from the room. He shut the door and turned around to face the wide-open sweatshop of a newsroom.

A rush of adrenaline coursed through his body as he hurried back to his cubicle. He almost skipped through the maze of desks and waist-high dividers until he reached his seat. He plopped into the leather and ran his finger along the phone extension directory he'd scotch-taped to the wall of his space, adjacent to a photograph of him with his parents. It was a graduation photograph. He'd never paid attention to the fact that nobody was smiling in the black-and-white three-by-five image.

Linh found the travel desk extension and punched the numbers on his phone. He cradled the receiver against his neck. It rang twice.

The woman who answered was pleasant sounding, like a flight attendant reminding passengers to buckle their seat belts. "Travel," she said. "This is Harriett."

"Hello, Harriett. This is Jimmy Linh in the newsroom. I've got a travel request. It's rather urgent."

Harriett giggled. "They all are, Mr. Linh," she said. "How might I help you?"

The words sped from his lips. "I'm going to Vietnam for a story," he said. "It's my first big assignment. It's about Ma Trang, which translates to White Ghost. The legend says the ghost has been traveling up and down this one path for more than a decade and snatching people. So, Gertrude Wombley, the editor, you're acquainted with Gertrude Wombley, she—"

"Mr. Linh," said Harriett. "Mr. Linh."

Linh exhaled. "Yes?"

"I'm so pleased for you, but I needn't know anything but where you need to travel and when," she said. "My apologies."

Linh felt warmth flood his cheeks. "Of course," he stuttered. "I should apologize."

"No worries," she said. "Are you flying to Hanoi or Ho Chi Minh?"

"Hanoi."

"When would you like to depart?"

"As soon as possible, please."

"Return?"

"Five days. No. Wait. Four days. Yes. Four days."

"Four?"

"Yes."

"Will you be overnighting in Hanoi?"

"Yes."

"Driver?"

"Please."

"I'll make a couple of phone calls and be right back with you," she said and hung up.

Linh pressed the switch hook and took a deep breath. He was dreading the next call, but he had no choice.

He pressed the numbers and rocked back and forth in his chair as the phone rang. Once. Twice. Three times. The line clicked and Linh unconsciously held his breath.

"*Chào*," said Linh's father.

"*Chào,*" replied Linh breathlessly. "I need your help."

His father sighed. "I am busy. Can this wait until after work?"

"No," said Linh sheepishly, "it cannot."

"Okay then," said his father. "What is so important you bother me at work?"

"I need a phone number for Uncle Due."

"My brother?"

"Yes."

"Why?"

"I'm going to Hanoi."

"For what?"

"Work."

Linh's father chuckled condescendingly. "Work? You don't work. You tell stories. You don't make anything. You don't—"

"*Father*," interrupted Linh, "I don't have time for a lecture right now. I have to get on a plane. Could I please have his number?"

Linh heard his father put his hand over the phone and call to Linh's mother. In muffled Vietnamese his father spat out his disapproval of his son's career, his life, his trip to Vietnam. He was preaching to the choir. Linh's mother surprised him by suggesting they give Linh the number.

"He's going home regardless," she argued. "Maybe Due can talk sense into him while he's there."

Linh rolled his eyes. "*Ba*," he said loud enough that the reporter in the cubicle across from him shot him a dirty look before turning back to his work.

His father pulled his hand from the phone. "Okay," he said and gave Linh the number. They hung up. Linh sat there with his hand on the receiver, thinking about the conversation.

Not once did his father ask why work was sending him to Vietnam. It was because he didn't care, Linh believed. Unless he was working for the family business, any other employment was unimportant and a waste of time.

Linh moved his hand to dial the long-distance number

his father had given him for his Uncle Due when the phone rang. He picked it up on the first chime.

"*London Morning Reflector*," he said. "This is Jimmy Linh."

It was Harriett from travel. "Mr. Linh, I have your travel arrangements."

"That was quick. Thank you."

"Of course," she said and gave Linh the details for his flight and hotel. "A car will meet you at your arriving gate. He'll have your name written on a placard. Remember it's six hours ahead in Hanoi. Plus it's a thirteen-hour flight, so you'll be landing at approximately two o'clock in the afternoon local time. I've got you booked in Hanoi for four nights. There are no international brand hotels, but I think you'll be pleased nonetheless. The driver will pick you up at the hotel in time for your return flight next week."

Linh was scribbling down the information as quickly as he could transcribe it. Flight numbers, phone numbers, addresses—all of it looked good. He thanked Harriett and hung up before checking his watch. He had five hours until his flight.

He looked at the number his father gave him, and dialed. It was early evening in Hanoi.

A soft, kind voice answered the phone. "*Chào ban*," said Uncle Due.

"*Xin chào Bác*," said Linh, greeting his uncle and asking him how he was. "*Ban khoe không?*"

"Jimmy?"

"Yes, Uncle," Linh said. "I hope you are doing well."

"I am good. Why are you calling? Is your father healthy?" Despite the opposite tones of voice, Due was like his brother in his direct approach. Linh remembered he didn't suffer fools any more than his own father would.

"Yes," said Linh. "Everyone is healthy. I am calling because I am coming to Hanoi tonight."

"Why?"

"For work."

"Your storytelling?"

Linh took a deep breath before responding to the gut punch. "Yes, my storytelling. I was hoping you could meet me and help me with it."

Uncle Due paused before answering. "I could do that," he said. "You arrive tonight?"

"I arrive tomorrow afternoon. I have a car taking me to my hotel. I could have him bring me to you instead and we could get straight to work."

"How much?"

Linh crinkled his nose. "How much what?"

"How much are you going to pay me?"

"We're family," Linh stuttered. "You're my uncle. I just figured—"

"You have to pay me," said Due. "I bet your storytelling boss gave you money."

"I have money," said Linh. "I can pay you."

"One thousand pounds."

"One thousand? That's—"

Due interrupted. "One thousand."

Linh sighed. He was already wondering if calling Due was a mistake. He actually knew the answer. "Okay. One thousand."

Uncle Due agreed. He gave Linh his address and wished him safe travels. Linh was relieved his uncle hadn't asked him about the topic of his reporting. He knew his uncle would think less of him than he already did, if that were possible. He'd also want more money.

Linh reached into his drawer, pulled out a handful of spiral reporter notebooks, some disposable ballpoint pens, and a brand-new Ultra Compact Pearlcorder L400 Micro audio cassette recorder. He'd spent most of his first month's salary on the hi-tech device and hadn't used it for a story yet.

He slid the supplies into his brown leather satchel and pushed himself from his desk. He slung the bag over his shoulder and headed for the exit. He had to pack. He had to get to the airport. He had to focus. Something in the back of his mind told Jimmy Linh his adventure was going to be life changing.

— 8 —

Philadelphia, Pennsylvania
April 18, 1980

Nick Womack's head was pounding. His tongue was thick with the hangover he hadn't quite sweated out the night before. He didn't want to answer the phone. He rolled over, semiconscious, and grabbed the receiver.

"Hello?" he grumbled through the fog. His eyes were shut. He wasn't even sure if he was holding the phone close enough to his mouth or if he was actually holding the phone at all. The cord was wrapped around his arm.

The voice on the other end was gruff. "I'm calling for Nicholas Lincoln Womack."

Womack smacked his tongue against the top of his mouth and winced against the thumping bolts of pain flashing across his forehead and between his eyes. He tried to place the caller but couldn't.

"Is this Nicholas Lincoln Womack?"

Womack blinked his eyes open. Only two people ever used his middle name, and his mother was dead. He elbowed himself onto his back and untangled himself from the phone cord.

"Who is this?" he croaked, still bewildered by the

remaining alcohol in his system.

"Is this Nicholas Lincoln Wo—"

"Yes," said Womack. "Who is this?"

"Please hold," said the voice. "I have General Reed for you."

General Anthony Reed. When Womack's phone rang and there was a job to do, it was always Reed calling. Womack rubbed the sleep from his eyes and listened to a series of clicks before a familiar voice boomed through the earpiece, sending another bolt of pain thundering through his head.

"Nick," said the general, "you got me?"

Womack sat at attention. "Yes, General."

"I know you've been waiting on a call," he said. "Sorry I haven't gotten in touch sooner. I know it's been a couple of months."

"It's been four months, six days, and a few hours," said Womack, clearing the phlegm from his throat. "But who's counting?"

The general laughed. He was a brick wall of a man, compact and powerful with a barrel chest and silver crew-cut hair trimmed high and tight. There were deep creases across his forehead that told the story of a man who fought in battle himself and bore the internal scars of sending other men to die.

He'd commanded Womack a decade earlier, and when Nick decided to get out, it was General Reed who'd provided him a steady stream of off-the-books work and income. The men owed each other more than they could ever admit publicly.

"I've got a job for you," General Reed said. "Five men, including you. That's the usual team, I suspect. You leave tomorrow."

"Where?"

"This isn't a secure line," said the general. "You can find your intel on the steps."

"Got it," said Womack. "I'll call the boys. I'll pick up the package. We'll be en route."

"Good." The line went dead.

Womack threw his legs over the edge of the bed and raked a handful of Tylenol from the bedside table. He downed them without water and fought the headache to his closet. He was dressed in a minute, slid a dark green Eagles ball cap on his head, and was out the door.

He was within walking distance of the drop location, so despite the predawn chill, he marched with purpose west along Spring Garden Street. He stuffed his hands into his jacket pockets and balled them into fists. It couldn't have been more than fifty degrees, which was ridiculous for April.

"I really gotta move south," Womack mumbled as he crossed Kelly Drive and moved north of Eakins Oval. "Key Largo sounds good about now."

A young couple jogged past him. The man was carrying a Walkman cassette player in his right hand as he ran.

Womack shook his head at the yuppie. "Two hundred dollars for a tape player," he said to himself. "Lunacy."

He started humming Stevie Wonder's "Higher Ground" as he approached the Philadelphia Museum of Art. He started up the steps slowly at first, but increased his pace as he moved higher up the incline. He reached the top of the steps and leaned over to catch his breath. He sucked in air and coughed against the rush of cold filling his lungs. His temples throbbed.

Womack winced and stood up straight, planting his

hands on his hips. He cursed himself for succumbing to the urge to run the steps like Sly Stallone. Stupid. Just stupid. He was preoccupied with the pain racking his head and didn't notice the bell-shaped man approach him from the side.

"You like Ansel Adams?"

Womack spun around to face the man, who had a black backpack slung over one shoulder. He smiled at him. "I do. I understand I just missed the exhibit."

"That's too bad," said the man, pulling the pack from his shoulder. "His *100 Photographs* was quite the show."

"So I've heard," Womack said. He actually had heard about the exhibit at the museum. He'd thought about going to see it over Thanksgiving the year before but never got around to it.

The bell-shaped man dropped the pack onto the stone ground and turned to waddle away. Womack watched him navigate the seventy-two steps with his short, pudgy legs. The man didn't look back once he'd begun his descent.

Womack picked up the pack, jostled it onto both shoulders, and walked down the steps opposite the way he'd approached. It took him fifteen minutes to get home and empty the pack's contents onto his dining room table.

On the table was everything he needed for the mission: false passports, cash in various currencies, maps, contacts, and a detailed timeline. They were going to Iran.

The mission, as best Womack could tell, was large scale. It was approved at the highest levels of government and involved the rescue of the fifty-two hostages held inside the United States embassy in Tehran.

His team was one of three off-the-books sets of

operators who would join the military mission to free those held since 4 November 1979. It was called Operation Eagle Claw. There were eight helicopters, six C-130 transports, and an undisclosed number of personnel employed for the extraction.

Womack and his men would use their Canadian passports only if needed. They'd enter Iran aboard an unmarked military aircraft disguised as a cargo plane delivering humanitarian aid. The team would disembark at an airstrip in Mashhad. They'd find needed equipment there and would base in the northwest region of the country before moving to the departure point for the action on 24 April.

His headache dissipated as he looked at the maps and read through the plans that were available at his classification level. There were a lot of gaps. It seemed to Womack he was either out of the loop on a lot of intelligence or it was a bad plan. He couldn't tell which. The seven-figure payday he'd share with his team was more than enough incentive to shove his misgivings to the back of his mind.

Womack moved to the easy chair and started calling his team members one by one. Each of them agreed to meet at the airport within three hours for their trip. Womack checked their names off one by one and made sure the false paperwork contained the appropriate photographs.

He didn't trust many people, but the four men with whom he'd fought and bled were among them. They were better than brothers. He'd picked them.

William Cosgrove was the most experienced. He was a sharpshooter with an equally accurate wit. The team called him Wilco.

Jack Ferguson was the demolition specialist. He was also deadly with a knife. Or a ballpoint pen. He was the most ruthless of the group. They called him Ferg.

Ben Luster was a mountain of a man. His thick, wiry beard and Popeye-sized forearms were all anybody noticed about the operator. Womack called him Shine. Most others called him sir. He knew Shine better than most people knew themselves. Shine knew him too. They'd spent time together in some awful places, places that would have broken lesser men. In some ways it had broken them.

The youngest member of the team was its most enthusiastic and most fearless. Wolf was the nickname for Rob Wolverton. He was in his mid-twenties and had only caught one tour in Vietnam. He liked to say the one tour was all the women could handle. Wilco liked to remind him the women could handle whatever he'd been willing to pay them.

Womack, who didn't have a nickname, stuffed the material back into the pack. He checked his watch. He'd leave for the airport in ninety minutes. He had a lot to do to get ready.

— 9 —

Hòa Bình, Vietnam
April 18, 1980

Lieutenant Trevor Brett still had dreams. They were the worst part of his life post-VX-99. In the past twelve years, he had learned to obey the voice in his head. He'd come to cope with the ubiquitous hunger pangs that clawed at his insides. He'd even rationalized his need to kill. He was an animal. He was carnivorous. He was a survivor.

But when he slept, the jagged edges of his life before VX-99, before the war, poked at his psyche. In his dreams, Lieutenant Trevor Brett was a man again. He was kind. He was generous. He had a future.

As he slept in the dry riverbed on the eastern edge of the Da River, his past haunted him. It revealed what might have been if it weren't for Vietnam, if it weren't for the experimental drug he'd willingly injected into his body.

Brett's dream landed him in the red clay of Athens, Georgia. He was fourteen years old on his newspaper delivery route. He was pedaling his ten-speed royal blue Schwinn bicycle through his neighborhood. He rocked the bike back and forth as he worked his way up a hill.

His heavy newspaper bag was strapped across his back and made it tough to maintain his speed on an incline.

Brett could smell the magnolias blooming, their scent mixing with the sweet honeysuckle that grew in clumps along the fences that separated the wide green lawns of his hometown. He reached into the wide mouth of the bag, fished out a rolled paper in one hand, and flicked it up onto the brick path that led to Stacey Arbuckle's house. Stacey Arbuckle. She was the Bo Derek of eighth grade but without the cornrows.

Brett craned his neck toward the Arbuckles' house as he passed it. He searched the windows for a glimpse of Stacey. He finally turned forward in time to see her headed straight for him on her bike. They were feet from colliding. She screamed to Brett and he swerved to avoid her. Their bikes missed, but Brett wobbled and couldn't regain control. The heavy newspaper bag swung wildly to one side and pulled Brett down with it.

His bike tumbled on top of him as he bounced and skidded on the asphalt. He came to a stop on his back against the raised concrete curb that separated the street from the sidewalk.

Before the pain of his skinned knees and shoulder consumed him, he looked up to see Stacey standing over him. She was straddling her bike and leaning forward on the handlebars.

"Are you okay?" she asked. "Do you need help?"

Brett clenched his jaw against the first wave of stinging pain from his injuries. He felt tears welling in his eyes, but he fought them. He refused to cry in front of Stacey.

"I'm okay," he said through his teeth. "Just some scrapes. Are you okay?"

"I'm fine. You look hurt. You should come inside. I

can clean up your knees for you at least."

Brett started to refuse but thought better of it. Stacey had invited him into her house. Of course he'd take her help.

The door to Stacey's home opened and Trevor Brett limped into another place altogether. His dream had taken him three years down the road. His hands were on Stacey's hips. Her arms were looped around his neck. Her face was buried in his neck as they swayed slowly back and forth on the dance floor.

"I love Dionne Warwick," Stacey whispered as she lifted her lips to his ear, "but this song is so sad."

"What do you mean?" Brett asked.

"She's singing about a lost love," Stacey said. "How she and her former lover pass each other on the street. He left her. She's still hurting, so she doesn't want him to see her."

Brett laughed and slipped one hand from her hip and into his tuxedo pants pocket. "You get that from the song?"

"Trevor"—she ran her hand up the back of his neck, sending a chill down his spine—"of course I do. That's what the lyrics say. It's not a secret."

"I just listen to the rhythm," he said and pulled her closer to his body.

Stacey lifted her head from his neck and looked him in the eyes. "Promise me something, Trevor."

"Anything."

"We'll never be like that."

He leaned in and kissed her forehead. "Like what?"

"After high school, when we're at college," she said, "that we don't drift apart. That we don't break up and then ignore each other. Promise me."

Brett laughed at the absurdity of it. He knew she was the best thing in his life, would be the finest girl he could ever hope to meet. He'd never drift from her. Never.

"I promise," he said.

She smiled, her eyes glistening before she closed them, and she opened her lips to kiss him. It was a long, soft kiss. Stacey was a good kisser. Brett drew his hands to her cheeks and gently held her face until he felt a strong thump on his shoulder.

It was one of the dance monitors. "No public displays of affection, young man."

Brett turned back to look at Stacey, but she wasn't in chiffon anymore. Her eyes weren't inviting. She had stepped back from him. Her arms were folded tightly across her chest.

They weren't in the dance hall either. This was a college campus. Brett recognized it as the University of Georgia. He was standing outside Stacey's dormitory.

"The truth is," she said, "I can't wait for you."

Brett's heart was pounding against his chest. He balled his sweating hands into fists. "I don't understand," he said. "Everything was fine."

He stepped toward her. She stepped back.

"You're going off to war," she said. "You know I don't agree with that. I don't—"

Brett felt his pulse quicken. "I don't have a choice," he said, straining not to explode in a burst of confused anger. "I was drafted, Stacey. I ran out of student deferments. What was I supposed to do?"

"I love you, Trevor," she said, her voice beginning to warble. "But I can't be here while you're there, wondering if you'll come back alive or if…"

"If I'll die?"

Pooling tears in her eyes ran down her cheeks. She took another step away from him.

Brett raised his voice. "You've got to be kidding me."

Stacey's eyes darted from side to side. "Keep your voice down, Trevor."

He took another step toward her as if ready to pounce. "We've been together since we were in middle school," he snarled. "You think that because we're not going steady anymore, you'll stop caring whether I live or die?"

"I-I-I don't know what to think," she stammered. "I just know I can't have my heart broken more than it already is."

Brett exploded. "*Your* heart?" he spat. "*Your* heart? *What* heart? You're heartless, Stacey Arbuckle. It's a good thing I never loved you."

The words spilled from his lips without Brett thinking about what they meant. As soon as he'd said them, he wanted to take them back. He couldn't. His rage wouldn't allow it. It was too late regardless. The damage was done.

Stacey took a step forward. She pointed a shaky finger at Brett. "You're the monster," she snarled. "You're the one who killed us. Not me. You're the monster. You're the killer."

She glared silently at him for a moment, her eyes searing a final image into his memory. Then his first and only love turned away and marched back to her dorm. A pair of friends held the door open for her, and she disappeared from his life forever.

Her voice, that unearthly, guttural voice, didn't spew venom from the Stacey he knew. It was laced with a poisonous vitriol he'd never heard from her before. And it was the last time he heard her voice before he left for basic training and a one-way ticket to the rotting

Southeast Asian jungle.

"You're the monster," she'd said to him. "You're the killer." The words rang in his ears for weeks. They stuck with him. They tortured him. They spoiled every good memory of the woman he'd intended to marry.

She was the one with whom he planned on sharing a life. He'd graduate with his degree in finance and get a job working in banking. They'd buy a house, maybe in Atlanta or Charleston, and they'd settle down. They'd have children and grow old together. Each was the other's better half.

But the war ruined that. The war and the draft destroyed their dreams. They sent him to war. They led her to walk away. They led him to lie and tell her he'd never loved her. They forced her to call him a monster. "A monster," she'd said in that feral-sounding voice he'd hoped to never hear again.

Of course, he did hear it again. It was the voice in his head after he slipped the VX-99 into his veins. It was the woman's voice who first commanded him to kill. It was the voice that ground through his thoughts every waking moment of every day as he hunted and fed. Trevor Brett had promised Stacey Arbuckle he'd never leave her. Instead, she'd never left him.

Get up, she ordered. *Enough sleep. You need to kill,* she said, awaking him from one nightmare and dunking him into another. *It's getting late. You need to find food.*

Brett's eyes snapped open and adjusted quickly to the midday sun beating down on the dirt of the dry bed. He was curled into a fetal position, hidden by the tall grass and trees that lined the snaking dirt path that led from the hills to the river.

For a moment, he could see an afterimage of Stacey in

his mind. Then it was gone.

Brett rolled onto his knuckles and crouched on his heels. He blinked the dream from his head and drew a deep breath into his lungs. The smell of fish and fresh fertilizer filled his nostrils as they flared. He exhaled and filled his lungs again before throwing his head back to wail. The screech was earsplitting and vocalized the pain of a dissatisfied inhuman monster.

Stop crying, said the voice. *Hunt.*

— 10 —

Frederick, Maryland
April 18, 1980

Dr. Justin Starling was standing in the doorway of Major Rick Gibson's office. He rapped on the open door. "Can I turn on the lights?"

Gibson, sitting behind his desk with his back to the door, wheeled around to face Starling. "I don't know," he said, glowering. "Can you?"

Starling ignored the sarcasm and flipped the switch. The overhead fluorescent clinked and flickered to life. It cast a sterile glow across the large sparsely decorated space. "I have something to show you."

Gibson narrowed his eyes against the light. "What?"

"I think we've made some progress. It's not a breakthrough per se, but it's significant."

The major ran his hand across his mouth. He grunted. "What?"

Starling took a step farther into the office, his hands dipped into his lab coat pockets. "I understand we have little time left, Major. Even an incremental advance could be enough to change—"

"You're wrong," blurted Gibson. In one seamless

move, he pushed back the chair and stood, leaning on the desk with his elbows locked. The overhead lights aged him and gave him the appearance of a man who hadn't slept in a week. In truth, he hadn't slept in three days.

He stepped around the desk and quickly closed the distance to Dr. Starling. "This is it. We're out of time. Unless we find a human subject without command's help, we're terminated. It's crystal clear."

Starling pulled his hands from his pockets and used them to advocate for his argument as he spoke. "I respectfully disagree. They didn't terminate us effective immediately. They gave us three days. That means there is a window. Now, if you're not willing to crawl through that opening and—"

Gibson raised his hand to stop the scientist. "Don't patronize me, Starling. You're a hired hand. Nothing more. You don't get how it works. I can't blame you for that. Your naiveté, however, is taxing. Have you figured out how to stabilize the cocktail without a human subj—"

"Close," said Starling. "Very close. I've tried an entirely new approach. I started from square one."

Gibson's frown relaxed. He tugged on the bottom of his uniform to even out the creases. "What did you do?"

"You need to come with me."

Gibson sighed and extended his arm, telling Starling to lead the way. Starling nodded and turned, stuffing his hands back into his pockets as he moved into the corridor outside the office. At each secure entry, he scanned his card and held the door for Gibson. The two of them wound through the maze back to the secure corridor leading to Starling's primary laboratory.

Starling ran his identification card and then entered a numeric password into a keypad that resembled the face of a telephone. There was a hiss and a metallic click that signaled the door was unlocked.

The men entered a locker room and removed their clothes. Both stripped to their undergarments and slipped into hospital scrubs. Starling entered another code and the men stepped into the exterior lab classified as BSL-3.

Biosafety laboratories were designed to isolate potentially dangerous biological agents. They were one of four levels. BSL-1 was the lowest level of biosecurity. BSL-4 was the highest.

Once in the BSL-3 lab, Starling entered a code to lock the door through which they'd entered. There were two technicians working in that lab. Neither of them paid attention to Starling or Gibson as the men stepped past them and through another secure doorway that resembled the type of throughway one would find on a military ship.

Once that door was closed and locked, the men were in the secured suit room. Inside the room, waiting for them, was a pair of lab assistants whose job it was to help researchers don a new type of biohazard suit.

The heat-sealed positive-pressure suits were called demilitarization protective ensembles. The DPEs had been designed only a year earlier for maintenance workers at chemical weapons sites. Gibson, with help from some higher-ups, was able to procure dozens of the single-use suits for his clandestine purposes.

The only catch was that the suits, while state of the art, weighed fifty pounds and required help from dressers. The cumbersome process took at least a half hour. The last step was putting on the three-layered rubber gloves.

Once suited up, the suit's purified air came from long hoses that would connect inside the BSL-4 as soon as the men secured the lab. Until then, and during transition from the BSL-4 back to the changing room, the suits offered a self-contained breathing apparatus with up to ten minutes of breathable air.

The dressers checked the suits' heart monitors before giving the okay. They activated the air, the suits filled and puffed like balloons, and the men moved into the secure shower area.

Starling entered another series of codes and the men moved into the final room, the BSL-4 laboratory, where the bulk of the VX-99 Berserkr work took place. The men connected their hoses and slowly moved to an encased bench on the far side of the twenty-by-twenty lab.

Gibson keyed the radio transceiver in his suit. "This had better be worth it."

Starling offered a weak smile. "You told me I hadn't thought of everything. You were right. I hadn't tried hormones."

"Hormones?"

Starling moved to the bench and slid his gloved hands into work holes in the protective glass wall. "We're trying to take VX-99 and modify it. We still want the genetic changes that make for the perfect soldier, but not to the degree that we activate the primal, reptilian urges you unwittingly unlocked the first time around. All of the good parts about being a monster without the bad."

"I already know this, Starling," said Gibson. "What's new?"

"Our problem was taking some of the mitigating attributes of the cocktail we engineered and finding a way to make them stick to the VX-99 at a cellular level."

"Get to the point."

"Hormones may be the answer," said Starling, his

excitement leaking through the DPE. "Hormones are essentially chemical messengers. They're secreted into either the blood or extracellular fluid. Both travel through the body in search of cells. When they reach those cells, the hormones affect how they function."

Starling turned to the glass and used a remote system to adjust a large microscope on the work desk. Then he stepped back and offered the spot to Gibson, telling him to take a look.

"Each hormone targets a cell that has a receptor for that hormone," Starling explained. "It's like a lock and key, except it's not."

"Explain," said Gibson.

"While hormones target their receptor cells, they can affect neighboring cells too, cells that aren't intended to receive whatever it is that hormone is carrying," said Starling. "Not only that, but there are ways we can impact the cells at a molecular level. They're actually molecules themselves. One is called an agonist. The other is an antagonist."

Gibson moved to look at the microscope's display. "So what am I looking at?"

"You're looking at the modified VX-99 structure adhering to an endocrine cell. It's sticking."

Gibson turned to Starling, his eyes wide. "What does that mean?"

"It means we have a potential delivery system. The VX-99 wouldn't hold our modifications before. That was the problem. We couldn't alter the original compound at its basic level. If we attach it to a hormone and then adhere the cocktail, which I've successfully done, we could theoretically induce the best of VX-99 without suffering the worst of it."

"So the hormones act like glue?"

Starling's face lit up. "Exactly, sir. Exactly."

"What's the catch?"

"We still need a human," Starling admitted. "I can test it in primates or other mammals, but I can't be certain the naturally occurring hormones would act identically in other species. I can hypothesize. I can't be certain."

Gibson frowned, his jaw set. "So we're no better off than we were?"

Starling shifted in his suit and looked down. He shook his head. "I disagree. We have new information to give the decision makers. This is a big deal."

Gibson pointed his gloved finger at Starling's chest. "You yourself said this wasn't a breakthrough, Doctor. How can I sell this to the decision makers if the man who made the discovery doesn't think it's a breakthrough or a game changer?"

Starling leaned in to Gibson's finger and eyed him in a way a civilian shouldn't eye an officer. "It's significant, Major. It's significant enough I dragged you through BSL-4 protocol to show it to you on a microscope. It's not a breakthrough, though. That can only take place in a human. I'm convinced of that. They said you needed actionable information to change their minds. This is actionable."

Gibson stepped back and nodded. A smile crept across his face. He keyed his radio. "Finally," he said. "You're showing some backbone to go with that brain of yours. It's about time."

Two hours later, Gibson sat alone in his office. The only light in the room was the glow of his computer screen. He typed his appeal.

EYES ONLY, CLASSIFIED
PROJECT BESERKR USAMRIID TRIALS
New substantial progress.
Molecular structure is stable when attached to hormone. VX-99 rendition is stable.
Hypothesize the need for active VX-99 culture for synthesis to occur.
Request live test subject repeated.
Request for deadline extension.

Gibson sent the message and waited. If command denied his extension, it was over. He chuckled thinking about it. Under the pressure of a ridiculous seventy-two-hour deadline, his Stanford-educated genius had made a breakthrough. He'd been able to stabilize the combination of the updated VX-99 and the new Berserkr cocktail. They'd worked for years without success. And in less than a day, Starling had figured it out.

That should be worth something to the string-pullers higher up the chain of command, the men to whom Gibson had to answer. They knew VX-99 had value. They'd told him as much, even as they ridiculed what it had done to the team of Marines in Operation Burn Bright in July 1968.

Gibson reached down to his right and unlocked a file drawer underneath his desk. He slid open the drawer and withdrew a thick file folder, which he dropped onto his desk and opened up.

In the dim light of the computer monitor, he again read through the postmortem intelligence report from Burn Bright.

Gibson scanned through the briefing, as he had countless times before. He always hoped to find something he'd never noticed before. He was always disappointed.

The facts hadn't changed in a dozen years.

All thirty-two men inserted into the jungle via a CH-47 Chinook were dead. At least, they believed all of them were dead. It was nearly impossible to determine which body parts belonged to which men. Some of them were unrecognizable as human.

Graphic black-and-white photographs might as well have been full color. The images were splattered with the dark color of blood. It was everywhere. Gibson's stomach lurched, but he pressed forward.

Officially, thirty Marines were listed as KIA. Two of them, Rick Fern from Texas and Trevor Brett from Georgia, were officially MIA and presumed dead. Neither their bodies nor their dog tags had been recovered during the hasty retrieval mission sixteen hours after the insertion.

The retrieval team wasn't there to recover men who'd given their lives for their country. The team was dropped into the jungle to make certain no evidence of the VX-99 remained. They were the ones who snapped the grisly photographs, the proof that VX-99 had worked *too* well.

Almost immediately, Gibson had been tasked with finding an alternative to the DNA-altering concoction. Funding was limitless for seven years. Then the war ended. The immediate need for supersoldiers or monstrous Marines disappeared with the final choppers evacuating Saigon.

Gibson suddenly had to fight for every dollar, for every test tube and petri dish. His work wasn't critical to those in charge. Maybe that would change, he thought, if he could prove to them he'd cracked the code.

His eyes stopped at a photograph of a young Marine. He'd looked at the photograph so many times before. And it struck him every time. The Marine looked like a child. Fresh-faced, hope in his eyes, confidence in his jaw.

Gibson always wondered what those final moments were like for the Marine. What did he feel when he injected VX-99? What raced through his mind as his body changed and his fellow Marines attacked him?

Gibson's computer beeped with an alert. There was a new message from command.

EYES ONLY, CLASSIFIED
PROJECT BESERKR USAMRIID TRIALS
Request for live subject pending.
Extension granted until 1 May.

Gibson sighed. At least it was something. He ran his hand across the photograph of Lieutenant Trevor Brett and closed the file. As was the case with Operation Burn Bright, he resolved this operation needed his personal touch. He had an idea, somewhere he could turn to test the new theory. It was unconventional but necessary.

He picked up the receiver on his phone and dialed an internal extension. The phone rang once before a woman answered.

"This is Major Gibson," he said. "I need a secure line to another installation."

He gave the operator the number and waited for the series of clicks that indicated she'd switched his extension to an encoded line. There was a brief dial tone followed by the rapid analog ticking of the operator inputting the number. The phone on the other end of the line rang three times, and a familiar voice answered.

"Colonel Long," said the man.

"Colonel Long," replied the operator. "I have a secure call for you from USAMRIID."

"Securing line," Colonel Long replied. There was a beep and another series of clicks. "Line secure. Please proceed."

"Thank you," said the operator. A short tone indicated she'd disconnected from the call.

"Rod," said Major Gibson, "it's Rick."

The colonel laughed. "Rick? Good to hear from you. How's the family?"

"Excellent, thank you. Yours?"

"Wonderful," said Colonel Long. "What's it been? A year?"

"Two, I think."

The colonel sighed. "Time flies. I assume you aren't calling to reminisce, given we're on a secure line."

"Roger that, Rod."

"What do you need?"

"You still running Project Judas?"

Colonel Long cleared his throat. "Officially?"

"Unofficially."

"Roger," said the colonel. "From time to time, depending on the circumstances. You need some assistance?"

"Roger."

"Officially?"

"Unofficially," said Gibson. "But I need the paperwork to look clean."

"For you, Rick, not a problem," said the colonel. "How fast do we need to make this happen?"

"Yesterday," said Major Rick Gibson. "I need it yesterday."

— 11 —

Hanoi, Vietnam
April 18, 1980

The humidity was suffocating. Linh stepped from the plane and tore his tie from his neck and folded it neatly before slipping it into his jacket's breast pocket. It was too hot for the jacket, but he was embarrassed by the instantaneous rings of sweat that had soaked through his dress shirt by the time he'd descended the steps from the aircraft.

He fumbled with his brown satchel and walked across the boiling tarmac to the terminal. Linh swore the soles of his shoes were melting on the blistering ground. Instead of the cool relief he expected, Linh was met with a warm gust of air as he entered the loud, crowded space. He looked up at the low ceiling and spotted an old fan with wide, dusty blades slowly spinning and creaking above the din of passengers awaiting loved ones.

The collection of sounds was almost deafening, and Linh wondered if he'd made a mistake. After a long, uncomfortable flight next to a pair of Frenchmen smoking putrid Gauloises cigarettes, he was already exhausted. The humidity, noise, and mix of body odor that washed over him as he shuffled only made it worse.

He tightened his grip on the bag and pinballed his way through the crowd to search for his driver. Harriett had told him to look for a sign with his name on it. Linh tried taking short breaths through his mouth to avoid the suddenly overwhelming stench that hung in the stale indoor air. Once he'd cleared the initial swarm, he found a row of drivers holding up pieces of paper with names scribbled on them. He scanned the row of casually dressed men and found one whose placard read "Jinny Linh". Close enough.

"I'm Jimmy," he said to the leathery-faced chauffeur. "Jimmy Linh."

The man nodded and reached for Linh's satchel. "I'm Huynh."

"I'll keep my bag, thanks," Linh said, "but I do have a suitcase at baggage claim to pick up."

Huynh waved at Linh to follow him. He was chewing on a stalk of sugar cane as he maneuvered expertly through the throngs of travelers moving their way in all directions. Linh struggled to keep pace and caught up with Huynh when he reached the baggage carousel.

"You have one bag?" asked Huynh, the thick stalk hanging from his lip like a cigar.

Linh nodded. "Instead of going to the hotel, could you please take me to my uncle's house? It's not far."

Huynh shrugged. "Your money. We will go where you want."

Twenty minutes later Linh's bag was the last to arrive. Huynh yanked it from the carousel, popped the handle, and rolled it back into the thickly oppressive heat.

Linh sucked in a breath of air and felt it in his lungs. By the time he'd reached Linh's beige 1962 Peugeot 404, he was wiping the sting of sweat from his eyes.

"You look like you're from here," said Huynh, opening the door, "but you're not from here. You sweat too much."

Linh slid into the backseat and set his satchel next to him. "I was born here," he said. "We moved when I was little. I haven't been back in a while."

Huynh chuckled. The deep creases of his crow's feet melted into the corners of his eyes. "No kidding, Jinny."

He shut the rear driver's side door and climbed behind the wheel. He honked the horn and forcefully merged into the slow-moving traffic trying to leave the airport. Huynh grabbed the stalk from his mouth and pointed it back at his passenger, waving it up and down.

"So what do you do, Jinny? Why are you here sweating and stinking so bad?"

Linh leaned over to sniff his armpits. Was it him? He couldn't tell. He caught Huynh's near-toothless grin in the rearview mirror. "I'm a reporter. Can you turn on the air-conditioning?"

"A reporter? Of what? Roll down your window."

"News."

"What news is here in Vietnam, Jinny?"

Linh cranked the window as low as it would open. The warm breeze offered minimal relief. "It's Jimmy."

"Jinny."

Linh rolled his eyes. "I'm working on a story about a village legend," he said. "Maybe you've heard about it."

Huynh rolled the sugar cane around in his mouth. "I hear lots of things. Lots of stories. People sit in your seat there and tell me all about their lives."

"Ma Trang," said Linh. "It's the story of—"

"I know Ma Trang," said Huynh, the smile melting

from his face. "It's not a legend. It's truth."

Linh leaned forward in his seat. "How do you know?"

Huynh stuffed the stalk in his mouth, pressed the clutch, and shifted the four-speed manual into third gear. "Everybody knows. Ma Trang is real."

Linh leaned over and rifled through his satchel. He pulled out the Ultra Compact Pearlcorder L400 Micro audio cassette recorder and pressed record. "Can I ask you a few questions for my story?"

Huynh shrugged. "Your money. We do what you want."

"Tell me everything you know about Ma Trang."

Huynh jerked the wheel and changed lanes to pass a pickup truck. He accelerated and glanced at Linh in the backseat. "I know you don't want to find him."

Linh shifted in his seat, used his arm to wipe sweat from his forehead, and moved the recorder to the seat back to the right of Huynh's shoulder. "Why?"

Huynh looked back at Linh as if he'd said the most idiotic thing he'd ever heard. "Because he'll eat you."

Linh didn't say anything. Despite his inexperience, he'd already learned that silence was uncomfortable. An interview subject always felt compelled to talk to end the silence. If he sat there without speaking, the driver would elaborate. After thirty seconds he did.

"He's American," said Huynh. "He was a fighter during the war. He was killed, but he didn't die."

"How is that possible?"

"That's what makes him Ma Trang," said Huynh. "Did you give me the address?"

Linh reminded Huynh where they were headed. "What makes him Ma Trang, the White Ghost? Why do people think he is a ghost?"

Huynh downshifted and slowed in the worsening traffic. "He's not a man," he said. "His skin is pale. His hands and feet are claws. His teeth are sharp like knives. His mouth is not normal."

"How so?"

Huynh held his fingers like he was plucking a bulb from a socket and held it to his lips. "They are round like a…like a…what do you call the bloodsucker in the river. *Con dĩa?*"

Linh searched his mind for his Vietnamese vocabulary. "A leech?"

Huynh snapped his fingers. "Yes. A leech. His lips are like a leech."

"You said he eats people?"

"Yes."

"How do you know this?"

"I said to you already, everybody knows this. Nobody goes near the Da River from Hòa Bình to Thung Nang. Only villagers and fishermen go there, and they know they could die."

"Have you ever seen the Ma Trang?"

Huynh shook his head. "No," he said. "My cousin's wife has a brother who died. Ma Trang ate him. Five years ago. Five or six years ago. Very sad."

"If I wanted to talk to people who've seen Ma Trang, where would I go? What village?"

"I said to you people who see Ma Trang die. So good luck talking to dead people."

Linh sighed. "Okay," he said, "how about talking to dead people's families? Where would you suggest?"

"Hòa Bình is a big village. You could go there. Xóm Bưa Sen is a tiny village. That is where my cousin's wife's brother lived. You could go there."

Huynh flipped the turn signal, downshifted, and turned right onto a narrow street lined on either side with three-story-high apartment buildings. He narrowly avoided a pair of men on bicycles and eased the Peugeot into an empty spot against the crumbling curb. He slipped the car into park and shut off the engine before turning around to face Linh.

"This is the address you gave me," he said. "You get out here."

"Okay." Linh reached for the door handle.

Huynh stopped him. "You pay me first," he said. "A little extra too for the story."

Linh reached into his satchel and pulled out a wad of the petty cash he'd gotten from work. "How much?"

Huynh glanced at the cash in the mirror. "British money?"

"Yes. Is that all right?"

"Sure. I'll take all of it."

Linh resisted and scowled.

Huynh broke into laughter. "I'm kidding, Jinny the reporter. I'm just joking. Ten pounds is fine."

Linh exhaled nervously, smiled, and handed the driver his money. He shouldered his way out of the backseat and stepped back into the stifling humidity of Hanoi in April.

Huynh delivered the suitcase and offered his hand. "Good luck with your story. I hope you don't see the ghost."

"Thank you," said Linh. He grabbed the suitcase and lugged it onto the sidewalk. His uncle's apartment was on the third floor. He licked beads of sweat from his upper lip.

"Great," he mumbled. "Heat rises."

— 12 —

Thirty thousand feet above Iran
April 19, 1980

Nick Womack moved the headset microphone closer to his lips. "We're getting close, gentlemen," he said, drawing the attention of the four other men on board the ridiculously long and uncomfortable flight from Willow Grove Navy Base in Horsham, Pennsylvania.

"Time for a quick briefing," he said. "I'm going to tell you what little I know."

"About time," grumbled Ferg.

"Yeah," chimed Wolf, the young one of the group. "We've been flying in the dark here."

Wilco laughed. "You're always flying in the dark, Wolf. Doesn't matter how much light we give you."

Wolf stuttered, hitching as he tried to find the right comeback. "Yeah," he said. "Well…"

Wilco punched him in the shoulder. "Proving my point."

Shine cleared his throat and adjusted his mic. His resonant voice boomed into the others' headsets. "All right, fellas," he said. "Enough. Listen to the boss."

Womack nodded at the burly Shine. "So we'll be landing in northeastern Iran. Once we deplane, we'll have transport waiting for us. It's a short trip to a safe house, where we'll gear up."

Wolf interrupted. "The agency has a safe house in Iran?"

"Roger that," said Womack. "My understanding is it's a black site, so there may be another team gathering intel while we're there. Regardless, we stay focused on our task."

Womack pulled a stack of papers from a manila folder tucked underneath his legs. He kept one set for himself and handed the rest to Shine. Shine took one, as did the rest of the team.

Womack held up his packet. "First page is a map. Take a look. We've got distances, key sites, emergency rendezvous locations. Memorize this. Copy?"

The men agreed in unison. They flipped the page, following Womack's lead.

"This page is a schematic of the US embassy in Tehran," he said. "This is a layout of the different floors. The subsequent pages give you electrical, plumbing, ventilation, et cetera."

"So what exactly is the mission?" asked Wolf.

"He'll get to it," said Wilco. "You're more impatient than a virgin on prom night."

"Were you a virgin on prom night?" snapped Wolf.

"Only until your mother—"

"Cut it out," said Womack. "Wilco, c'mon, brother, you're better than that."

Wolf protested. "And I'm not?"

Womack glared at him, answering his question without saying a word. He smirked. "May I continue?"

He didn't wait for a response. He cleared his throat again and keyed the mic.

"The mission is the extraction of fifty-two American citizens held against their will by a violent opposition. We are one of several teams tasked with the operation," explained Womack. "We'll get a sitrep and briefing on the ground. I'm told we'll have a run-through. I don't yet know what our particular task will be. It's likely TBD. Questions?"

"We get a full complement of toys?" asked Wilco. "The usual stuff?"

"Roger that," said Womack. "Full complement. Everybody's personal tastes taken into consideration, as per usual."

Ferg raised his hand. "I got a question about timing. We're in-country today. When is the op?"

"Five, maybe six days," said Womack. "That's all I know. I think this op is coming together quick. It's complex. A lot of politics."

"Which is why we're Canadians on a humanitarian mission," said Ferg.

"Yes."

"That's better than the time we were Swiss filmmakers." Wilco laughed. "Still can't believe we pulled that off."

The men chuckled their agreement. Womack ended the trip down memory lane.

"I'll be straight up honest with you, gentlemen," he said. "This mission has a lot of moving parts. We don't know what all of those parts do. I sense a lack of organization here, a ready-made Charlie Foxtrot. We need to be tip-top and ready for anything. Understood?"

The men nodded. They understood.

"Any other questions?" There were none. "Okay then," Womack said. "Study up."

Womack flipped his microphone away from his mouth and closed his eyes. He'd already studied the map. He'd memorized the various blueprints of the embassy in Tehran. In his mind, he visualized the mission.

He could see his team roping from the chopper onto the embassy's roof, taking out hostiles as needed. They moved silently from the top of the building to the interior, sweeping hallways and rooms until they found the hostages.

He imagined a brief but effective firefight. No friendlies harmed. Collateral damage minimal. Hostiles toasted. A quick extraction from the rooftop. A fast flight out of Iranian airspace.

Quick. Silent. Violent.

The plane rumbled and jostled Womack in his seat. He tightened the shoulder harness and sat up straight against the jump seat. His lower back was sore and his neck ached. Military transports weren't the first-class cabin on Pan Am, that was for sure. It was more like riding Greyhound without air-conditioning, in the back of the bus, next to the bathroom, after stopping for dinner at a Mexican food buffet. Add to the discomfort the lack of alcohol in his system and Womack wanted to strap on a parachute and jump.

But flying sober in a loud, rattling tin can was part of the job. It was free transport. And he was with the only family he knew. Womack opened his eyes, content with the vision, and scanned his men. They were a good team. Wilco and Wolf were children at times. Wolf had a way of lowering the otherwise adult Wilco to his adolescent level. At least they provided some comic relief. There was that.

Ferg was studying the packet, flipping back and forth among the scaled drawings. He was the smart one. Womack had told him long ago he should have his own team. He was a born leader who could easily branch out, work a deal with any of the intelligence agencies who relied on off-the-books operators. There was a glut of work and not enough good men to do it.

But Ferg wasn't interested in that, he'd explained to Womack. He liked following orders. He enjoyed the mission execution but not its planning.

"I don't get it, Jack," Womack had said more than once. "You could be making a mint. Instead you're letting me do it."

"I get paid plenty. Tell me where to go, what to save, and who to kill," he'd said to Womack. "That's what I like. No need to mess with a good thing."

Womack was grateful for Ferg's lack of ambition. It made his job easier to have a right hand at his side.

Shine was studying the map on the front page of the intel packet. His lips were moving as his eyes scanned the page. Womack couldn't make out what he was saying, but he'd often noticed Shine mouth words as he read. When he wasn't studying for a mission, he was devouring dime-store Westerns. It was escapism, pure and simple. Better to be in an imaginary world where the good guy always won than in the real one where he didn't.

Louis L'Amour was his favorite: *To the Far Blue Mountains*, *Bendigo Shafter*. L'Amour probably made his fortune off of Shine. From one story to the next, there was almost always a dog-eared paperback in his hands. He'd sit there, mouthing the words, scratching his beard, flipping the pages. Over the years, he'd started holding the book farther away from his eyes. Nobody had the nerve to suggest he wear glasses.

Wilco had his eyes closed. He was smacking his chewing gum, occasionally blowing and popping bubbles. An expert marksman, Wilco was the least serious of the men. He was the first to make light of a situation, however dark it might be. Womack had considered that Wilco was certifiably crazy. He didn't take anything seriously, it seemed, except for drilling bullets into the enemy from any and all distances. Womack had never seen a shot like Wilco. It was worth the headache that was William Cosgrove to have his valuable deadly aim at his disposal.

Wolf, on the other hand, was an idiot. His youth was no excuse, Womack thought. Wolf was stupid. He asked too many questions. He was foulmouthed and sex addicted.

Womack had considered replacing him repeatedly, but just when he was convinced Wolf was a liability, the kid would redeem himself. He'd single-handedly saved Wilco and Ferg during an ambush in Damascus. Twice, he'd ignored heavy incoming fire to extract targets and salvage missions.

Wilco had joked that Wolf was so fearless because he was stupid and didn't know better. He was probably right. Regardless, Womack could never bring himself to kick the youngster to the curb no matter how lacking his intellect might be.

He had a good team. They complemented each other. Where one was weak, another was strong. No matter the mission, they moved as a well-oiled machine. As the plane lurched and dipped for its descent, he was confident this mission would be no different. Check that. He was mostly confident. As the plane rattled against another bout of turbulence, Womack chewed the inside of his cheek.

He couldn't rid his mind of the nagging suspicion Operation Eagle Claw's architects were missing something. Something was off.

The plane dipped lower and Womack felt the landing gear deploy. They were getting close. Too late to do anything about his misgivings. They were in Iran. They had a job to do. They had people to save and a nation to protect.

— 13 —

Da River, Vietnam
April 19, 1980

Trevor Brett was flat on his stomach on the riverbank. His face was inches from the surface as he drew long slurps from the water. The ripples in the cloudy water dissipated and revealed Brett's grotesque reflection. He recognized the monster staring back at him as himself, and though he tried as hard as he could, he wasn't able to remember what he'd looked like before VX-99.

He knew he didn't have the pouty, sucker lips. His hair was shorter. His skin had more color. His nose was thinner. That he knew. In the back of his mind he knew that.

Brett drew back his lips, revealing his angular, razor-sharp teeth where they met his inflamed gums. He drew a clawed finger to his mouth and touched the teeth, pressing the digit against one of the fangs. He pushed downward as hard as he could until he felt the tooth puncture the skin, poking through and drawing blood. The blood pooled in his mouth, finding its way to his tongue, and he reflexively puckered. His lips closed tightly around the clawless finger and passionately sucked the wound.

The voice purred. *Mmmmmm,* she said. *Don't stop.*

Brett jammed the finger deeper into his mouth, his piranha teeth scraping the skin as he sucked and swallowed. He pushed his way back from the water and knelt in the mud.

That's so good, moaned the voice. *The taste of your own blood.*

He might have bitten off his finger had something else not caught his attention. Someone was close. A human. A child maybe. Brett yanked his finger from his mouth, to the disapproval of the voice in his head, and scanned the riverbank. He rolled his tongue around in his mouth, savoring the last remnants of salty, coppery-tasting blood. His eyes darted back and forth. Back and forth.

He'd caught the odor on a dank breeze. It was gone. Brett jammed his fists into the mud and gnashed his teeth. As quickly as he'd caught a whiff, the scent was gone.

Brett had evolved into an instinctive machine. His emotions were basic and raw. Elevated hormone levels coursed through his body. His sense of smell, sight, hearing, and touch were heightened. His world was as it had been for a dozen years. There were moments of muscle recall when Brett experienced a phantom burning sensation that mimicked the torturous, stinging heat that sparked through his body as the VX-99 swam through his body. His head would flash with pain. His heart would race. Then, much like the scent that had appeared and evaporated into nothing, the pain and heat and jolts of jarring electricity would vanish.

He'd lived a short cycle of hunting, killing, eating, and

sleeping since that first day in 1968, that day his platoon had eviscerated itself. The ones who died that day were the lucky ones. Their agony was short lived. It didn't linger.

Even had it not been for Operation Burn Bright and the ill-fated VX-99 mission, 1968 was a pivotal year for the Marines in Vietnam. Six weeks after Brett became what would be known as the White Ghost, Typhoon Bess put them on the defensive. In Da Nang, winds and rain caused mudslides, collapsed bunkers and trenches, and grounded air support.

In the wake of the storm, the Marines realigned their troops and resumed their aggressive offensive. The enemy, however, inflicted heavy casualties. In one September battle, the North Vietnamese killed forty-two Marines of Second Battalion, Seventh Marines, Company F. Later that month, Companies G and H lost another nineteen Marines. Seventy-three more were wounded.

No doubt, they could have used more men like First Lieutenant Trevor Brett, who'd first set his boots in Vietnam months earlier. As a United States Marine, Trevor Brett had been a natural.

That was what his drill instructor had told superiors at Parris Island during basic training. He'd said Brett had shown exceptional capabilities in a multitude of disciplines. He had been one of forty-two thousand six hundred and thirty-three men drafted into the Marine Corps during the Vietnam War. He'd been one of their best. So instead of sending him to the jungle as a noncommissioned jarhead, the Marines had sent him to a fast-tracked officer training program. They'd needed officers. They'd wanted to forge leaders from the best possible crop of recruits. Too many of them had already come home wounded or dead.

The Marines had found that officer, that leader, in Trevor Brett.

He'd never liked the idea of serving in the military, he didn't enjoy the prospect of killing people, and he wasn't a fan of spending more than a year in Southeast Asia. It wasn't any of those things that made him good at his involuntary job.

Instead, it was his focus that made him good. It was his ability to drown out the distractions, to follow orders, and carry out missions that made him good. He was physically superior to many of the other recruits. Tall and lean, he'd run cross-country and track in high school and at Georgia Tech in Atlanta.

He'd wished he could have run to Canada when Selective Service drew his number. He'd wished he could have run after Stacey Arbuckle when she'd unceremoniously dumped him and left the sound of her disgust ringing in his ears. Instead, he'd run around his neighborhood one final time, making sure to avoid the Arbuckle house, hugged and kissed his parents goodbye, and boarded a bus for Parris Island.

Maybe it was Stacey's brutal dismissal that allowed him to pour everything into his training. Maybe it was intelligence and guile that allowed him to excel. Maybe it was patriotism and a youthful, naïve belief he could make a difference.

He wasn't the best shot among his group of draftees. He was a marksman but not an expert. Where he rose above so many of the others was the speed with which he could disassemble and reassemble his weapon. He was twice as fast as the next fastest man with the M14.

Brett resisted, at first, the idea of becoming an officer.

The commission was nice, even if it was paltry compared to what young bankers were making, but the money didn't really matter. He wasn't certain he wanted the responsibility of other men's lives.

He could take point or have the back of the man next to him. It wasn't a question of bravery or the willingness to self-sacrifice. It was knowing that a platoon of men would rely on his judgment and act on his orders. It was a lot different from being the captain of the track team. Nobody died running around an oval. Nobody lost a limb or an eye from running through an oak-lined course.

Still, he'd accepted the offer, and six months later, he was in Vietnam. The muck, the jungle rot, and the sudden torrential rains were too much for him. He hated every minute of it. Add to that the constant threat of death from the enemy or friendly fire or the rumors about Agent Orange and Brett was convinced he was living in Hell.

The first time he killed an enemy, he'd vomited afterward. It was an NVA sapper who'd used a bamboo reed as a snorkel. The enemy had swum through heavy debris in the Vinh Dien River and had placed an explosive charge underneath a bridge.

Brett's platoon was guarding the bridge. It was critical for troop and supply movement. He was the first to spot the sapper. He took aim and fired. His shots peppered the river from his spot guarding the bridge and traced a path until they tacked the enemy in the face. He convulsed at the surface before partially sinking into the rain-swollen river.

A Texan named Fern noticed the charge was set and managed to clear the bridge before it exploded and collapsed into the water below. He had his arm on Brett's back as the doubled-over lieutenant wiped the remnants of his regurgitated C ration from his face.

"Pretty good one-two punch," Fern said, a wide grin spread across his face.

Brett cleared his throat and spat onto the ground before swigging a pull from his canteen. He swished it around in his mouth and spit it out. "How's that?"

Fern wiggled his finger back and forth, pointing at himself and then Brett. "You and me," he said. "A good one-two punch. You saw the sapper. I saw the charge."

First Lieutenant Brett shrugged. "We didn't save the bridge," he said. "That was our job."

"Yeah." Fern frowned. "Well, we ain't dead. I'll take that. They want to punish us or something for staying alive, have at it."

That was exactly what Brett thought was going to happen five days later when his commanding officer summoned him to an encampment fifteen kilometers away. Despite another two successful missions since the bridge deployment, he was certain they'd lose their R&R or they'd draw worse duty than was already assigned. Instead, he was surprised at the smile greeting him when he dipped into the tent at a forward operating base in a clearing atop a strategic hill not far from the border.

"Permission to enter, sir," said Brett.

"C'mon in," said the full bird colonel leaning on a map table at the back of the tent. "Join me back here, Lieutenant. I want to show you something."

Brett apprehensively moved to the center of the tent. He stood at attention and Brett snapped a salute. His eyes were straight ahead, but he could see another man standing behind the table. He was Army.

"At ease, Lieutenant," said the colonel. "Brett, this is

Major Rick Gibson. He works with all branches of the service as part of our medical research teams. He's only here for a couple of days."

Brett glanced over at Major Gibson. There was something off about him. The man wouldn't look him in the eyes. He didn't like it.

"So this isn't about the bridge?"

The colonel narrowed his eyes. His brow furrowed. "The bridge? No, son. It's not about the bridge. You did what you could there, is my understanding."

"Yes, Colonel."

"This is about Operation Burn Bright," said the colonel. "It's a unique and important opportunity for you and your men."

"Burn Bright is a first-of-its-kind inoculation," said Gibson. He pulled a vial from his pocket and held it up. "It's cutting-edge science."

Brett's eyes danced between the two men. "What kind of science?"

"It's biochemistry," said Gibson. "We believe it lessens or totally eliminates the risks associated with exposure to Agent Orange."

"I thought the risks were rumors," said Brett. "I thought they—"

The colonel held up his hand. "Let the major finish."

Brett nodded silently and clenched his jaw.

"There is a risk," said Gibson. "That much is true. We can't define exactly what that risk might be. We'd rather not get that far. Instead, we'd like to mitigate them entirely. To do that, we need to study the pharmacological effects of Burn Bright in the field."

Brett looked at the colonel and then back at Major Gibson. "On us."

"Yes."

"Me and my men."

"Yes."

"How many of us?"

"All of you."

Brett turned his attention squarely to his colonel. "Is this a request, sir, or an order?"

The colonel cleared his throat. "It's an order."

Before Brett could respond, the major interjected, "We'd like your cooperation with this critical assignment. If you'd please step closer to the map, we'll show you where we'll conduct the trial."

"Here's the good part," said the colonel. "You complete this assignment and we send you home early."

Brett's eyes widened. "Early? How early?"

"Six months." The colonel motioned for Brett to step to the table and then ran his hands across the map as if he were straightening a bedsheet. On the map was a large red circle. It marked a village not far from his team's current location.

"You'll insert here," pointed out the colonel. "You'll fast-rope out of the Chinook to the LZ. We're not planning on putting down there. There is a lot of enemy activity."

Brett tapped the map. "Is that rice paddy?"

"Yes," said the colonel. "We'll drop you at the edge of it. It's maybe knee or waist deep. You'll have to move through it. Once you've cleared it, there's a ridgeline here." The colonel ran his finger back and forth along the topographical representation of their target. "Just beyond the ridge is the village."

"What will we find there?"

"We've hit it a couple of times," said the colonel. "So

a lot of the green cover is gone. Still, recon aircraft images are showing there's a nice little gathering there. We expect you'll see some resistance."

"Is there a strategic component to this village?" asked Brett. "It seems like it's not really contiguous to—"

"The VX-99 is the strategic component, Lieutenant," answered Major Gibson.

"V what?"

Gibson held up the vial, presumably for effect. "VX-99. It's what you'll be injecting into your bloodstream before moving into the village. This is an area that likely has lingering Agent Orange particulates. We think it's a good place for our testing."

"So we're injecting it? It's not a pill or something?"

"Correct," said Gibson. "All thirty-two men in your platoon will receive syringes. Buddy up into sixteen teams. One man stands watch while the other breaks the plastic tip and jams the needle into a vein. The wrist or forearm is preferable. Once you've punctured a vein, depress the plunger until all of the VX-99 is in your system. Then switch."

"When do we do this?"

"Tomorrow. Ten July."

"What kind of side effects are there?"

Gibson shook his head and shrugged. "Minimal."

"What are they?"

"Headache. Maybe some nausea. A little burning sensation at the injection site. Nothing more than that."

"Then what?"

"You provide additional intelligence on that village and take out what resistance you meet."

"No, Colonel," said Brett. "What do you do to us afterward?"

"Simple," answered Gibson. "We take blood samples. We thank you with cold beer and hot food. You move on. We punch your ticket back to the States one hundred and eighty days earlier than it was when you walked into this tent."

"All right then," said Brett. He stood at attention and saluted. "All right then, I'll tell my men. Anything else, sir?"

"That's all, Lieutenant."

Brett snapped to attention and saluted. The colonel returned the salute. "Dismissed."

More than forty-three hundred and eighty days later, Rick Gibson still hadn't kept his promise to Trevor Brett. Brett was still in the jungle. More than that, he'd become part of it. He was one of its dangers.

— 14 —

Near Hòa Bình, Vietnam
April 20, 1980

Jimmy Linh was listening to his uncle, but his attention was on the swollen, raging Da River. It ran parallel, north and south, to TL 317, the highway that took them into Hòa Bình. They'd left a little more than two hours earlier. The ride was rough. The river and the men and women working alongside it, even in a monsoonal rain that had dogged much of their trip from Hanoi, were a nice distraction from the road and Uncle Due's lecture.

Due was driving with one hand on the wheel. The other was wagging a finger nonstop at Linh. No doubt, Linh's father had gotten to him and given him a laundry list of talking points. Linh noticed the finger was moving with the same metronome-like precision of the windshield wipers that swung back and forth with a comforting squeak.

"You are too smart to tell stories," said Due. "You have a business mind. You're like your father and your mother. You should be running a business. You should be making good money and thinking of a future. You can't be..."

Linh tuned him out. He'd heard the argument before. He could almost recite it. It didn't matter except that it did. Linh wanted his family's approval; he wanted its support. Enough was enough.

He stopped his uncle's soliloquy and drew a raised brow of offense. "Uncle," he barked, "I hear you. It changes nothing. I am here to tell stories. You either help me and stop berating me with my father's words, or you pull over, stop, and let me out."

Due's already pouty lips turned down at the corners. His eyes widened, and without taking his eyes from the road, he shifted into neutral and slammed on the brakes. The car fishtailed and came to a squealing stop.

Linh was looking at his uncle, not at the road ahead. "Seriously? You're just going to leave me here? I—"

Due glanced at his nephew and pointed to the road. "Look."

Linh followed his uncle's finger and looked at the road ahead. It disappeared into a slop of mud and debris. There was no driving around it.

"I guess you're getting out here whether I stop talking or not," said Due. "You need to pay me now."

"Pay you?"

"Pay me," said Due. "One thousand."

Linh rolled his eyes and pulled the cash from an envelope in his satchel. He handed it to Due, who counted every single bill. He stuffed it in the glove box at Linh's knees and locked it.

Linh craned his neck to look beyond the road. "There must be a path around it. We can't be stuck here, can we?"

Due shrugged. "We are."

Linh shouldered open the passenger's side door and

stepped out of the car. He was immediately slapped with thick, cold raindrops that drenched his head and shoulders by the time he'd rounded the hood of the car. He planted his hands on his hips. The mud sloped into a mound that must have been at least three or four feet thick. More of it oozed with purpose from the broken retention wall to the right of the roadway. It was an impassable mess.

Linh ran his fingers through his hair and shook the water from his fingers. He looked back at his uncle through the windshield wipers, but the curtain of rain made it difficult for him to see him. He trudged back to the driver's side and motioned for Due to roll down his window.

"What?" Due asked through a thin crack.

"What do we do?"

Due laughed. "We? Funny. *You* walk."

Linh knuckled water from his eyes. "You're not coming with me? You're going to let me walk the remaining mile alone?"

Due rolled his eyes before rolling up the window. He turned off the ignition, reached into the backseat, and emerged from his car with an umbrella. He popped it open and shut the car door. He mumbled something about his nephew "the storyteller" being a baby and marched ahead, trying to avoid the deepest part of the mud pit.

Somewhat taken aback at his uncle's change of heart and derision, Linh stood at the car, watching Due pick his way past the roadblock. He wiped his face with his hands and picked his soaked shirt from his chest.

Due stopped and turned. "You coming?"

Linh nodded and bounced forward, toward the muck.

He held tight to his leather satchel, trying to keep its flap tightly wrapped across the top. "I'm adjusting my bag. I can't get it too wet."

Linh sighed and stepped off the road, trying to maintain his balance as the mud sucked at his feet. He slipped but caught himself with his hand. Still he slid a couple of feet sideways down an embankment. A rotting tree stump caught the side of his foot, preventing him from tumbling down into the underbrush that separated the road from the riverbank. He steadied himself and looked up to find his uncle laughing at him. The pounding rain and rush of the river below drowned out his uncle's taunts. It was just as well.

Linh clawed his way back to the road on the other side of the mudslide and found solid ground on the road. Once he was back on the pavement, Linh picked up his pace and jogged to catch his uncle.

"Thanks for waiting for me," said Linh.

Due shook his head. "You want me to come," he said, holding the umbrella low over his head. "Then you don't want me to go too fast. I don't understand."

Linh opened his mouth to respond but thought better of it. His uncle, however acerbic, was here with him. He'd offered his home, he'd gotten up early to drive to the jungle, and now he was slogging through a deluge to keep him company. Uncle Due didn't even know why they were going to Hòa Bình. He'd not asked and Linh hadn't volunteered it.

"Do you know why we're here?" he asked his uncle. "Why we're doing this?"

Due stepped around a large puddle. "So you can tell a story."

"You haven't asked what story I'm telling."

"Does it matter?"

"It's about a legend."

"An untrue story, then."

"Not necessarily," said Linh, walking ahead of his uncle so he could see the man's reaction to what he'd say next. "I'm writing a story about Ma Trang."

Behind the curtain of water dripping from the umbrella, Due froze. His eyes opened wide. His jaw dropped before he pressed his lips tightly together. He stared at his nephew without responding.

Linh immediately regretted having said anything. He swallowed hard. "What?"

"Ma Trang is not a legend, nephew," said Due. "It is real. The American White Ghost haunts this land. He seeks revenge on our people."

"You know about Ma Trang?"

"Everyone knows about Ma Trang."

Linh shrugged. "Well," he said, "that's my story. I'm here to talk to people who know about the White Ghost, and get a picture of it."

Due narrowed his eyes and tilted his head like a dog before erupting with laughter. He threw his head back, seemingly for comic effect; his shoulders shook back and forth.

Linh clenched his jaw. His uncle was making fun of him again. Linh turned, wiped the rain from his eyes, and walked away from the laughter. It was better not to talk about anything with Uncle Due. The man was worse than his father. He was judgmental and condescending.

As Due finished his fit, Linh looked toward the river. The rain was beginning to lessen. It wasn't much more than a thick drizzle. The river was angry. It was moving fast. A pair of fishermen stood on its banks, nets on the shore. The men were talking to each other with their hands, evidently frustrated by their inability to ply their trade.

Linh stopped and nodded toward the men. "I'm going to talk to them."

"I'm going to stay here," Due said.

Linh moved toward the embankment. "Suit yourself."

He carefully worked his way down the steep gradient, stepping on rocks to help his footing. He reached the bottom and walked cautiously to the pair of fishermen. He waved and smiled, hoping his cheer would put them at ease. He spoke to them in Vietnamese, using the pre-war dialect they likely spoke.

"Hello," he said. "My name is Jimmy Linh. I am from the United Kingdom."

The fishermen glanced at one another. Both men were older, their faces creased like the dry riverbeds that branched outward from either side of the Da. Their eyes were narrowed by the sun, their leathery necks unprotected by their wide-brimmed hats and traditional rounded-collar shirts.

One man was taller and thinner than the other. He was holding a net with both hands. "What do you want, Jimmy Linh?"

Linh measured both men as best he could. They'd know if he was lying or beating around the bush. There was no doubt. It was best to be straight and honest up front.

"I'd like to ask you about Ma Trang."

Both men stepped back, closer to the water. The one holding the net shook his head. "Why?"

Linh reached into his wet leather bag and pulled from it the microcassette recorder. He held it up to the men and pressed the record button. "I'm a reporter for a newspaper. I'm writing about Ma Trang."

The shorter man pointed at Linh. His fingers were curled toward his palms, arthritis having disfigured them. "It's not safe, you know," he said. "We don't say the name. It's bad luck. What is that?"

"It's a tape recorder. Why is it bad luck?"

The man's eyes widened with genuine fear. "Because he hears it," he said, his fingers trembling. "He thinks you're calling him, offering a sacrifice. Is that taking my picture?"

Linh looked at the device in his hand. "No. It's recording your voice." He took a step toward the men. "Could we talk about him without using the name?"

The taller one shrugged. "You've already said it. You should go."

Linh held his hands up in surrender. "Okay," he said. "I'll go. One question, please. Who is he?"

"An American," said the taller one. "He fought in the war. He died a horrible death. Now his ghost comes to haunt us. He's not himself anymore."

"What do you mean?"

The shorter one drew his hands to his mouth. "His lips and his teeth," he said. "They're not human. His lips are round. His teeth are fangs."

"And he is very fast," said the taller one. "He runs like a panther. His joints make a noise when he runs."

The shorter one made clicking and popping noises with his mouth. "Like that," he said. "It's like the bones don't fit the joints."

"And his hands are like claws," the taller one added.

Linh stood quietly, soaking in the information. He'd asked one question. They were answering twenty.

The shorter one nudged his friend. "I saw him once," he said. "He was eating something. I could hear the slurping sounds. His skin was white like rice. He was a…"

Linh finished the thought. "White ghost."

The men nodded in unison. The short one waved his hands at the embankment behind Linh. "You said it again. You need to go. Now."

Linh thanked the men and deliberately climbed back up the embankment. The rain had stopped; the mist was subsiding. He reached the top and wiped his muddy hands on his pants.

Uncle Due was leaning on the collapsed umbrella. "Any luck?"

"Yes," said Linh. He nodded toward Hòa Bình. "But they told me to leave."

"Why?"

Linh started walking. He stuffed his hands into his pockets, trying to adjust the damp clothing on his legs. "I said the name Ma Trang. They told me it was bad luck and that saying the name summons the ghost."

Due opened his mouth to respond, but before he could say anything, a loud shriek pierced the air. It was primal and chill-inducing. The call echoed, and before the last of the reverberations had ended, another scream ripped through the dank, humid air. The second was more terrifying than the first.

It was impossible to know from where the cry came. It could have come from a mile away or twenty meters. Linh's stomach turned. An involuntary shudder rippled through his body.

"What was that?" asked Linh, already suspecting the answer was one that would both excite and frighten him.

Uncle Due looked his nephew in the eyes. "You mean

who was that?" he said. "And I think you know the answer."

— 15 —

Black Site Installation NSS-1018, Northeastern Iran
April 20, 1980

Nick Womack was never much for sand. He didn't like beaches unless they were topless, he wouldn't play games with hourglasses for timers, and he sure as night didn't like the Middle East. It wasn't as bad as the jungle, but it was close.

"It's freakin' everywhere," he complained. "I got sand in cracks I didn't know I had."

"I'd rather the desert than the jungle," said Wolf. "I've seen enough of Charlie and boot rot for a lifetime. Hit me."

Ferg's expression squeezed into a tight ball of disapproval. "You're at nineteen," he said. "You really want another card?"

"Hit the man," said Wilco. "Idiot wants to bust. Let him bust."

Fern shrugged and dealt the next card faceup. It was a two of spades. "Mother—"

"Ha!" said Wolf. "I'll take being an idiot who wins over a righteous SOB who loses any day."

Wolf reached to the middle of the large round table

and wrapped his hands around the pot. Wilco grabbed his wrists.

"How'd you know?" he asked Wolf. "You cheating? That's the sixth hand in a row you've won."

Wolf wiggled free of Wilco's grasp. "I ain't a cheat," he said. "I just know what's coming. That's all. I know what's left in the deck. We're almost finished with the deck, and a two hadn't come up yet. It was bound to happen."

Wilco grunted and flopped back against his seat. "Figures."

Shine, who'd been quiet for the two hours they'd been playing cards, rocked his neck back and forth. It cracked repeatedly. "I'd rather play Texas Hold 'Em," he said. "This game is crap."

Womack laughed. "I'd rather be working," he said. "I'm sick of playing cards and eating lamb and hummus."

Wolf nodded toward the small kitchen adjacent to the table. "There's a cabinet full of C rations." He chuckled. "I bet you'd get your first pick. Hams and muthas?"

Womack glared at Wolf, pushed himself from the table, and stood. They'd been at the black site for a day. It was a small nondescript farmhouse a good click or two from anything else. There were two other buildings on the compound. They housed the bunks. The main house, where they were playing cards, was the only one with working electricity and fans. The only bathroom was an outhouse next to the goat pen.

Despite pre-arrival information indicating another team, or two, would be housed at the site, nobody else was there except for a single military liaison and an Iranian translator. Womack figured the translator was more likely an agency asset.

Their initial briefing was vague and uninformative. The liaison had essentially told them to sit tight, get some rest, and await further instructions. He'd left with the translator about an hour later and hadn't returned.

"I'm not liking this," said Womack, pacing back and forth. "Something's not right. Either the job ain't the job, or they've got bigger problems. When's the last time we sat around playing cards?"

Ferg got up from the table and walked into the kitchen. He pulled a pitcher of water from the small refrigerator. "This been treated?" he asked, holding up the pitcher.

"Supposedly," said Wolf. "It's your deal, Shine."

Ferg poured himself a glass of water and walked over toward Womack. "Here's the thing, boss," he said. "You don't like sitting around. You don't like lack of intel. Most of all, you hate the desert. I think that's your problem."

"I agree," said Wolf.

"Make that three," said Wilco. "You'd rather be covered in cheese and dunked into a rat den than be in the desert."

Shine shuffled the cards and nodded. "True."

Womack smirked. "All right," he acknowledged. "I'll give you that. When I die and go to Hell, there'll be sand instead of fire. It's more than that."

Ferg motioned to Womack with his glass. "Go on."

"I think this op is FUBAR," he said. "I think they know it. They just haven't admitted it yet. My gut's telling me we're gonna spend a week here and then make the round trip without action."

"We still get paid, though," said Wolf. "So who cares?"

Silence.

Wolf's voice cracked. "We still get paid, right?"

Womack sighed. "Yes," he said. "We get paid."

Wolf exhaled with relief. "Good. I was gonna say…"

Womack rolled his eyes and marched to the front door of the house. He unlatched the crude mechanism holding the door shut and pushed himself outside into the bright light of the afternoon. As much as he hated the sand, he couldn't stand another minute of sitting inside without something to do. Plus, he'd already lost all of his cash to Wolf.

His boots squeaked against the soft white sand as he marched toward the goat pen. There were eight of them working a small patch of weeds. The pen was on a partially irrigated piece of land. There was dirt, some grass, and a couple of struggling olive trees. A large galvanized bucket was positioned underneath a rusty spigot.

Womack watched the goats for a few minutes. A couple of them had their faces buried in the tub, drinking what was left of the scummy water. Another goat was trying, unsuccessfully, to find shade underneath the spindly olive branches. One goat stood in a corner of the pen, bleating into the desert. It was a pained cry, almost like a child's scream. Womack winced at the sound. Images flashed in his mind. They were images he tried to bury, but couldn't. The goat bleated again and Womack squeezed his eyes closed. He inhaled and took a deep breath. The wailing animal reminded him of prisoners he'd seen in Vietnam and elsewhere. They were the weak ones. They'd crack instantly and confine themselves to a corner of their cell. They'd curl into a fetal position or sit flat on their heels, rocking back and forth as they mumbled incoherently. They'd eat and drink things not meant to be eaten or drunk. They knew their lives weren't their own anymore. He'd seen them do terrible things to themselves to regain a sense of emotional control.

People, he'd come to realize, were animals at their core. No matter how civilized society became at its surface, underneath the veneer Womack believed there to be primordial ooze. Stripped of their finery and haircuts and manicures, people were elemental flesh bags prone to doing bad things to one another. Under stress, when pushed against a wall, in desperation they would revert to the basest instincts of self-preservation. He'd seen it in war. He'd seen it at home. Humans were no different from goats in that respect. Womack's thoughts drifted back to the present as one of the smaller goats clopped over to him, its devilish eyes blinking.

The goat shook its head and tried speaking to Womack. "Meh-eh-eh. Meh-eh-eh."

Womack reciprocated with his own nasally interpretation. "Meh-eh-eh-eh-eh."

The other goats seemed uninterested in the visitor, but the one animal, the tiniest of all of them, was intrigued. Womack smiled at the animal, leaned down, and ripped a handful of weeds from the dirt. He balled his hand into a fist and reached out to the goat. It nuzzled his hand, sniffing, exploring. Then it opened up and bit down hard on the operator's hand.

"Ow!" Womack cried out and reflexively drew back his hand. "You little son of a rich mother sucker." Womack, for all of his bad habits, wasn't one to curse. He found it lazy. It was more fun coming up with other ways to express his displeasure.

The goat planted its feet in the sand at the edge of the pen and held its ground. It stared at Womack, its ears pivoting back and forth. It was plucky. Womack liked that.

"What do you think, goat? We stuck here for nothing? Or does the big general in the sky have something better for us?"

The goat stared blankly. Its nostrils flared in and out. "Meh-eh-eh."

Womack opened his fist and held the weeds flat in his palm. The goat looked at the bounty, sniffed it, nudged it with his nose, and then used his lips and teeth to pick it from Womack's hand. The animal stepped back, chewing through the food. Another goat, much larger than Womack's new friend, wandered over to the fence line. It bleated at the smaller goat and then at Womack.

The operator leaned against the post nearest him. "Too late, brother." He chuckled. "Little dude here beat you to it."

Womack ripped open the Velcro on his thigh pocket and pulled out a silver flask. It was coated in sand. Womack held the flask with one hand while he wiped it clean with the other. He unscrewed the top, took a sniff of the well-aged contents, and toasted the goat.

"Here's to biting the hand that feeds you," he said and took a long pull from the flask. He swallowed the nectar, relishing the burn as it trailed down his throat. "Ahhh," he said. "That's the stuff."

Womack took another swig, swishing the whisky around in his mouth, letting it swim around and between his teeth. He instantly felt better about their situation. Wolf was right. They were getting paid. What did it matter if they were holed up at a black site for another week?

As long as they got home alive, every man in one

piece—Womack reminded himself that was the most important thing.

— 16 —

Frederick, Maryland
April 20, 1980

Dr. Justin Starling stared at the sedated man strapped to the gurney. "Where did you find him?"

"Fort Leavenworth."

Starling kept his eyes on the patient but spoke to the only other person in the room, Major Rick Gibson. "I don't understand."

"He's a deserter," said Gibson. "Your breakthrough with the hormones opened some doors that were previously closed."

"It wasn't a breakthrough. It was a—"

"Semantics, Dr. Starling. Did you take any English courses when you were at Stanford?"

Starling didn't answer. He dipped his hands into his lab coat pockets and stepped to the side of the gurney. The man's chest was rising up and down. His breathing was slow and even. A long thin tube was taped to the back of his hand, where an intravenous needle was delivering the liquid sedative. Soon, they'd switch out the supply bag, and a consistent drip of VX-99 Berserkr would mix with the man's blood. He was their live subject.

Starling looked up from the guinea pig. "So you finally convinced them? After years of denying you a live subject, they just handed one over?"

Gibson swallowed hard, looked at the floor, and nodded.

"With all due respect, Major, I don't believe you."

Gibson pulled his arms behind his back and puffed his chest. He cleared his throat and stepped to the young scientist. He was a good three inches taller than Starling and took advantage of his domineering presence as he looked down at his personal conscript.

"You really are naïve, Doctor," he said. "Our world is what we make it. We have that ability, you know, to forge a world in which we'd *like* to live. In the course of that endeavor we must break down barriers, or walk around them if they are otherwise seemingly impenetrable."

"So you walked around it."

"I know people who know people." Gibson oozed condescension. "That happens when you work as hard as I do, when you forge relationships with like-minded people."

Starling's eyes narrowed. "What's Project Judas? The classified requisition form was stamped Project Judas."

Gibson ran his tongue across the front of his teeth. "It's what you think it is."

Starling motioned toward the guinea pig with his pocketed hands. "Is it what *he* thinks it is? Does he have any idea about what's going to happen to him? Did he volunteer for one thing only to be injected with another, like those Marines in Operation Burn Bright?"

Gibson flinched before the grimace on his face eased

into a smile. He stepped back from the scientist and chuckled at Starling's sudden gumption. "He's fully aware of the deal we presented him. He agreed to undergo an experimental procedure that might kill him. It might not. If he lives, and after the testing is complete, his record is cleaned. He gets an honorary discharge."

Starling nodded. "So he doesn't know that even if he survives, he'll never be the same person. He won't..."

"Won't what?"

"Won't be a *person*."

Gibson shrugged. "The survival of the many requires a sacrifice of the few."

"How can you be so cavalier about this, Major? I thought you'd learned from the disaster twelve years ago," Starling said, looking at the unconscious lab rat on the gurney. "We're talking about a man's life here."

Gibson's shoulders relaxed. He brought his hands from behind his back and laced his fingers together at his chest. His tone softened. "I find this newly discovered moral high ground refreshing," he said. "But don't forget that you knew exactly what we were doing when you signed up. When I paid off your student loans, when I gave you a stipend five times that of other postdoctoral programs to which you'd applied, when I provided for you the most exceptional, cutting-edge laboratory this side of Geneva, you had no complaints."

Gibson inched closer to the scientist and put a hand on the young man's shoulder. "Unlike the traitor on this table, I told *you* everything about what your job involved. I warned you there would be lines we'd cross. I also explained that in my line of work, the end will always justify the means. Always. Our job is to keep our country safe; it's to minimize casualties; it's to forge the best version of ourselves."

Starling swallowed hard. He stared at Gibson before lowering his eyes. "By engaging the worst version of ourselves."

The words stung. Maybe because of the way Starling said them. Maybe because they were true. Rick Gibson knew, when he had trouble falling asleep at night, that his work had become an obsession.

He questioned his own methods. He wondered, especially when he sat in the dark, holding the picture of his young family, if he'd lost himself. It was difficult to see the forest for the trees. Gibson was so determined to right the wrongs he'd created in Vietnam that he was slipping deeper and deeper down the rabbit hole.

It didn't matter. It wasn't enough for Major Gibson to stop now. He couldn't stop. Then there could be no light at the end of the long dark tunnel he'd dug.

He rolled the metaphors around in his head. Forest, hole, tunnel. All of them were dark and difficult to escape from. That was where he was. He glanced over at the patient, the man who'd refused to serve his country for fear of death but was now willing to risk his life at the end of a needle. For a moment, a split second, an instant nearly too short to measure, the major softened.

Was it remorse? A bolt of morality? A voice in his head telling him he was misguided?

Whatever it was, it evaporated as soon as it formed. The sensation was gone.

Gibson squared his jaw and nodded toward the door. "Are you ready to do this or not? If not, you can leave right now. I'll find someone else."

Starling's eye twitched. He bit his lower lip. His chest expanded with a deep breath. "Fine," he said, "let's do this."

Gibson nodded and stepped to the door. He pressed a button on the wall, triggering the intercom. "We're ready," he said, leaning into the two-way speaker.

Thirty seconds later, the secured door hissed open and two MPs entered the room. After saluting Major Gibson, one moved to the head of the gurney and the other wrapped his gloved hand around the wheeled pole to which the IV bag was attached.

The men rolled the traitor from the room and into the maze of corridors. Gibson and Starling followed. As they approached the BSL wing, the major put his hand on the scientist's shoulder and stopped him.

"We are doing good work, Justin," he said. "If this works, you can take the credit for saving countless American lives. Countless."

Starling frowned. His eyes were glossy, reflecting the bright fluorescent light that illuminated the long corridors of the facility. "What if it doesn't?" he said. "Then what have I done?"

Gibson pursed his lips. He scratched the top of his head. "Then," he said, "you followed orders."

The major pushed past Starling and used his key card to enter the outer lab. He didn't speak to the scientist again until they'd completed the long BSL process and were in a secondary BSL-4 that was adjacent to the one where the samples were held and testing was conducted.

This space, unlike the room next door, was not set up like a laboratory. Instead, it resembled an operating room. It was bathed in bright light. The concrete floor and walls were painted a glossy white. The stainless steel bed, or table, in the center of the square room was bolted to the floor, as were two thin pedestals on either side. Atop the pedestals were thick leather cuffs that matched four larger such straps at the foot of the table.

There was a series of machines at the table's head, and mounted on the ceiling and walls were five CCTV cameras. Each camera had a long omnidirectional microphone extending beyond the lens.

Gibson, wearing his heat-sealed positive-pressure DPE, entered the room, connected his suit to the oxygen supply, and directed the MPs to move the patient from the rolling gurney. The men did as instructed and lifted the unconscious volunteer onto the stainless steel altar. The suited MPs moved with the grace of astronauts collecting moon samples. One MP strapped cuffs to the thighs and ankles. The other extended limp arms onto the pedestals and applied the cuffs. From the overhead camera, the man looked like the *Vitruvian Man* as drawn by da Vinci. Starling moved to a glass-fronted refrigerator at one end of the lab and removed a pair of clear bags from the top shelf. They both contained a milky-colored liquid.

Gibson nodded at Starling, disconnected from the oxygen hose, and used his pass card to exit the room. He worked his way through a series of doors before securing himself in a small anterior room. One wall was a large glass panel that looked into the BSL-4 operating room. Gibson connected to the air supply, unkinked the tubing attached to his suit, and checked the videocassette machine to confirm it was recording. He pressed a small switch on the wall and held it down with his gloved finger.

"Proceed," he said to Starling, speaking into an

intercom system through his mask. "We're recording."

Starling removed the anesthetic bag from the mobile pole and replaced it with the two bags he'd removed from the refrigerator. With all of the lines pinched, he slowly connected a Y valve to the bags and to the intravenous tube that flowed into the back of the patient's hand.

When he confirmed the lines were secure, he looked over to Gibson. His eyes were wide. He was sweating inside his hood.

Gibson rekeyed the intercom. "Proceed."

Starling licked the sweat beading on his upper lip, awkwardly nodded toward Gibson, and unclipped the lines. He checked both feeds to be certain the drip was functioning. It was, as were the biometric diodes attached to the man's chest, stomach and groin.

Starling backed away from the patient and turned toward a clock on the wall. He moved to the clock and pressed a button that initiated a timer.

"All right," said Gibson into the intercom. "Starling, join me in here."

Starling walked to the door, unhooked his air, and a minute later was next to Gibson in the observation booth. "What about the MPs?"

"They're staying put," said Gibson. "We need them in there, just in case."

The MPs stood equidistant from the gurney, one on each side. They were armed. Both of them had their eyes fixed on the unconscious patient on the table between them. Both of them jumped when the man's eyes popped open and a loud, guttural moan croaked from his wide-open, foaming mouth.

The man's eyes were dilated, the pupils filling all but an infinitesimal ring of white at the edges. His nostrils were flexing unnaturally, his chest heaving up and down, his tongue wagging from the side of his mouth. His head jerked back and forth, and he began struggling against the leather binds. He let out another pain-soaked moan. Soapy foam bubbled from his mouth and trailed down the side of his face.

Gibson was transfixed. His attention moved from the glass window to each of the five monitors that displayed the various cameras. He could see the man's body fighting what he and Starling had introduced into his system, fingers flexing in and out, toes curling unnaturally. From the overhead view, the subject's body seemed to flash from one cramped position to another, jerking and convulsing.

Starling stepped to the glass and placed his glove on it. "Is this supposed to happen?"

Gibson shook his head slowly. "I don't know."

The man's body shuddered. His fingers extended and trembled. His back arched and he slammed the back of his head onto the stainless steel. The MPs stepped back at the metallic bang. One of them drew his weapon.

Gibson keyed the mic. "Lower the pistol," he said. "Do not fire unless I issue the command."

The MP stepped back another step and kept both hands on the weapon as he lowered it toward the floor. His finger eased off the trigger.

The patient banged his head against the table again, this time leaving a marked indention in the stainless headrest. *Bang. Bang. Bang.* Each successive thrust backward into the table was more aggressive than the one before.

Starling shifted, turning his shoulders and head to Gibson. His face was pale, almost gray with fear. "He must be hurting himself," he said, his voicing arcing an octave upward. "What is happening?"

"Just wait," said Gibson. "Just watch."

Starling pointed to the biometric monitor to their right. "His pulse. It's too high. He'll have a stroke."

"Just wait."

The thrashing intensified. The patient's hips swung wildly from side to side. Blood oozed from underneath the restraints at his wrists and dripped to the floor. The bright red splatter seemed to glow against the alabaster-colored concrete. It drew Gibson's attention away from the deafening convulsions on the table. *Drip. Drip. Drip.* Gibson could faintly hear Starling grumbling his concerns, but he wasn't listening. *Drip. Drip. Drip.*

The blood is the key, isn't it? What is happening to his blood?

Then the guinea pig spoke.

It was more of a growl than anything else, but his words were clear and discernible. He was still thrashing back and forth and up and down, but he lifted his head forward. His chin almost touched his chest and he looked straight at Gibson, as if he knew, as if he'd been coherent this whole time.

His voice was guttural and thick with phlegm. "What did you do to me?" His voice was low at first, like an idling engine. Then he spoke again, more loudly. Spit flew from his swelling lips, and Gibson could see his teeth for the first time. They were somehow different, smaller and razor like. Together his top row of teeth resembled a serrated knife edge.

"What did you do to me?" he bellowed, his eyes still set on Gibson. "I'm on fire," he screamed. "I'm burning from the inside. What. Did. You. Do?"

He arched his back again and shuddered as if a bolt of

lightning was coursing through his body. He wailed in agony. He whipped his head back and forth, spraying a froth across the room, and cried out one more time before his body went limp and he exhaled. His lungs rattled. The biometric display flashed an error. The rooms were silent.

Starling was the first to speak. "Is he dead?"

Gibson didn't respond. He was watching the blood drip to the floor. He was paying attention to the man's fingertips.

"Is he dead?" Starling pressed.

The fingers were still. The MPs were shaking. Gibson could hear them sucking in too much oxygen.

Starling again. With more desperation. "Did we kill him?"

Gibson held up his finger, silently asking for a moment. He keyed the mic. "Slow your breathing, gentlemen. In and out slowly. In and out. You're going to deplete your air supply. In and out."

He looked at the blood. It wasn't red anymore. Not really. It was something else. Not red. Not quite red.

Starling put his hand on Gibson's shoulder. "Is he—"

A finger twitched on the patient's right hand. A second twitch. A third.

"He's not dead," whispered Gibson through his mask. "He's changing."

The entire hand was twitching. No. It was morphing. The knuckles seemed to distend and pop as his fingers curled into claws. His feet arched and extended. The pads of his heels shifted backward, and his toes elongated into what looked more like talons than digits.

His back arched again, but this time his hips dislocated and realigned themselves at his pelvis. His shoulders and elbows cracked and slipped into unnatural-looking positions. His brow drew forward, intensifying the depth of his eyes. His lips were swollen into a sucker, and his cheeks were drawn thin. And his skin. His skin was almost translucent. It was losing its pigmentation by the second. Veins bulged at his biceps, across his forehead, and along his neck.

He was no longer human. He was superhuman. When he stopped convulsing and his morphology appeared complete, he leaned to one side and roared as he freed his right arm from the restraint. An instant later his left arm was free.

Before the MPs could react, he'd used his claws to tear through all four leg restraints. In one swift movement he twisted his body and jumped from the table. Perhaps sensing the tension of the intravenous line, he looked down at his hand and pulled out the IV. Then he threw back his head and wailed.

The MP who'd drawn his weapon was the first victim. Without a command from Gibson, he managed two shots at the attacking monster before a pair of swipes exsanguinated the poor soldier. As his half-suited body melted to a heap on the floor, the second MP emptied his .45 into the beast. It did nothing.

The animal looked down at the tight pattern of wounds in its chest and dug a finger into one of the wounds, fishing out a mangled round. It held the bullet between its thumb and forefinger and studied it before it flicked it at the MP and pounced. In a single miraculous leap it had crossed half the distance of the lab and tore the man open like a Christmas present.

Then it turned its sights on the glass window. The beast crouched low and jumped at the glass, slamming into it. It screamed as it connected with the window, its body smearing its discolored blood on the glass.

"He wants to kill us," cried Starling. "What did we do? What did we do? What did we create?" He dropped to his knees, crying and praying for forgiveness.

Gibson, on the other hand, was unfazed. He stood at attention at the window as the monster repeatedly smashed itself into the four-inch-thick bulletproof glass. Again and again it reared back and exploded into the window. Its eyes never left Gibson.

"I think we failed," Gibson said calmly.

"You think?" Starling cackled amidst a Hail Mary. "Really, Major? Really?"

"We failed because this, I think, is no better than Burn Bright," he said. "He's not a fearless death machine we can control. He's just…"

"He's a monster," said Starling, still on his knees. "He's an abomination. We've killed three men today. Three men!"

The beast was tiring. It had lost a lot of blood. Its attempts at breaking through the glass were increasingly weaker.

Gibson sighed. "This is a disappointment," he said dispassionately. "A very big disappointment. Clearly the hormonal theory was incorrect."

The major stepped across Starling to the bank of monitors. Next to the biometric display was a key and an encased green button. Gibson turned and looked at the flailing monster one more time before turning the key, flipping open the case, and depressing the green button.

As he did, a thin, tea-stained mist appeared at the ceiling of the BSL-4 operating room. The mist thickened and billowed, swimming down the walls until it reached the floor. Within thirty seconds the mist had filled the room. The monster, lost in the fog, was invisible.

Gibson checked his watch. Two minutes later he turned the key to its initial position and the mist thinned before vacuums on the walls of the operating room had sucked away the last tendrils of it. The monster was flat on its back on the floor. Its arms and legs were splayed at grotesque angles. Blood pooled from underneath its body, leeching across the floor.

"Get up, Dr. Starling," he said to the blubbering scientist. He offered Starling a hand. "We have work to do. We need to know what went wrong so that when we get another live subject, we can fix the anomalies."

Starling looked up at Gibson through his mask. His eyes were swollen and red. His face was soaked with tears and sweat and snot. "What?"

"Help me grab the body. We need somebody to perform an autopsy on this thing," he said. "The faster, the better."

— 17 —

Hòa Bình, Vietnam
April 20, 1980

Jimmy Linh and Uncle Due stood in front of a thatched hut, waiting for someone to answer. They'd called out a greeting. Linh heard shuffling inside. The residents were home.

Linh's hands were on his hips. "They'll come," he said out of the corner of his mouth. "Just wait."

They'd arrived at the house after others in the village had pointed them there. The people living in that house would be the ones to interview. They could talk about the White Ghost. They knew the terror it caused as well as anyone. That was what everyone told them.

Besides, it was getting late, and none of the villagers wanted to stand outside listening to the familiar, bone-chilling call of the Ma Trang. None of them had uttered the name during the conversations. It was bad luck, they'd reminded Linh and his uncle. Very bad luck.

Linh waited patiently several steps from the door. Uncle Due was tired of waiting.

"*I'll* knock," he said. "Step aside." Due huffed and

stomped to the door. He pounded on it with the side of his fist.

"What do you want?" called a woman's voice from the inside. "Who are you?"

The woman's Vietnamese was a dialect with which Linh was less familiar. His face must have betrayed his inability to translate. Due rolled his eyes at his nephew.

He spoke slowly in his native tongue. "We are here to talk about the Ma Trang," said Due, throwing caution to the wind. "We know the White Ghost has hurt your family."

The door cracked open and a small woman looked up through the thin opening. "You said the name," she said. "You shouldn't do that. You need to go."

Due stepped forward. "We just have a few questions," he said. "My nephew came a very long way to speak with you."

The woman looked past Due to Linh. Her eyes scanned him up and down. She pursed her lips. "How long will this take? You cannot stay."

Due turned to Linh. "How long will this take?"

"Ten minutes," said Linh. "No more than ten minutes."

"Ten minutes," said Due.

The woman eyed both men and pulled the door wide. "Come in," she said. "Ten minutes."

Unlike most of the other homes in the area, the woman's home was not on stilts. It was on a wooden platform that extended beyond the frame of the house and served as a porch. Linh followed his uncle and stepped from that porch into the dim interior of the home. The familiar smell of incense hit him immediately as he cleared the threshold.

In the corner of the open room was an altar, a trio of bamboo sticks smoldering at its center. Two children were cross-legged at the altar, their heads bowed in prayer. Neither of them acknowledged the visitors until the woman called them.

"Come here," she said. "These men want to talk about something."

The children pushed themselves to their feet and quietly shuffled to the center of the room. Both were wide-eyed. The boy was taller than the girl, but Linh figured they were the same age. It was something about the way they carried themselves. They almost seemed to be two halves of a whole.

"Yes, Grandmother," said the boy. "What do they want?"

"They want to talk about the howl we heard," she said. "They have questions about your parents."

Due whispered the translation into Linh's ear. Linh nodded and spoke directly to the boy as he pulled the cassette recorder from his bag. He pressed record and held it in front of him.

"My name is Jimmy Linh. What's your name?"

Due started to translate, but the boy stopped him.

"I understand the question," he said. "My name is Chi Dinh. This is my sister, Lan. We are twins. This is my grandmother."

"Tell me about your parents," said Linh.

The boy nodded at Linh's recorder. "Tell me about what you have in your hand. Are you taking pictures?"

"No," said Linh. "This records your voice. That way, when I write my story, I make sure I get all of your words right."

The boy reached out his hands, cupping them. "Please let me hold it."

Linh didn't hesitate. Anything to make the child feel at ease. He knelt down and handed the boy the recorder. He pointed out the internal microphone. "That's what hears you when you speak."

The boy pulled it to his mouth and blew air through his lips, making a motorboat sound against the recorder. His eyes brightened and he smiled. "Can I hear it?"

"Of course," said Linh. He showed the boy which buttons to use to stop the recording, to rewind, and then to play.

The boy held the device to his ear and then to his sister's. Their faces glowed with wonder. They giggled and laughed. The boy kept replaying the motorboat sound over and over. Several minutes passed before he handed back the device.

"Thank you," he said. His sister echoed the gratitude.

"Of course," said Linh, bowing to the children. "May we talk about your parents?"

The children's joy vaporized and they nodded in unison. A wave of guilt washed over Linh. He took a deep breath and pressed record.

"People in your village tell me both of your parents are gone," he said softly. "I am very sorry."

The boy tried to smile. It didn't stick. "My father was taken first," he said. He then relayed the gruesome details of the attack, at least what he knew of it.

Linh looked at the grandmother and then back to the children. "And you don't think it was a land mine?"

The boy shook his head. "No," he said. "Land mines don't strip bones clean. I've seen people hurt by land mines. Everything looks like it exploded because it did.

My father didn't explode."

"And your mother?"

"She was washing clothes," said the boy. "It attacked her there."

"Mother fought back," said the girl, tears welling in her eyes. "She tried to live."

Linh offered a weak, crooked smile. "I'm sure she did."

"I know she did," said the girl. From underneath her shirt, she pulled out a leather necklace. On the end of the necklace was a long curved ornament. It resembled a tooth or a claw. She held it with her fingers.

"What is that?" Linh asked.

"It was the monster's," said the boy. "It belonged to the White Ghost."

The boy's grandmother flashed him an angry glare. "You should not say the name. You know not to say its name."

Due translated the grandmother's admonition for Linh. "We should go," he added.

Linh shook his head. "Not yet." He turned back to the girl. "May I hold it, please?"

The girl looked at her brother. He nodded. She pulled the leather loop from around her neck and over her head and handed it to Linh. Linh handed her the recorder.

Linh gripped the necklace like a bag of loot, holding it in front of his face, watching the claw or tooth swing back and forth. "What is it?"

"A claw," said the girl.

Linh took the claw in one hand and weighed it in his palm. It was heavy but not dense. He took it between his fingers and held it up to get a closer look. It was a claw. Linh could see thin layers of keratin, like a stack of thick fingernails fused on top of one another. It wasn't bone, though it resembled the color and striation of a horn. It was sharp, with barely visible serrations on its underside. At its base, the pearly-colored claw turned black. The darker color was dried blood.

"May I take a picture of this?" asked Linh.

The girl nodded and Linh looped the necklace over her head. He took back his recorder and tucked it under his arm as he fished through his satchel for his camera. He pulled out the camera and draped its strap over his neck. The camera was a Nikon FTN 35mm camera and loaded with Kodak Tri-X low light 400 ASA film. He'd borrowed it from a photographer at the paper.

"Before I take the picture," he said, "I do have a couple more questions."

"You've stayed longer than ten minutes," said the grandmother. "You should be going now."

Due translated. Linh nodded. "Three more questions. That's all. I promise."

The grandmother frowned but relented. Linh thanked her. Due grumbled.

"When was the last time you saw the—it?"

The boy's eyebrows furrowed with confusion. He shook his head. "Nobody sees it until it's too late," he said. "I've never seen it. I've heard it."

"I've heard it too," said his sister. "We heard it today. This morning."

"I heard it too," said Linh. "It's frightening. How often do you hear it?"

The boy shrugged. "It comes and goes. Sometimes we don't hear it for weeks or months. Sometimes we hear it every day."

"When we hear it," the girl added, "people disappear."

"How many people have disappeared?"

"Too many," said the boy. "I can't count them. As long as I've been alive, we've feared it. I don't remember a time without it."

"Is there anything else you'd like to say?" asked Linh. In his short career, he'd learned that last open-ended question was the best thing he could ask. It often provided the best responses, giving the interview subject the best opportunity to mention something important about which Linh hadn't thought to ask.

"No," said the boy. The girl shook her head.

Linh nodded. "Thank y—"

"I have something to add," said the grandmother. "There's something I'd like to say."

Linh smiled at Due's translation and told the woman to offer her testimony. "Please," he said, "whatever you'd like to add."

"What Chi Dinh tells you is not true."

Linh stepped back. "What?"

The grandmother stepped toward the reporter. She lowered her voice and spoke slowly. "The boy is wrong. Somebody has seen the monster and lived."

The boy shook, hushed in disbelief. "Who, Grandmother? Who saw the monster?"

The woman took a deep breath and sighed. She folded her arms across her chest. She swallowed and opened her mouth to speak before closing it again. Her chin began to tremble. Tears leaked from the corners of her eyes.

"It was me," she said. "I looked into its eyes. It looked into mine."

"When?" asked the boy.

"You saw it?" asked the girl.

The grandmother opened her arms and motioned for

the children to move to her. They quickly slid to her side and wrapped their arms around her. All three of them were crying. Linh felt sweat suddenly blooming on his brow and on his upper lip. He averted his eyes from the family hug, but an invisible magnet pulled him back to it. He was at once compelled to leave the house and delve more deeply into what the woman had experienced. Despite his misgivings, the reporter in Linh took hold. He checked the recorder to insure the device was still on, and he stepped to the woman. He put one hand on her shoulder and rubbed back and forth with his thumb.

"When did this happen?" he asked. "When did you see the White—it?"

Due, whose face was drawn with disbelief, translated his nephew's question. The woman, her eyes squeezed shut as she held tight to her grandchildren, licked her lips and spoke deliberately. It was as if she were relaying a fairy tale.

"This was years ago, before my son and his wife were killed. It was early morning," she said. "The sun was barely visible through the trees. Birds were chirping. The mist was steaming from the river. I needed a bucket of water to cook. Our plumbing wasn't working. In the days after the war, our plumbing didn't work many days."

"It's still not good," said the girl.

The woman chuckled through her tears. "You're right," she said and kissed the girl's head. She stopped for a moment and took a deep breath, her nose buried in the girl's thick black hair. She exhaled with a loud sigh.

"You were alone?" Linh asked.

The woman nodded. "I was alone. My husband died in the war with the French. That was a long time ago. So I have done many things alone since then. Getting water from the river is just one of them. I've done it so many times."

Linh wiped his brow clean of sweat and waited for the translation. "What happened?"

"I was walking through the grass to the water," she said. "I had the bucket in one hand and was swinging it back and forth. It made a squeaking sound. So at first, I didn't notice the noise coming from the riverbank."

"What noise?"

"It sounded like the bucket squeak at first. Then it was more like a cry or a whimper. I stopped swinging the bucket as I got closer. Then I saw it. It was the back of the monster. It was crouched low. Its elbows were moving back and forth and back and forth. I couldn't tell at first what it was or what it was doing."

Linh glanced over at Due. His uncle's face was ashen. He uttered the translation softly and with hesitation, as though he wasn't certain he was using the right words to describe what the woman was saying.

"I thought it was a fisherman," she explained. "But its joints didn't look right. Its knees and elbows were bent at odd angles. Then I saw its skin. It was so white, I could almost see through it. I knew I should turn and run back to the house, but I couldn't look away. I couldn't stop looking at the monster."

Linh checked his recorder again. It was still working. "What was it doing?"

"It was eating something," she said. "I mean, it was eating someone. I could see it holding an arm. It was eating it. It was chewing and slurping and making awful sounds."

"That was the squeaking you heard?"

The woman shook her head, tears again filling her

eyes. "No," she said. "The squeaking was coming from the person it was eating. The person was still alive. He was trying to scream but couldn't. I can still hear the sound in my mind. *Squeak. Squeak. Squeak.*"

The boy leaned away from the woman's hold and put his hand on her cheek. "What did you do, Grandmother?"

She didn't look at the boy when she spoke. Instead, her gaze was distant. Her mind was trapped on the riverbank, feet from the feasting Ma Trang. "*Squeak. Squeak*," she said above a whisper. "*Squeak. Squeak.*"

The boy moved his other hand to her face, holding it gently on both sides. "Grandmother," he said, "Grandmother."

The woman blinked from the vision and returned her focus to the boy. "It saw me," she said. "I gasped when I realized it was eating a man. It turned. There was blood on its face. It had small sharp teeth and a sucker mouth stained with blood."

Linh swallowed then spoke. "It saw you?"

The woman nodded. "It growled at me and I ran," she said. "I ran through the grass, carrying the bucket. I tripped and fell. I was sure it would catch me and kill me. It didn't. It didn't chase me."

"Did Father know?" asked the girl. "Did Mother know?"

The woman's lips and chin quivered and she hung her head before shaking it back and forth. "No," she said. "I never told anyone. I was afraid people wouldn't believe me. I was afraid they would say I was crazy." The woman drew her hands to her face and sobbed.

Due interjected. "That doesn't make sense. Everybody knows about it. People would believe you."

The woman dropped her hands and looked at Due, the years of anguish carved into the lines along her brow and cheeks. "This was almost twelve years ago," she said. "Nobody had heard of the monster then. Nobody."

Due pressed. "Then why didn't you tell people later, once there were sightings and people started dying."

The woman nodded. "I should have," she admitted, "but then people would ask me why I kept silent. They would blame me for the deaths. They would punish me. Instead, the heavens punished me for being silent. The heavens forsook me and took my son and his wife."

The children looked up at their grandmother with confusion and then hurt. Both turned from her and moved to each other. The boy and girl embraced one another, both of them convulsed with emotion.

Linh felt a thick lump in his throat. His breathing was hard to control. He blinked back tears. "Why are you telling us now?" he choked.

The woman took a deep breath, filling her lungs with air, and exhaled through pursed lips. "I am telling you because I want everyone to know the monster is not a ghost. That man, that thing, whatever he was or is, is not a ghost. It is not human, but it is alive. It is *alive.*"

— 18 —

Hòa Bình, Vietnam
April 20, 1980

Lieutenant Brett was crouched low in the high grass, waiting for dusk. The voice in his head had suggested he wait for the sun to drop. Men and women would be tired; they'd be focused on nightly chores and wouldn't be aware of their surroundings.

Easy pickings, she'd said.

His ears pricked and he pulled the necklace from his mouth and held a nose between his fingers. There were feet trudging along the dirt. There were four feet. They were distinct. It wasn't an animal. There was no rhythm to the rise and fall. Brett was certain the steps belonged to two people. His ears filtered out the ambient sounds of the river and the wind in the trees.

It was two men. The steps were too heavy and too far apart to be women.

Brett raised himself from his crouch, his knees clicking as he shifted his weight. He scanned the horizon just above the grass. Nothing. He turned his body, using his fists to balance himself on the damp ground as he pivoted. Still nothing.

He blinked and refocused and then drew in a deep breath through his flared nostrils. A cacophony of odors threatened to overwhelm his sense of smell. The earlier rains had dulled some odors and freshened others, making them particularly acute. Mixed with dung and jungle rot, he sensed fish and soap. A large cat was close. A tree infected with termites was dying. Brett sucked in another waft of humid air, and there it was. Sweat. Sweat mixed with a fragrant cologne or deodorant. It was men all right. No doubt. And they were getting closer.

Brett picked his way through the grass, sliding his calloused hands along the thin blades as he moved. The click and pop of his joints was masked by a sudden gust of wind that blew directly at him and then swirled before dissipating. The trees above swayed, their leaves rustling against one another.

He reached a clearing and stopped. Lifting himself up, he again scanned his surroundings. This time he saw the men. They were on the road now, maybe a hundred yards from the clearing. They were walking toward him. Neither man was speaking.

One of the men was older and walked with a hunch. His steps were heavier. He was squatty with thick fingers and favored his right side. He was the weaker one. The other man was taller and thinner. His gate was even and quick despite his long legs. He carried a brown satchel on his left side. Brett could smell the wet leather.

Go now, urged the voice in his head. *Kill them both. Attack the taller one. Get him out of the way. The older one won't have the strength to fight.*

Brett popped his lips and dug in his heels. The men were walking toward a car parked on the road. The car was empty. He closed his eyes and listened.

Keys jingled in the older man's pocket. It was his car. Brett judged the distance between the men and the car. He could cut them off on the road. They'd have nowhere to run. To one side was a steep incline leading toward the mountains. On the other side of the road was a drop toward the river.

Go, urged the voice. *Go now.*

Brett leapt forward on his hands and galloped across the grass. His joints snapped and clicked as he raced to the road. Saliva pooled in his mouth.

The older one will be tough and fatty, said the voice. *The younger one, though. Lots of juicy, fresh muscle. Warm, lean meat. It's been so long since we've had two meals at once.*

Brett lunged with his powerful legs and then pushed forward with his hands and arms, moving swiftly to the road. It was a clear shot to the narrowing gap between the men and the car. The only hindrance was the occasional pool of mud that sucked at his hands and feet as he moved. Brett was getting closer, advancing on his prey, as he'd done so many countless times before.

He could still taste the flesh of the first person he'd killed after the VX-99 had taken hold and his fellow Marines were dead. He could smell the man's fear.

It had been weeks after injecting the VX-99. Aside from manifesting the omnipresent voice, the one that wouldn't let him rest, the drug had amplified all of his senses. It had started with shimmering arcs of colored light clouding his vision. Then his body had caught fire. The sensation of thousands of stinging bees had spread across his skin from the inside. As quickly as the pain had enveloped him, it was over. And the world became remarkably, impossibly vivid. From the sound of bugs crawling to the stink of his pit-stained uniformed, he'd been born again. The taste of coffee had filtered across his tongue. He could feel the throbbing pulse of blood through his veins.

It had been liberating and debilitating. For the first few days, the newly invincible VX-99 version of Lieutenant Trevor Brett had wandered aimlessly through the jungle, up and down peaks, and at the edge of rivers, trying to cope with the sensory overload. Without a direct threat, as he'd found in his fellow Marines immediately following the VX-99 injections, Brett was able to ignore the urges of the voice and the demands of his hunger.

You must hunt, she'd growled.

What was left of pre-VX-99 Brett, that part of him that clung perilously to human morality, fought the more primal, single-minded tendencies as valiantly as it could. When he finally succumbed to his voracious appetite, he'd chosen to ignore the voice's command to find a human. Instead, he'd pounced on a Vu Quang ox, a bovine and one of the world's rarest large mammals.

It had been chewing on underbrush in a heavily wooded area, using its long tongue to pull the broad green leaves into its mouth. It was oblivious to Brett's presence. He, however, could smell the musk emanating from its long straight hair that thickened on the insides of its forelegs and belly.

Brett had focused on the thick pulse at the side of its neck, just beneath its jaw, and he pounced. The animal had seen him at the last moment, its round pupils reacting to the oncoming threat. Its brown irises had appeared almost orange as it froze in fear, a leaf hanging from its mouth. It had squealed as Brett grabbed it along the thick stripe that ran across its back from its neck to its tail. Brett had dug in with his fingers, feeling the pop as they punctured the animal's skin. He'd done the rest of the deadly damage with his teeth.

The animal, however, had not satiated his hunger. The pangs had grown worse, more consuming, more mind-altering, until he could think of nothing but killing and feeding on a human.

Brett had found the man near the village of Hòa Bình. Of course, he hadn't known the name of the village. He'd only known there were a lot of people from which to choose. He'd smelled them: men, women, children, infants, a veritable fresh meat buffet. He'd clung to the trees near the Da River, resisting the urge for as long as he could. Early one morning, as the fog lifted from the Da, he'd had enough. He'd needed to kill.

The voice had purred in his head. *It's time*, she'd said. *You've waited long enough.*

Then it had begun.

Each successive kill was easier than the one before. Countless times he'd attacked, slaughtered, and fed. Now he raced toward his newest targets, a pair of unsuspecting travelers walking into a trap. He was yards from intercepting them.

***

Uncle Due saw it first. It was a flash of white amidst the tall grasses off the side of the road. A gust of hot wind blew toward the grass, sending a whoosh past his ears. Underneath the fanning of the blades and the rustling tree branches, Due thought he heard a sound that resembled knuckles cracking. The sound, and not the wind, produced a chill on the back of his neck.

The white flash was bolting through the grass straight

toward them. He could hear it grunting as it advanced. Due stopped on the road, short of the mudslide that had stranded his car. His instincts told him to run, to turn and run as fast as he could. Instead he was frozen from a strange mixture of curiosity and fear.

Is this the White Ghost? Have we found it? Has it found us? How is that possible?

Due considered his options. He had none. The White Ghost was too fast, too big, too strong. He'd never be able to outrun the beast if it were coming for him.

If it were coming for him…

From the corner of his eyes, he could see Linh was oblivious. The reporter was deep in thought. His heavy leather satchel was draped across his body like a messenger bag and bounced on the small of his back as he moved. His Nikon was still around his neck. Linh had insisted on taking photographs of the woman and her two grandchildren. He'd gotten a close-up of the claw before they left.

Linh was such a disappointment. He was a smart boy, did well in school, and was the perfect person to inherit his father's business. It was preordained his nephew would finish his studies at university and then join the company. He would work in every job. He would learn the trade inside and out. His father, Due's brother, could retire. He could travel. He could enjoy a life that had not been easy.

Instead, the boy chose to tell stories, to be an observer of other people living their lives. That wasn't work. That wasn't a trade. It was a weak excuse for a hobby, let alone a job. And here it was, this storytelling, this ridiculous storytelling, had landed them both far from real civilization and in the clutches of a fabled predator.

Due caught a glimpse of the monster's face as it leapt above the grass line. He opened his mouth to say something, to warn his nephew. He didn't. In that split second, he thought it better to stay quiet. Linh was closer to the monster, standing off the edge of the road at the mudslide.

If the beast attacks Linh, it will give me time to—

He couldn't do it. He couldn't sacrifice his nephew to save himself.

As the monster leapt toward Linh, Due called to him, his own feet still cemented to the road. "Linh! Behind you!"

Linh turned to look at his uncle, his face screwed tight with confusion. "Wha—"

As he spun, Ma Trang descended on top of him, knocking him to the mud. The two of them slipped into the soft brown mound, tumbling over one another. Limbs flailed, splattering mud against the nearby rocks and spraying it into the air. Due couldn't move. His legs, and his conscience, wouldn't let him. He watched in horror as the Ma Trang rose from the mud, its ghastly sucker lips drawn back, revealing piranha-like rows of teeth. The monster's pale skin almost glowed in contrast to the black mud.

Linh slipped beneath the mud. Due couldn't see him. He couldn't see him at all as the Ma Trang took a violent swipe downward with his clawed hand.

***

It all happened too fast. Linh had heard his uncle call his name in the same instant he felt a sudden jolt on his right side. Something or someone had tackled him, knocking him into the thick, pasty mud covering the road. The shock of the hit had knocked the wind from his lungs, and despite landing in the mud, his shoulder and head hit something hard. A burst of stars had exploded in his vision.

At first, Linh had thought it was an animal that attacked him. Maybe a tiger? Whatever it was, the beast was feral. It was dense with muscles and had fetid, hot breath Linh could smell despite the foul aroma of the mud.

But he'd instantly dismissed the tiger theory when he felt the grip of a man's hand around his arm, twisting and pulling, as the two struggled to gain traction in the mud pit. The animal was grunting and growling. Linh could hear pops and clicks and what sounded like teeth snapping as he kicked and squirmed deeper into the mud.

That mud was initially his savior. The animal couldn't grip Linh. It couldn't gain its footing. Instead it was nearly as helpless as Linh.

Linh sucked in a deep breath and threw himself backward into the mud, pulled his knees into his chest, and mule kicked the beast in the square of its chest as it tried to pounce on top of him. It was in that moment, as Linh slipped beneath the mud, that he knew what it was he was fighting.

Ma Trang.

Linh hoped his blurry vision was the culprit, that he wasn't truly struggling against an invincible monster. He knew that wasn't the case. He tried squirming backward from the Ma Trang, but it caught the strap of his satchel and yanked it with such force that it flipped Linh onto his stomach, facedown in the mud. As he struggled to breathe, a sudden force of pressure hit him squarely in the back, and a burst of white-hot pain stung his right shoulder. Linh surfaced long enough to gulp another swallow of air before he sank beneath the mud again. The animal was grappling for his feet. Linh kicked and danced free of its grasp, and as he tried pulling himself away, his hand wrapped around the thick shard of a tree branch caught in the mudslide. Linh pivoted to his back and used his elbows to push himself above the mud. Once he was sitting upright, he quickly raised his right arm and forcefully drove the shard downward toward the Ma Trang.

Linh couldn't see. Between his blurred vision and the mud coating his face, he was virtually blind. He knew he'd connected. He felt it and heard the Ma Trang scream in pain. The grandmother was right; this was no ghost. It was flesh and blood.

The blow gave Linh a moment to scramble free of the Ma Trang's grip. The beast, still waist deep in the mud, wailed. Its cry was earsplitting and unearthly. Linh covered his ears as he caught his breath. The animal grabbed at its wrist, holding it above the filth, its fingers curled toward its palm.

Then it turned its attention from the wound. Ma Trang turned its demonic, reptilian eyes to Linh. The pupils were yellow, thin slits. Its chest was heaving. A spiderweb of dark blue veins stretched against its chest.

The chest. What is hanging across its chest? Is it a necklace? And what is hanging from it? Are those…body parts?

Its nostrils flared. Its leechlike sucker lips popped open and closed before a wide smile spread across its face.

A smile? It's smiling?

The world slowed and Linh suddenly felt the urge to

vomit. His stomach heaved and the sting of bile rocketed up his throat. All he wanted was a story about a legend. Instead, he was about to become part of the legend.

Amidst the searing pain across his shoulder, headlines flashed in his mind.

Reporter In Search Of Ma Trang Finds What He's Looking For, Dies Horrible Death

British Journalist Becomes Subject Of His Own Report

Gertrude Wombley, his editor, would have a field day. She'd be thrilled at the publicity for the paper. She wouldn't care it took his life to gain it. She'd probably even pay for the cost of an elaborate funeral just to promote the story even more. That was, she'd pay for the funeral if there was anything left of him to bury.

Linh knew he was taking his last breaths. The White Ghost was gathering its strength for one final attack. It pushed itself to its feet and stood, mud dripping from its head and shoulders. It flexed its fingers in and out. In and out. The joints clicked. In and out.

The reporter searched the mud for another weapon. Anything. Anything at all. All that wormed its way through his hands was lumpy black mud. He closed his eyes and said a prayer. Maybe he should have joined the family business. There were no flesh-eating monsters.

His muscles tensed as he awaited the final lunge. It never came. Instead he heard an engine rev and tires screech. He opened his eyes in time to see Due's car slamming into the Ma Trang, sending it flying fifteen feet from the edge of the road. The monster's wide-open eyes and slack jaw imprinted in Linh's mind, and he scrambled to his feet. His uncle was waiting for him, screaming at him to get up and get in the car.

***

With a surge of adrenaline, Due scurried from the road and ran through the grass, past the mudslide and to his car. His nephew, surprisingly, was putting up a fight. Due thought he was a goner when the Ma Trang had swiped at him with those gargantuan claws. Somehow Linh had fought back. Due pushed his way, breathlessly, through the grass and emerged on the other side of the mudslide.

As he ran the short distance to his car, he turned and saw the monster rear back and grab one of its wrists. It wailed a bloodcurdling scream that almost knocked Due off balance. He kept his feet and, using his hands, he worked his way around the front of the car to the driver's side door.

He fumbled for the keys in his pocket and then struggled to find the right one to slip into the door lock. Once he'd managed it, he dropped into the driver's seat, cranked the ignition and slipped the car into reverse.

Due didn't know what had come over him. He didn't even have time to think about his actions. He didn't plan them. He just executed them. Some subconscious survival/hero mechanism kicked into gear and he slammed on the gas with the transmission in reverse.

The tires struggled to grip the wet dirt and spun, squealing and emitting a thickening cloud of smoke from the burning rubber. He pressed harder on the gas and they caught. The car jumped backward and Due used his rearview mirror to aim straight for the beast.

He prayed his nephew wasn't in the way. There was no other choice. He didn't have time for anything other than to slam the car into the mud in the hopes of hitting the Ma Trang. The car lurched as he hit the front edge of the slide, but it held its momentum and speed.

"Yes!" Due cheered as he felt the heavy thump against the rear left corner of his car. He slammed the brake and the car skidded before stopping in the mud. He drove open his door and jumped to his feet, slipping against the thick dark slime.

He didn't see his nephew anywhere. He scanned the mud pit, the hillside, the grass. "Jimmy," he called. "Jimmy, get up! Get up!" He took another step into the mud. It was at his ankles. "Jimmy!"

His nephew's hand reached up from the mud, and then his mud-covered face appeared. Linh pushed himself to his feet and slopped his way toward his uncle. Due grabbed Linh when he was close enough and pulled him to the car. He tossed Linh into the backseat and hurriedly moved into the front.

Behind them they could hear the beast's high-pitched cry. Due shifted the car into gear and pressed the accelerator. The engine whined, but the car didn't move.

"We're stuck," said Due, panicking. "We're stuck."

"Rock it back and forth," suggested Linh. He was coughing and trying to free mud from his nostrils. "Forward and reverse. Forward and reverse."

Due did as his nephew suggested. It wasn't working.

Without saying anything, Linh kicked open the rear driver's side door and rolled around to the rear of the car.

Due almost stood in his seat and yelled back at Linh, "What are you doing?"

Linh coughed and leaned onto the trunk. The camera was swinging around his neck. "Pushing."

Due glanced in the rearview mirror. He didn't see the Ma Trang. He shifted into drive and slowly depressed the accelerator. Linh was grunting. Due pushed harder with his foot until the wheels caught and the car jerked forward from the mud. He looked back in his side view and saw Linh covered with the spray.

"Get in," Due yelled through the open back door swinging on its hinges. Linh wasn't coming though. Instead he had his back to the car and was looking out toward the grass.

Due shifted his weight and turned around to look out the back window. Standing in the grass, next to a tree, was the Ma Trang. His clothes were muddied and tattered. Due's heart leapt into his throat. He swallowed past the knot and swung back around to Linh, who was frantically wiping his camera clean.

The idiot is taking a picture?

"Get in!"

Linh recapped his lens and limped toward the car. His right arm was bloodied and it was dripping from his elbow as he moved.

Due checked the rearview again. The Ma Trang was still there, but he was moving toward them again. He began running and then dropped onto his hands and used all four limbs to propel himself toward the car.

"C'mon," Due said as Linh reached the backseat. Due had his foot pressed to the floor before Linh could close the door. The car accelerated and Due wrapped both of his hands around the steering wheel. He leaned forward in his seat, rocking back and forth, urging the car to move.

In the rearview, the Ma Trang was gaining ground. It had passed the mud pit and was closing the gap. Due kept the pedal pressed to the floorboard as he drove north. His eyes were on the winding road ahead, until the car bounced and the wheel jerked to the right. The Ma Trang was clinging to the trunk, clawing its way toward the roof.

***

Brett didn't see the car hit him, but he felt it. It was a sledgehammer that knocked him from his feet as he launched toward the thin man in the mud. He breathlessly flew through the air and landed on his back in the grass. If it hadn't been for the mud, he'd have been mid-feast.

Despite the muck, he thought he'd gotten the thin one with a wide swipe of his hand. But instead of gashing the man's back, he'd caught the leather bag with his claws. The man was resilient and crafty. It made Brett want to kill him all the more. He caught his breath, gathered his strength, and made another run at them. He couldn't let them get away.

Run, said the voice. She was angry. *Faster.*

The car was accelerating and Brett was exhausted. Exhaustion was a rare feeling for a man who'd morphed into something invincible. There it was, thickness in his muscles and burning in his lungs. He fought past it and used the spring in his legs to explode toward the car.

He extended his body, flying almost horizontally as he landed with a heavy thud onto the trunk. The curled edges of his claws caught the lip of the trunk where it met the rear window, and he pulled with his biceps until he was comfortably on the back of the car.

The chunky, older man was driving. The thin one was in the back. That thin one. He'd been arrogant enough to stand in the mud and take a photograph.

Who is he?

Brett gripped the edge of the trunk with all ten fingers and pulled his chest forward. He reached back with one hand, balled it into a tight fist, and slammed it through the window. Glass exploded around him, slicing his arm. The blood was intoxicating, but he ignored it and reached deep into the car, fishing for the thin man. He pressed the side of his face to the glass and opened his eye wide. The man was there, bleeding himself, and curled on the floor behind the driver's seat. He'd made himself as small as he could. It wasn't small enough.

Grab him, cried the voice in Brett's head. *He's wounded. You can take him and the driver. Crawl inside the car. Get in there.*

Brett withdrew his arm from the jagged opening, drew back, and punched another hole into the glass. Now the opening was wide enough for him to squeeze through. He adjusted his grip on the trunk and then reached into the backseat.

He could smell the sweet odor of urine mixed with sweat. Someone was afraid. *They should be,* Brett thought.

The driver was screaming. The thin man was struggling, kicking his feet, as he had in the mud. Brett managed to grab the seat fabric and puncture it with his claws. He used the leverage to heave his head through the opening. He licked his teeth and drew in a deep breath before opening his pucker lips as wide as he could to wail as loudly as he could.

The shriek was bloodcurdling. He knew it. In the mirror in front of him, the driver's eyes were bulging; his skin was gray with fear. He was soaked with his own sweat. Brett reached his other arm through the opening, but as he did, he felt his weight shift violently to the left and then to the right.

His claws lost their grip and he slid from the opening. Brett tried holding onto the trunk, but couldn't. His claws scratched through the paint, but he tumbled from the car and rolled off the road and into the grass. The driver had swerved and knocked Brett from his hold. Now he was a hungry, bleeding heap in the dirt. Brett pushed himself to his feet and watched the car spit mud as it moved north along the narrow road. The men had escaped. The hunger in his gut was suddenly acute. He lowered himself to a crouch and licked his wounds. He rolled his blood-soaked tongue across the roof of his mouth, relishing the consolation.

If you ever see them again, said the voice, *you need to punish them.*

For once Brett liked what the voice had to say.

***

"I pissed myself," said Due. He took his eyes off the road to look at the broad damp spot on the fabric between his legs. "I can't believe I pissed myself."

Linh pulled himself from the floor and sat in the middle of the backseat. He carefully brushed window shards onto the floor. He reached out and put his hand on Due's shoulder. "I'm sorry."

Due snapped. "Sorry I pissed myself? Sorry my car is a mess? Sorry we almost got eaten by Ma Trang?"

Linh winced at the pain in his shoulder. "All of it."

Due glared at Linh in the mirror. "You should be sorry. You should be ashamed."

Linh's eyes narrowed. "Ashamed? I'm not ashamed. It was bad luck."

Due shook his head. He banged on the wheel with his hand. "No," he said. "Not the monster. You should be ashamed because of what you do."

Linh leaned forward. "What?"

"You bothered those fishermen while they worked, while they were trying to provide for their families," Due explained. "Then you invaded that woman's privacy. You made her cry. You made her tell you things her own grandchildren didn't know. Then you nearly got me killed because you stopped to take a photograph of Ma Trang."

"I don't—"

"You are a waste of a good mind, Jimmy Linh," said Due. "I'm telling your father. I'm telling him what happened. He will stop you from this foolishness."

Linh sat back against the seat and said nothing. He thought about his uncle's complaints. They were valid. He had stopped the men from fishing. He had unwittingly led the old woman to reveal her darkest secret. He had, indirectly, caused his uncle to piss himself.

Those fishermen, though, volunteered information without any prodding. The woman had chosen to open up about her past when the interview was over. She'd *invited* them into her home. And his uncle had been battling incontinence before the Ma Trang jumped them. His father had told him as much months earlier.

The truth was, Linh felt invigorated. Despite apologizing for nearly getting them killed and the damage to the car, this had been a remarkable day. They'd survived the attack, hadn't they? He couldn't wait to get back to his hotel and call Gertrude with the news. His fingers were itching to start writing. He almost couldn't feel the wound in his shoulder. Almost. Another round of adrenaline was coursing through him. He felt as alive as he ever had. Surviving the attack had been empowering somehow.

Linh leaned forward again, using the front seat backs

to draw close to his uncle. "Look, Uncle," he said. "I will pay for the damage to your car. I will pay for new pants. And I will give you gas money plus something extra for your trouble. I owe you that. I am grateful to you for coming with me and for helping me escape."

Due opened his mouth and wagged his finger. "You can't just—"

Linh cut him off. "But I'm not a disgrace. I am a reporter. I'm a *storyteller*. You can tell my father whatever you want, Uncle," he said. "It won't change my mind."

Due sat dumbfounded. He huffed and regripped the wheel with both hands before holding up two fingers. "Two thousand."

"Two thousand what?"

"Pounds. I need two thousand."

Linh chuckled.

Due shot his nephew a glance. "What?"

"I met a woman on the train," said Linh. "She's beautiful. She likes me. I'm going to try to call her when we get back to Hanoi. I want to take her out on a date. And guess what, Uncle?"

Due shrugged.

"She's white," said Linh. "Tell my father about that too."

— 19 —

Frederick, Maryland
April 20, 1980

Major Rick Gibson held the paperwork in his hands. He was at his desk. It was dark in the room aside from the spray of pale yellow light from a desk lamp. He leaned on his elbows and reread the US Federal Form sf-503. It was the official autopsy protocol for the military. The patient's name was absent from the identification box at the bottom of the form. Gibson wanted it that way. He didn't know the guinea pig's name when the man arrived at the installation from Leavenworth, and he sure as hell didn't want to know it now. Instead of the name, social security number, and rank, it listed his Bureau of Prisons number, 07424-080, his date of birth, 05/01/50, and his sex.

There were two main sections to the form. The first was the clinical diagnosis. The second was the pathological diagnosis. Gibson had overseen the transcription of both sections. Neither was entirely accurate. Neither told the truth of how the man died or the condition of his internal organs.

Gibson put down the document and slid it across the desk to Dr. Starling. "Take a look," he said. "I think that should cover us."

Starling looked at the paper for a moment before picking it up to read it. He shot Gibson a disapproving look as he read the false narrative. He'd been in the lab. He'd seen the procedure. The official sf-503 was a farce.

The procedure had been as much an autopsy as it was a necropsy. The attending forensic pathologist had called for the help of a veterinarian.

"The phenotypic changes from the normal human characteristics are remarkable," observed the pathologist. "The skin is almost absent melanin, similar to albinism. The hair on the scalp and in the pubic region has, however, retained its pigment. The eyes are inhuman."

"They're reptilian," the veterinarian had added. "Maybe amphibian. Note the upper lid above the conjunctiva and the lower lid. There are also suspensory ligaments that you wouldn't typically find in a human eye."

They'd measured and examined the claws on both the hands and feet, which they determined to be keratin, the same biological material humans use to produce fingernails and toenails. But they were thicker and multilayered.

The men had spent considerable time measuring the angles of the joints and their distention, but the majority of the exterior examination had been spent on the subject's lips and teeth.

"The lips are best described as a sucker," the pathologist had said. "They're swollen and rounded. The tongue is also enlarged. The teeth—"

"The teeth are similar to the black piranha," the vet had said. "That species, the *Serrasalmus rhombeus*, has among the most forceful bites. It's not just the teeth.

There's a mechanic to the way the jaw muscles are attached closely to the tip of the jaw. This slows the speed of the bite but provides tremendous force. That strong jaw and the finely serrated teeth allow the fish, or in this case the subject here, a unique ability to tear flesh."

The pathologist had shaken his head. "I've never seen anything like this," he'd said. "Where did you say you found this man? What was the chemical weapon to which he was exposed?"

Gibson had frowned. "I didn't say."

The vet had looked up from the body. "I've heard rumors about this," he'd said. "Some experimental super-soldier experiment that went wrong in Vietnam. It changed the men into monsters."

Gibson had grunted. "Huh," he'd said. "I hadn't heard that one."

Starling and Gibson had exchanged knowing glances. The young scientist had been standing in the corner of the examination room, having told his boss he didn't want to get too close. He'd seen enough of the mutant.

"Yeah," the vet had added. "I don't know much else. But it sounded worse than Tuskegee or MKULTRA."

"It does sound awful," Gibson had said. "Can we get on with the procedure? I'm anxious to see the histopathology."

"We need fingerprints and photographs of the outside of the body first," the pathologist had said. "That's standard pro—"

Gibson had shaken his head. "No photographs. No fingerprints."

"But—"

Gibson's eyes had narrowed. He'd spoken more forcefully. "No photographs. No fingerprints."

The pathologist had lowered his mask. "X-rays?" he'd asked, like a child wanting seconds of dessert despite knowing his parents would say no.

"No."

"We'll proceed to the blood and urine draw, then," the pathologist had said sheepishly. He'd raised his surgical mask and plucked a syringe from the table next to him. He'd drawn several samples before injecting another syringe into the bladder to draw urine.

"We'll be taking those," said Gibson. "All of them."

The pathologist and vet had obliged and began with the body cavity examination. Using a scalpel, the pathologist made a large Y-shaped incision from each shoulder and across the chest. He'd then sliced straight down to the pubic bone.

"Holy mother of—" The pathologist had caught himself as he'd pulled back the skin and exposed the rib cage. It didn't look like a human rib cage.

Gibson had stepped forward, toward the table. "What?"

"The ribs," the veterinarian had said. "They're flared, like an ape."

"Or a Neanderthal," Gibson had said. "The cage is large like an early, prehistoric human."

"Or an ape," the vet had repeated.

"The pelvis is flared too." The pathologist had been speaking quickly as he'd taken rib shears to split the cage and examine the underlying organs. "And it's much larger."

"So are the lungs," the vet had said. "The capacity must be at least thirty percent greater than the average person. Add to the that the musculature, this man or whatever it was, must have been remarkably strong, had incredible endurance, and was—"

"A killing machine," the pathologist had added. "This was a killing machine."

The men had quietly finished the rest of the examination, weighing the organs, rechecking the eyes, and removing the brain to weigh it. In addition to the unmarked vials of blood and urine, they'd taken skin and organ samples and provided those to Gibson and Starling. Both men had been as white as the dead patient on the table by the time they'd finished.

Sitting in Gibson's office hours later, Starling seemed unsurprised by the fictional sf-503 in front of him. He looked up at his boss. "I have the blood results."

Gibson's eyes widened. "You didn't tell me."

"You didn't ask, Major."

"So?"

Starling sighed. "So, after looking at the samples microscopically, I can tell you why it didn't work."

"Do I want to know?"

Starling shrugged. "It didn't work because the attachment didn't occur as I hypothesized."

Gibson's brow sagged. He frowned. "So you were wrong."

"Not exactly," said the scientist. "From what I could determine, and again this is preliminary, the attachment failed because we introduced it simultaneously with the VX-99."

Gibson pinched his eyes and shook his head. "How else would we do it? We have to inject simultaneously."

"No," said Starling. "That's not entirely true. We would have to inject the cocktail to a subject that already had VX-99 in his system. The cellular mutations would already have had to take place. The hormones do carry the cocktail. But if the VX-99 isn't already there, if the cells haven't previously accepted their fate, so to speak, there's no VX mutation to which the cocktail can attach."

"I see."

"Which means we'd need to inject someone with VX-99 and then wait for the changes to occur," said Starling. "Then, and only then, could we truly test the theory."

"That's a problem," said Gibson.

"Other than the obvious ethical violations, why?"

"We don't have any more VX-99."

"What do you mean? It's all gone?"

"We stopped synthesizing it in 1968," said Gibson. "The VX-99 you've been using for your experiments was what we had left. That final test, with the deserter, was the last of it."

Starling jumped to his feet. "Why would you use the last of it? That's crazy. Without any more pure VX-99, we can't do anything. We're finished."

Gibson chuckled. "First, I find your sympathy for my immoral program to be disingenuous, Dr. Starling. Second, your test was our last shot at this regardless. It didn't matter. We're shut down."

Starling rubbed his chin before running his hands through his hair. He grasped at the ends of the strands as if to pull them out. "You're right," he said. "Ethically and morally I'm glad we're finished. Especially after what we did to that man today. But scientifically, I'm conflicted. I want to solve the problem. I want to prove the hypothesis. Now I'll never get that chance."

"That was a refreshingly honest answer from the naïvely moral policeman," said Gibson. "You can stick around a few days to clean out your belongings, delete files, and destroy samples. I'll give you a good recommendation. You can go get a job working for the Centers for Disease Control or some benevolent foundation somewhere."

Starling nodded. "Thank you. I guess it's too bad all of those Marines killed each other in Vietnam. If they hadn't, you'd have your live sample and you'd have an endless supply of VX-99."

The scientist rapped his knuckles on the desk before stuffing his hands back into his lab coat. He spun around with a nod and left Gibson alone in his office. Gibson slid the autopsy into a manila file folder, unlocked his desk drawer, and slipped the file inside.

He picked up the phone and called his wife, dimming the desk lamp as he did. The phone rang once before she picked up.

The major pressed the receiver close to his lips. "Hi, honey," he said softly. "I'm sorry I haven't called. It's been a long day here. I'll be home shortly."

His wife asked if he wanted her to warm a plate in their new microwave oven. It had been an anniversary gift.

"No, thanks," he said. "I'm not one hundred percent convinced those radioactive things are safe."

She giggled at him and told him to drive carefully. "I love you."

"I love you too," he said. "Give the boy a kiss for me."

Gibson hung up the phone, his hand lingering on the receiver as he thought about the last thing Starling had said before leaving his office.

— 20 —

Hanoi, Vietnam
April 21, 1980

Jimmy Linh sat at the desk in his hotel room. His fingers rested on the keys of a small portable typewriter he'd lugged in his suitcase. He was almost finished with his article.

The Ma Trang is not a ghost. It is flesh and blood. And it's both blood and flesh it seeks in a place where legends are apparently real.

"That's good stuff," he said to himself. He winced against the pain in his shoulder. The quartet of gashes was long but not deep enough for stitches. He'd taken a shower and cleaned the wound. As soon as a nearby pharmacy opened, he'd gotten bandages, some Neosporin, and a large bottle of aspirin.

He checked the article one more time and picked up the phone next to the typewriter. He followed the instructions on the phone and, using his notes, dialed an international number. It rang a dozen times. He was about to hang up when he heard a groggy voice on the other end.

"Hullo? Who is this?"

"Gertrude," said Linh, "it's me, Jimmy Linh."

"Jimmy who?"

"Jimmy Linh. The new reporter," he said. "I'm calling you from Vietnam."

She cleared her throat. "Jimmy Linh? Do you have any idea what time it is?"

Jimmy paused. He bit his lip. He shouldn't have called her at home.

"That wasn't rhetorical, Jimmy Linh the new reporter. What time is it?"

"I think it's three o'clock in London."

Gertrude sighed and grunted. "All right, Jimmy," she said, her voice still laced with sleep. "What is it that's so important you called me at my flat at three o'clock in the morning on bloody Monday?"

"I found the Ma Trang."

"The what?"

"The White Ghost. The reason I came here. I found it."

She chuckled. "You *found* it."

"Yes. I have an article and a roll of film I'll have flown to you."

She chuckled again. "You have an article *and* film. Jimmy Linh the new reporter has an article *and* film of this mythical beast."

"Yes. I can read it to you. And it's not mythical. It's real."

"Go ahead," said Gertrude. "Read away."

"Okay," Jimmy said. "I wrote it quickly, so if you have notes, then—"

"Just *read* it, Jimmy."

"It's not often, if ever, a man looks into the eyes of a killer, smells its hot breath, feels the sting of its claws, and lives to tell about it," Jimmy said, his hands trembling as he held the freshly typed article. "In the sweaty jungles of a country still reeling from decades of war, I saw the monster firsthand. I can tell you its breath was rank with rot, and its claws sliced through my skin like hot butter. Its name is Ma Trang, Vietnamese for the White Ghost, and it has terrorized the mountains and valleys along the Da River for more than a decade.

"The legend of the Ma Trang says the creature is the ghost of an American serviceman who died in that country's military action, which ended in 1975. The Ma Trang is seeking its revenge. It hunts them. It kills them. It eats them. It has been stalking prey for as long as twelve years, according to those with whom we spoke.

"The Ma Trang, according to local reports, is responsible for the deaths or disappearances of hundreds, if not thousands, of people along a path that runs from Son La southeast into the mountains near Hòa Bình. It was in that small village of Hòa Bình that we met a family whose lives the monster destroyed and where I met the beast myself."

"Stop," said Gertrude. "You don't need to read any more."

A punch of nausea hit Linh in the gut. "Why? Is it not good?"

Gertrude laughed. "No," she said. "You silly fool. It's fantastic."

"Really?"

"Yes, really. Is it true?"

Linh wasn't sure what she meant. He was a reporter. Of course it was true. Why wouldn't it be true?

"Yes," he said. "It's all true."

"And you really have pictures?"

"Yes."

"Good," she said, suddenly invigorated. "Put the film in a container and the article in an envelope. I'll see to it a courier picks it up from you directly within the hour. We'll develop the film, tweak the prose a bit, and have it in Tuesday's edition. Excellent work, Jimmy Linh. Truly outstanding. Take the day to sleep, spend tomorrow in Hanoi on me, and then come back on Wednesday ready to work. I'll have travel rebook you a late flight out on the twenty-third."

"Thank you," Linh said. "May I ask you a question?"

"Of course," she said. "You've already awoken me at three in the morning."

"Why did you ask if what I wrote was true?"

Gertrude laughed so hard, Linh had to pull the receiver away from his ear. "Oh, silly new reporter, Jimmy Linh. You wouldn't believe how many reporters write things that aren't."

Jimmy thanked her again and hung up. He could barely contain himself. His heart was pounding; his palms were sweaty. It was like he'd just gone out on a first date. That reminded him.

He reached into his satchel, still damp from the rain, and pulled out his notepad. Not thinking about the time, he dialed the number scrawled in flowery handwriting. It rang only twice.

"Hello?"

Linh took a deep breath. "Molly?"

"Yes?"

"It's Jimmy Linh, from the train."

"Oh," she said. "Good morning. Or should I say good

night? What time is it?"

"Did I wake you?"

"Yes," she said, "but it's no problem. It's nice to hear from you."

"Nice to hear you," Linh said then slapped his forehead with his palm. What a stupid thing to say.

"Not to be rude," she said, "but why are you calling me so early, Jimmy?"

"I'm so sorry," he said. "I shouldn't have called. I'm in Vietnam. The time difference. I didn't consider it before dialing."

"Vietnam? How interesting."

"Quite," he said. "You'll be able to read about it tomorrow in the paper."

"Which one?"

"The *Reflector.*"

"Very good."

There was an awkward silence before Linh gained enough courage. "Would you like to have dinner?"

Molly giggled. "In Vietnam?"

Linh's face flushed. He rubbed his palms on his thighs. "No. I'm sorry. In London. Thursday night?"

"I'd love that."

"Very well then," said Linh. "That's wonderful news."

She giggled again and then yawned. "Yes, it is."

"I should let you get back to sleep," he said. "I'll ring you when I land."

They hung up and Linh wondered why he'd been so nervous. She'd approached him and not the other way around. The date was a sure thing. Still, Linh was a rookie at more than just his job. Asking a woman on a date was almost as daunting, he thought, as facing the Ma Trang. Almost.

There was a knock at his door. Linh jumped from his seat and peeped through the eyelet. It was a courier.

"Just a moment," Linh said in Vietnamese. "I'll be right with you." He gathered the article and the film canister and put them into an envelope. He addressed the envelope to Gertrude Wombley and carried it over to the door.

He gave the courier the package, signed it over, and watched his big break leave in the hands of a stranger. He prayed it would find its way to Gertrude and he'd get his big headline. Since he'd last slept, he'd plodded through a mudslide, interviewed a grieving mother and her two grandchildren, nearly died at the hands of a monster, written a masterpiece of modern journalism, and booked a date with a pretty woman.

It was a good day.

— 21 —

Frederick, Maryland
April 22, 1980

The computer sounded an alert, a single short tone that told Major Rick Gibson he had a new message. He walked across his dimly lit office to his desk and sat in front of the monitor. He bit his lip as his eyes focused on the display. He'd not yet told command about the VX-99 cocktail failure. He was waiting as long as he could and hoped they'd be patient.

EYES ONLY, CLASSIFIED
PROJECT BESERKR USAMRIID TRIALS
Dial into secure call ASAP.
Subject: Operation Burn Bright Rumint

Rumint? *Operation Burn Bright Rumint?*

Rumint was military shorthand for rumor/intelligence. It primarily meant gossip. Gibson reread the message a second and third time. He had no idea what command wanted to discuss.

He pinched the bridge of his nose with one hand and picked up his phone with the other. The operator connected him to a secure line and then to command.

A brusk voice answered the call. "Gibson? This you?"

"Roger that, General. I received the message."

General Anthony Reed huffed. "We have a real situation on our hands. I need you to tell me you knew nothing about it."

Gibson swallowed hard. "Go ahead."

Had they learned about the failed trial? Had Starling ratted him out?

"There's a report in a British newspaper that has pretty firm evidence we've got an MIA hunting people in Vietnam."

Gibson swallowed again. He dipped a finger inside his collar and tugged. "Hunting? How do you mean, sir?"

"You have a fax machine?"

"Roger."

"Probably better if I send you a fax," said the general. "That way you can see the picture yourself."

"The…picture?"

"I'm sending it now," said General Reed. "What it looks like is that one of your VX-99 super freaks didn't die after all. He survived and he's been killing people for, well, since he became whatever the hell he is."

The fax machine in Gibson's office rang, it picked up, and it started printing the document. "You're saying this was in a British newspaper?"

"The *London Morning Reflector*. Some reporter went to Vietnam and found the creature. Says he was almost killed. Talked to other people who say they saw it, who lost family to it."

"And there's a picture?"

"It's grainy," said the general, "but it's a picture of something all right. It looks more realistic than that

Patterson Bigfoot film from a couple of years ago."

Gibson glanced over at the paper curling into a scroll as it emerged from the fax machine. He rolled over to the machine and unraveled the warm, shiny fax paper with one hand. He could read the headline upside down.

GHOST OF AMERICAN GI HAUNTS,
TERRORIZES,
EATS VIETNAMESE VILLAGERS

"Good lord," Gibson muttered. "This is—"

"Bad," said the general. "It's bad. The president's already been informed. He's asking questions to which he doesn't really want to know the answers. Micromanager that POTUS seems to be, he wants to know everything about VX-99. He's already got his hands full with the hostage crisis. This is FUBAR."

Gibson squeezed his eyes shut. His mind was swimming.

"Tell me you didn't know about this, Gibson," said the general. "If I find out that you—"

"Of course I didn't!" Gibson snapped before taking a breath. "My apologies, General," he said calmly. "I didn't know. We believed the entire platoon to be dead. There were a couple of MIAs. But with the way the bodies were ripped apart, there was no way to account for everyone definitively."

"So there could be *two* of these things?"

"No," Gibson said. "Not possible. If two survived the initial fray, one would have killed the other. No doubt."

Gibson looked down at the emerging fax. He could see the photograph, however grainy and blurred by the facsimile ink. He knew instantly the monster captured in that image was one of his. It was a Burn Bright guinea pig. Somehow, one of the Marines had managed to survive as something other than human.

The fax quit printing and Gibson ripped the long sheet from the machine. He asked the general to hold while he scanned the article. He couldn't believe what he was reading. It was like science fiction, implausible science fiction.

The White Ghost? Hundreds or thousands dead? Unreal. Completely unreal.

The more he read, the less anxious he became. He had an idea.

"It's one of ours," Gibson said. "No doubt."

"How do we fix this, Gibson?"

"We find it. We capture it. And we use it to test our new cocktail."

The general laughed. "Capture something that's been roaming free for a dozen years? Then bring this killing machine back to American soil? You make me laugh, Gibson."

"I'm not joking, General. Our latest test failed. We're out of VX-99. This miraculous discovery gives us new hope in finding the right combination of chemicals to create the ultimate warrior."

The general mumbled under his breath for a moment. "Your test failed, huh? You failed to mention that."

"I hadn't had an—"

"Spare me, Gibson. I know what you're about. I know this is your passion. Or obsession. I admire your grit."

"Thank you, General."

"I think I can get the right people on board to make this happen," said the general. "I think I could probably have a team in-country by the end of the day, tomorrow morning at the latest. You send me everything you have about these VX-99 tests and what you think happened to them. If we find him, we'll get him back to you. Then, whatever happens…"

Gibson nodded. "Happens."

The men hung up and Gibson unlocked his file drawer. From it, he pulled a thick binder of documents. Among them were the files for two men, both of whom were listed as MIA in the aftermath of Operation Burn Bright.

He laid them side by side on his desk and simultaneously opened both of them to the front page. To the left he looked at the photograph of Rick Fern. The man looked like he had a wad of chewing tobacco in his mouth. His lower lip protruded slightly beyond the upper one. To the right was Trevor Brett. He was the young lieutenant in charge of the platoon. Gibson remembered meeting the young Marine in a tent where he'd handed over the vials of VX-99. It was a moment that frequently made it difficult for Gibson to sleep at night. The insomnia wasn't because of what he'd done to a platoon of Marines who'd pledged their lives to their country. It was because his operation had failed.

For a dozen years, Gibson had lived with the knowledge that his legacy was a failed experiment. He'd spent countless dollars, seemingly limitless hours, and much of his adult life in the pursuit of changing the future of warfare.

He'd studied man's predilection for armed conflict. From the earliest Neanderthals there were weapons. Studies had found forty percent of the Neanderthal skulls discovered had fractures.

Warfare itself was prehistoric. There was

archaeological evidence of a battle in Nataruk in Turkana, Kenya, more than ten thousand years ago. Remains revealed the violent deaths of two dozen people. Some contained embedded stone projectile tips.

From the Neolithic age to the advent of copper weapons in the Bronze Age, to Germanic warriors of the Iron Age, weapons advanced but men did not. Barbarism seemed to fester more deeply within societal fabric as one war dissolved into the next. It was the worst once the twentieth century had fully taken hold. Record numbers of people died in World War Two. As many as eighty-five million lost their lives in just six years. It was by far the worst war in human history.

Gibson knew he could not end war. He could not change man's desire to conquer and rule. He could, however, lessen the death toll. He could save lives. He could shorten wars. All he needed to do was amplify the genetic code that made men the beasts they truly were. The deadlier these super warriors could become, the faster any armed engagement would end.

To this point, he'd failed in that mission. Now, somehow, when it was darkest, dawn was upon him. He had a second chance. A white ghost was giving him an opportunity for redemption.

Rick Gibson smiled as he ran his hands across the files. His eyes danced between the photographs.

"It's one of you," he said. "One of you magnificent grunts is going to change the world. I have no doubt about that. Sooner or later, you're going to change the world."

— 22 —

Black Site Installation NSS-1018, Northeastern Iran
April 22, 1980

Nick Womack folded his arms across his chest. His jaw was set. "What do you mean we're off the assignment?"

"Yeah," said Wolf. "We've been sitting here with our thumbs up our—"

"Shut it, Wolf," snapped Womack. "I'm handling it."

The men were standing outside the main house. The military liaison had called them outside to discuss an update on their assignment. He'd left the Iranian translator inside the house at the card table.

"We're not going to need you for Operation Eagle Claw," said the liaison. "That's the only intel I can give you. I'm not authorized to divulge any more—"

"That's not acceptable," said Womack. "General Reed personally hired us for this mission. We're part of the extraction element. We've been briefed. We know the plan."

The liaison shook his head. "You're not part of the extraction anymore," he said. "You'll be paid for the time you've spent here, of course. That I can assure you."

"I need to talk with General Reed," said Womack.

"He's not going to like this. We've been sitting out here with our thumbs up our—"

"General Reed is the one who pulled you."

Womack took a step back and dropped his arms to his sides. "What?"

"General Reed is the one—"

"I think we get that," interrupted Ferg. He was cleaning his thumbnail with the tip of his knife. "What Womack is trying to say is *why?*"

The liaison shrugged. "You'd have to ask him," he said. "Answering you is above my pay grade. He'll be calling you shortly."

"You know this mission of yours is going to fail," said Womack. "The plan barely had legs before you cut us."

Wolf made a slicing motion with his hands. "You hacked off the feet," he said. "Nothing to stand on now, brother."

"What are you?" interjected Wilco. "The echo chamber?"

Wolf rolled his eyes. "I'm just saying—"

"I didn't cut you," said the liaison. "I made that clear. I didn't hire you. I didn't fire you."

Womack bit his lip. He balled his fists. He wanted to punch the smug little gofer. Instead he motioned to his men. "C'mon. Let's pack up and figure out what's next."

They marched back into the house as a satellite phone chirped. It was a black brick of a phone mounted to a wall in the kitchen. Womack headed straight to the phone and answered it.

"Speak of the devil," Wolf mumbled. He pursed his lips when Womack looked over his shoulder and flung a dagger of a glance.

There was ambient noise warbling in the background,

but he could clearly hear General Reed on the other end. His voice was unmistakable.

"This Womack?" asked the general.

"Roger that, General. I understand there's a change of plans."

"Sorry to do this to you, Nick," he said. "I really am. You'll get paid the day rate for the time you've spent in that dreadful desert."

"Understood. When is the plane home?"

"Home?" asked the general with a chuckle. "Nobody said anything about you going home. I thought you knew."

Womack pressed the phone closer to his ear and held his palm over the other to more clearly hear the general's voice. "Knew what, sir?"

"You're going from the desert to the jungle."

The operator wanted to puke. "The jungle?"

"Vietnam, son. You're taking that team of yours in-country. I don't trust anyone else with it. It's of critical importance."

"Not to question your decision, General Reed, but this jungle mission is more important than rescuing the hostages?"

"It is, Nick. You'll better understand it when you get the briefing packet I've had sent to your rendezvous point. As I said, it's of critical importance."

"What's the mission? Recon? Elimination? Extraction?"

General Reed paused. "Possibly all three. You'll understand when you get the intel."

"Roger that."

"Godspeed, Rick."

Womack thanked the general and disconnected from

the call. He slowly placed the transceiver onto the large brick-like cradle and let out a slow breath. "All right, men," he said, facing his team. "We're headed from the dry heat to the wet heat. Get your gear."

"Vietnam?" asked Wilco. "Again?"

Womack nodded. "Looks like it." He looked at the liaison. "When do we leave?"

"Transport is here in thirty," said the gofer. "Wheels up in ninety. Intel will be on the plane. You'll land in Laos and then chopper from Sam Neua to outside Hanoi."

"So you did know," said Wolf. "You lied."

A smirk spread across the liaison's face. "I didn't lie. I told you that answering you was above my pay grade. I never said I didn't know the answer."

"Semantics," said Womack.

"Se-what-ics?" asked Wolf.

Wilco laughed. "Semantics. It's Latin for 'Wolf is illiterate.'"

"Enough," said Womack. He stepped over to Shine. "You okay with this?"

Shine shrugged and rubbed the back of his own neck with his meat hook of a hand. "I gotta choice?"

"You always have a choice. If you don't—"

Shine interrupted. "You go, I go. That's all there is to it."

"All right then," Womack said. "We need to hit the road."

***

They'd been in the air less than a half hour into the seven-hour flight from eastern Iran to Long Tieng, Laos, when Womack opened up the folder for Operation Flame Out. There were matching dossiers for all five of the men. They'd waited for the okay to open theirs.

Womack keyed the mic on his headset. "Let's do this," he said. "Start with page one. Read everything. Wolf, if you need help putting sounds together, ask Shine."

The men laughed. Even Wolf cracked a smile at his own expense. The smile and laughter disappeared, however, as soon as the men began reading their assignment. It was a top secret document intended for special handling only. No foreign nationals were allowed access to the information contained in the following pages. That was customary. What was typed beneath it was not.

TOP SECRET SPECIAL HANDLING
NOFORN
USAMRIID 04221980-VX99
OPERATION FLAME OUT

22 April 1980

SUBJECT: VX-99 RESIDUAL CONTAINMENT

Background

On 10 July 1968, a Marine platoon under the command of Lieutenant Trevor Brett was assigned to a reconnaissance mission in an undisclosed location in South Vietnam. The Marines were inserted via CH-47 Chinook with specific instructions to target a remote village identified as harboring Vietcong.

The platoon's lieutenant, Trevor Brett, was tasked with distributing an experimental drug known as VX-99 to all Marines under his command. At a prescribed location prior to reaching the target, the men were to inject the experimental drug.

Under direction of USAMRIID, the Marines were told VX-99 was a prophylactic designed to minimize or eliminate the airborne effects of herbicide Orange sprayed across South Vietnam under Operation Ranch Hand.

The true nature/military purpose of VX-99 was, and is, classified. It is not an HO prophylactic.

The experimental drug did have unintended psychological and physical side effects, which proved fatal.
(SEE ATTACHED PHOTOS: PFC Michael Junko)

Thirty (30) Marines were KIA.

Two (2) Marines, Lieutenant Trevor Brett and Staff Sergeant Richard Fern, were MIA and presumed dead. One of them is no longer MIA. He is alive.
(SEE ATTACHED NEWS ARTICLE/PHOTO: *London Daily Reflector*)
(SEE ATTACHED PHOTOS: LT Trevor Brett, SSgt Richard Fern)

<u>Mission</u>

This is an activity under joint command of USAMRIID and CIA Special Operations Group.

You are to insert into North Vietnam via helicopter. Location is TBD within fifteen kilometers of Hanoi.

Travel to last known location of Brett/Fern.
(SEE ATTACHED MAP/NAVSTAR Coordinates)

Locate Brett/Fern. Capture and sedate Brett/Fern. DO NOT KILL.

Return Brett/Fern to TBD Landing Zone. Return Brett/Fern to USAMRIID.

Conclusion

Brett/Fern is property of the United States Marine Corp and the United States Department of Defense.

If your mission is compromised, the United States government, USAMRIID, and CIA SOG will deny all knowledge of your activities.

###

Ferg held up the open file in his thick mitt. "Is this for real? Thirty Marines KIA? Did the Brett/Fern thing kill them?"

"No kidding," said Wilco. "This has got to be some sort of joke. This mission file reads like—"

"That Sigourney Weaver movie." Wolf snapped his fingers. "*Alien.*"

The men grunted in agreement. Womack couldn't blame them. It didn't seem real. It was, though. General Reed wouldn't send him on some goose chase. Uncle Sam was paying too much money for that.

Womack raised his hand and quieted the men. "It's for real," he said. "This thing, whatever it is, is out there. No doubt. We need to track it, trap it, and bring it home."

Wolf laughed uncomfortably. "Why don't we just kill it, QSV style?"

Wilco and Ferg agreed. Kill it. Quick. Silent. Violent. No trapping. No transport.

Womack raised his hand again. "That's not the mission," he said. "That's not what we're getting paid to do. For whatever reason, USAMRIID wants this thing alive."

Shine keyed his mic for the first time. He hadn't said a word since they left the black site. "All due respect, boss, but you keep calling him a thing," he said. "He's a Marine. He's an American. It ain't his fault he followed orders. From the sound of it, he got lied to."

Womack pursed his lips and looked at his boots. He took a deep breath and sighed. "You're right, Shine. Absolutely right. It doesn't change the fact that this Marine isn't really human anymore. He won't hesitate to end you."

Shine nodded. "I get it. Just makes the jungle all the more hospitable."

Before Womack could respond, turbulence interrupted the smooth flight. The C-46A Commando twin-engine aircraft shuddered and its two-thousand-horse-power, radial-piston engines whined as the pilots took the aircraft higher into the Asian air. There were thirty-five empty folding seats in the cargo hold. Some of them flapped up and down as the plane rumbled and vibrated. The hydraulic winch hanging from the ceiling of the fuselage swung wildly back toward the rear of the plane as the nose arced sharply upward. Womack's stomach lurched. He worked to keep himself flat against the back of his seat. His eyes drifted to the large empty cage strapped to the port side of the hold, adjacent to the large cargo door.

"I'm telling you," said Wolf, his voice warbling with the movement of the aircraft. "It's like we're on the *Nostromo*."

Wilco, whose color had slipped to a pale white,

swallowed hard and looked at Wolf crossways. "The what?"

"The *Nostromo*. The spaceship from *Alien*. Except instead of seven people on board, we just have the five."

"There are two pilots," said Ferg. "That makes seven."

Wolf laughed. "Yep. We're all gonna die. Except for Ripley. Who's Ripley?"

"Does Ripley survive?" asked Wilco.

Wolf nodded.

"Then I'm Ripley," said Wilco.

"Figures," said Wolf. "Ripley's a woman."

The nose of the plane dipped, and the pilots leveled the World War Two-era plane above the storm brewing below. The rumbling subsided to a barely noticeable vibration. Womack let out a sigh of relief.

"Nobody's dying," said Womack. "We're doing what the general asked, we're getting home, and we're getting paid. Now get some sleep. There won't be any once we hit Laos."

— 23 —

Hanoi, Vietnam
April 23, 1980

Jimmy Linh pressed the phone closer to his ear. He wasn't certain he'd heard Gertrude's instructions. "You want me to what?"

"I want you to make another trip to the jungle," she repeated.

He'd heard her correctly.

"This story is cracking," Gertrude purred. "Our sales are smashing. I want more."

"But—"

"Jimmy," she said, "I won't have it. You promised me gold. You delivered. Now I want more gold."

"I—"

"This morning, I managed to cobble together a follow-up with some of the lesser photographs you snapped. There were only a few. I had one of our city reporters chat with an anthropologist. It's not enough. The people crave more."

"What exactly is the new angle?"

Gertrude sighed. "You're the reporter, Jimmy Linh. You figure something out. But I want you in the jungle. I want photographs. Go back to the scene of the crime, as it were. Interview more villagers. I want it for Thursday's paper."

"My flight is tonight."

"I'll talk to Harriett in travel," said Gertrude. "She'll wire you more money. Plenty for a fixer or a driver. We'll push you back a couple of days. Maybe you'll fly home Friday. If the story has legs, you may be setting up a bureau."

Linh was slack jawed. "I—"

"That was a joke, Jimmy Linh," said Gertrude. "I thought you'd be more peppy about this. You're on your way, Jimmy Linh. Really, the story was cracking. Sales are smashing. Smashing. Keep it up."

Gertrude Wombley hung up before Linh could say anything else. She was right. He should have been ecstatic. Instead, he was worried.

First, he didn't want to go back to the jungle. He'd survived one attack. If they stumbled upon the ghost or if it caught their scent or whatever, he didn't think he'd live to tell about it a second time. His unease crept up his chest from his gut. He tasted the acid in his throat.

Gertrude is asking me to commit suicide.

That wasn't the worst of it. He'd miss his flight that night and his date with Molly the next. That was a fate worse than death. She probably already thought him a flake for cutting their conversation short on the train and then calling her at odd hours. This would do it. Linh glanced at the phone and started to pick up the receiver. He stopped short.

"I'll call her when I get back," he mumbled. Instead he flipped the pages in his notebook to make another phone call he'd just as soon have put off. He dialed. It rang.

Uncle Due answered the phone in Vietnamese. "Hello?" His voice sounded weak, lacking the same force it had had when Linh had called him from London earlier in the week. He almost didn't recognize it.

"Uncle?"

Due sighed. "What do you want, Linh?"

"My story got published, and—"

"I know," said Due. "Your father called. He saw it in the paper yesterday. He's not happy."

Linh slunk against the back of the desk chair. "Why?"

"You embarrassed the family."

"I—"

"You wrote a science-fiction story," said Due. "That's what your father said. He is ashamed."

Linh pushed himself forward and stood at the desk. "It's not fiction," he said. "There were pictures. You were there. You saw the Ma Trang with your own eyes."

"He says the pictures are fakes. Like Bigfoot. He says a lot of people are telling him that."

"*You were there*, Uncle Due. Didn't you tell him you saw it too?"

"I don't know what I saw."

Linh clenched his jaw. His grip on the phone tightened. "You were there."

Due was silent. Linh could hear his breathing and the ambient noise of a television or radio in the background. A car horn blared.

"Uncle Due," said Linh, "I don't know what you're trying to do, but this is not make-believe. This is not a fairy tale or science fiction. You saw the Ma Trang almost kill me. Your car has scratches and a broken window. Those things are real. Didn't you tell my father that?"

"He didn't ask me."

"He didn't ask you what?"

"Your father didn't ask me any questions," said Due. "He just talked."

Linh bit the inside of his lip and slowly inhaled through his nose. "So you didn't defend me."

"I didn't say anything. I listened mostly."

"Okay then," said Linh. "Fine. You'll have another chance to figure out what you saw."

Due didn't respond.

"You need to go back with me."

The response was quick and definitive. "No."

"My boss," Linh said, "she wants another story. I need to go back to the jungle, back to the same place where we saw Ma Trang."

"No."

"I'll pay you."

"I don't need money. I'm tired."

"It would be enough to get a new car."

Due paused. It was almost as if Linh could hear the gears turning in his uncle's head. "A new car?"

"A used car," Linh clarified. "New to you. I have enough cash. More is coming."

"Your father says you are manipulative," said Due. "He says you are tricky. He's right. You didn't tell me how dangerous the last trip would be. You didn't say we would see the Ma…"

"We would what?"

"Nothing," said Due.

"I'm not going to argue with you about my father, Uncle Due. You know what you saw. You know what I'm offering. Take it or leave it. If you don't want to come, fine."

"Three thousand."

"Three thousand what?"

"Pounds," said Due. "I want three thousand pounds. That will get me a nice car."

"I've already paid you three thousand pounds."

Due chuckled. "You said take it or leave it. I'll leave it if you don't pay me three thousand pounds."

"Fine," said Linh. "Three thousand."

"Good," said Due. "I'll pick you up in an hour."

"Thank you." Linh started to hang up when his uncle called his name. He drew the receiver back to his ear. "You said something?"

"Yes," said Due. "I told your father about the white woman."

Linh dropped the receiver on the cradle without responding. His uncle was an ass like his father. Unfortunately, Linh needed him.

— 24 —

Near Hanoi, Vietnam
April 23, 1980

Womack kept his head low as he moved from the helicopter toward the collection of steel warehouses fifteen kilometers southwest of Hanoi. They'd landed in a field adjacent to the collection of rusting, crooked buildings.

He weaved his way through the tall grass and found the cracked concrete that led him to Warehouse 20-7. On the north side of the narrow flat-roofed structure was a single door. To the door's right was a keypad. Womack punched a six-digit alphanumeric combination with his finger, and a metallic click hummed until he yanked open the door. He backed against the frame and held it open for the rest of his men. They filed in and found themselves in a small dimly lit room.

Womack closed the door behind him. "Move, gentlemen," he said and wove his way to the wall opposite the entry door. On that door was what looked like a broken air-conditioning thermostat. Womack stepped to the thermostat, slid the temperature gauge, and popped the cover up on a hinge. Behind the thermostat was another keypad. He fingered the code. It triggered a pneumatic hiss, and part of the wall opened like a pocket door, revealing a bath of green light and the squawk and hum of a communications bunker.

"Spies rock," said Wolf. He passed Womack, held up his hand in the familiar rock and roll gesture, and strutted into the abyss of the bunker.

Wilco motioned at Wolf as he slid by Womack. "He's a moron."

"Yep," said Womack. "But he's *our* moron."

Shine lumbered through the opening. Ferg and Womack entered last.

"SOG gave you the codes to this installation?" asked Ferg. "That's pretty trusting of a group that trusts nobody."

"The code was set for our entry," said Womack. "Onetime use. If I tried it again, we couldn't get in." The opening hissed and the wall closed behind the men as they moved toward the hive of activity. There were at least a dozen men sitting at terminals, listening to radio traffic, pounding away at keyboards. One of the men, wearing a pale blue Hawaiian shirt and desert sand, military-style cargo pants, looked up from his work and marched over to Womack with his hand extended like a salesman on a call.

"Nick Womack?" he asked as he approached.

Womack took his hand and shook it firmly. "That's me."

"I'm Smith. I'll provide you with what you need."

Womack's eyes narrowed as he let go of the spook's hand. "Smith? Couldn't SOG come up with a better name?"

The man smiled, revealing the deep creases at the

corners of his eyes and in his cheeks. He was weather worn. It was hard to see in the green glow of the machines.

"Johnson was taken," said Smith. "So was Jones."

"I know they shipped most of your gear stateside since you came straight here from…?"

Womack smirked. "Another job."

Smith smiled. His white teeth glowed. "Gotcha. Okay, well, follow me to the back of the space here. I'll get your men kitted up and we'll get you on your way. Sound good?"

Womack nodded. He and his men followed Smith past the communication terminals to the far end of the long building.

"How long have you been here?" asked Wolf.

Smith glanced over at the young operator. "Me personally or the operation?"

"Either. Both."

"I've been here about nine months," said Smith. "I did three tours here. Just felt natural to come back."

Wolf nodded. "And this operation?"

Smith winked. "Officially it's not here. Unofficially we never left. This was originally set up by the French with the help of some friendlies in the north. It was a behind-enemy-lines setup that helped with intercepts, code breaking, that kind of thing."

Wilco grunted. "In the north during the war?"

"Yep," said Smith. "Crazy, right? Spitting distance from Hanoi. Nobody knew we were here. We've got tunnels to send and receive whatever we need. It's a fantastic asset."

"That doesn't exist," said Wolf.

Smith winked again. "*What* doesn't exist?"

Ferg leaned into Womack and whispered as they walked. "That wink is a little creepy. I think this dude has done some bad stuff."

"Agreed," said Womack. "Most of these SOG ops are creepy badasses. It's a given."

Smith spun and walked backwards as the group reached the corner of the building. "We've taken into consideration your personal preferences when putting together your care packages on very short notice. Each of these things is labeled."

Smith turned around and stopped at a pair of large collapsible laminate-covered tables. Atop the tables were five sets of gear. Each of the sets was boxed and marked by a strip of duct tape labeled with the corresponding operator's name.

Womack went to his box and started pulling out the goodies inside. He, and all of the men, were issued M1911A1 Colt .45s. They were slim but powerful single-action pistols. Each man also had three seven-round magazines.

"Love this weapon," said Wolf. "You know this is what Martin Sheen's character carried in *Apocalypse Now*?"

"Same as Robert Duvall," added Ferg. "But his had a pearl grip."

"Nothing like the smell of your useless trivia," said Wilco.

Aside from sidearms, extra ammunition, canteens, first aid kits, extra pairs of socks, K rations, and a rucksack in which to carry the haul, each operator had his own uniquely tailored weapon.

Womack was issued a .50 tranquilizer rifle. His job, when it came to it, was to hit the target multiple times. He picked up the lightweight weapon and turned it over in his hands.

"Ever fired one of those?" asked Smith.

Womack looked over at Smith and shook his head. "What's the drug?"

"M99," Smith said. "It's a semisynthetic opioid. Three thousand times more powerful than morphine."

"Huh," said Womack. "How many hits?"

"That's the tricky part," said Smith. "We've tried to calibrate the dosage based on what we believe the target's weight to be. We could be wrong."

"That's encouraging," said Womack.

"It's not an exact science, regardless. Tranquilizers don't affect everyone the same. We can't accurately predict whether one, two, or even three doses will have the same effect on you as it will on me. I can tell you, based on experience, that if you overdose the target, you'll kill him."

"So there's a sweet spot," said Womack. "We just don't know where it is."

"Sounds like you're talking about Wolf with women," sniped Wilco.

Womack frowned. "Mind your business, Wilco," he said. "You've got work to do over there."

Wilco nodded. "Sorry, boss."

Smith winked. "As I was saying," he said, "you just can't be sure how many hits it's gonna take. You also can't know exactly how long it will take for the drug to enter the bloodstream and sedate the target."

"Great."

"It's not ideal," admitted Smith. "If the target is attacking you, it's not like it's going to instantly stop. You need to hit it from a distance and have an escape route. Wolf, you get one too."

"Understood."

Womack looked at his men as they packed up their gear. Three of them had different primary weapons. They looked like a motley bunch.

Wilco had an M3 Grease Gun, a .45-caliber submachine gun. Similar in appearance to a mechanic's grease gun, the M3 had a hundred-yard range with a detachable thirty-round magazine. Wilco kissed the weapon as he held it in his hands. He looked like a child on Christmas morning, as did Shiner, who was checking his Stoner 63. The Stoner was an assault rifle capable of firing more than seven hundred rounds a minute. Shiner's model had a lightweight bipod that folded beneath the handle.

Ferg's weapon was maybe the most unique of all. His was a China Lake Launcher. It looked similar to a short-barreled shotgun, but was actually a pump-action grenade launcher. It had a three-round tubular magazine that unleashed explosive 40×46mm grenades. Each grenade, despite its relatively low velocity, could inflict serious damage with its percussive force and the twenty metal pellets inside it.

Once the men had packed their gear and strapped on their weapons, Smith led them to an elevator. He keyed in a code and hit the down button. The elevator door opened and the spook led the men inside the cabin with a wink.

Womack felt the men looking at him as they crowded into the elevator. He looked straight ahead at the door as it slid closed with a metallic *thunk*.

They descended for a few seconds to the sound of the lift's cabling whining, its gears grinding, until the box shuddered to a stop. Smith entered another code to open the door, and it pulled back to reveal a dank space no more than eight feet high.

It was lit by bulbs strung along wire and tacked to wood beams that framed a tunnel that reached endlessly in two directions. In front of the men was a Russian UAZ-469 truck. It was olive green, but without any military markings. The canopy that covered the cargo bed was torn along one side near the top.

"Is that ours?" asked Wolf.

"Yep," said Smith. "It's the best we could do on short notice. We're working with in-country assets here. It was an NVA general's ride at some point. I know it's not state of the art, but it'll accommodate the five of you plus one return passenger. And you shouldn't have any trouble with it in the jungle."

Wilco chimed in. "Don't you think it's too conspicuous?"

Smith shrugged. "What's not conspicuous, men? You're five hardened, pale-faced warriors traveling together in the north. Everything you do is conspicuous."

"Our job is being *in*conspicuous," said Wilco. "We're good at it."

"The truck won't be a problem," said Smith. "There's a ton of military surplus floating around Vietnam. Military left so much of it here when it bolted five years ago, this isn't going to turn any heads."

Womack offered his free hand to Smith. "Thanks for the help. Which way do we head?"

Smith pointed to the right. "That way. You'll be in the tunnel for maybe five kilometers. It'll put you straight onto a highway heading toward Hòa Bình. I'm told that's the general area you'll need to hit first. Turn left onto the highway and turn south. You've got a radio with a secure channel if you need me."

"Roger that," said Womack. "All right, men." He motioned to the truck. "Let's hit it."

— 25 —

Hòa Bình, Vietnam
April 23, 1980

Linh stared at the mudslide where he'd fought for his life. The mess resembled the remnants of a sand castle after the tide washed over it. He could tell something had happened there by looking at the slop, but there was nothing distinct about it.

"I thought you were a fool," said Due. "Now I know it."

Linh didn't acknowledge his uncle. He'd endured enough chastisement during the trip back here. He put his hands on his hips and sucked in a deep breath, puffed his cheeks, and released it.

"This really is stupid," said Due. "If you're trying to find the ghost, you're asking to die."

Linh glanced off toward the river below. "I didn't say I wanted to find the ghost. I said I need to produce another story."

"Are you just going to stand here all day?"

Linh rolled his eyes. "No. It's already getting late in the day. Let's go."

"I'm not going."

"What?"

"I'm staying with the car. I'll wait for you."

"But—"

Due raised his hands in protest. "You asked for a driver. I drove. Now shoo." He flung his hands in the direction of the village.

Linh didn't have the strength to argue. "Fine," he said. "I'll be back in a couple of hours."

Due huffed and walked back to his car. He swung open the door and dropped into the driver's seat. He cranked back the seat, folded his arms across his chest, and closed his eyes. Linh thought he saw his uncle crack open a lid for a second to see if Linh was still watching him.

The young reporter draped his satchel over his shoulder like a messenger bag and navigated his way around the mud without looking again at Due. The bag flapped against his back as he moved, and within minutes his sweat-soaked shirt was plastered to the small of his back.

Linh trudged along the edge of the road, his eyes dancing across the grass and densely packed canopy of trees that separated his path from the Da River. The river ran parallel to the road. The air was thick with humidity and the scent of rot. It was at once sweet and foul. It was the smell of death. The rancid, unmistakable odor was stained into his memory and was instantly recognizable. Linh had never seen a dead person before, but he'd seen plenty of dead animals.

He had been in year six of his schooling and was just eleven years old when dead dogs began appearing on street corners, in parks, and in back alleys near his home.

The dogs weren't only dead. They were mutilated. Sometimes it was days before the dogs were discovered or removed. Their scent lingered and hung in the air as a constant reminder to those, like Linh, who'd have preferred to forget.

At first, authorities chalked it up to dog fights. There were a fair number of angry strays that roamed his neighborhood and they'd been aggressive. The numbers of dead dogs, however, and their increasingly grotesque injuries, soon changed public opinion. Someone was hunting the dogs and torturing them.

Linh didn't have a dog as a child. His parents weren't interested. They were busy with the business, and a dog, they'd told him, was too much responsibility for a young boy. Still, he loved animals, and when he found one of the mutilated dogs in a gutter on his way home from school, he'd made a decision. He would do something about it.

Without his parents' knowledge, he'd visited the local Metropolitan Police station and offered his help. They'd told him he was too young. So he went to the neighborhood weekly newspaper and volunteered to write stories about the dogs in the hopes the attention might lead to the killer.

The older couple who ran the newspaper out of their flat was gracious. They'd told Linh they couldn't afford to pay him, but they'd publish whatever he wrote.

Linh immediately got to work. Every day after school, he'd stop by the police station and ask for any new reports about dead dogs. The constable on duty would take pity on the young boy and give him the information along with a warning to be careful.

Once a week for three months, Linh's articles about

the dogs, their injuries, and any clues he could find would appear in the paper under Linh's nom de plume, Francis James. He didn't want his parents to know.

The *London Daily Reflector* picked up and reprinted, with permission, the last of his articles in its new coverage of what it called *The Hunt For Jack The Dog Ripper*. The *Reflector*'s piece led to a suspect, which led to an arrest, which led to the conviction of a local auto mechanic.

Once he was behind bars, the killings stopped. It was then that Jimmy Linh knew what he wanted to do when he grew up. He'd seen the power of the media. He'd seen how he could make a difference.

He never got credit for what he'd done. He wanted to keep Francis James's real identity a secret. But when he'd applied for a job at the *Reflector*, in the back of his portfolio of work he included his series of articles from the community newspaper.

Gertrude Wombley had asked him, "How do I know you're Francis James? Anybody could claim it."

Linh had explained to her he'd chosen the name because Francis was the patron saint of animals. James was the patron saint of veterinarians. He'd also suggested that nobody other than the author of the articles or the killer himself would keep them in a scrapbook for more than a decade. He wasn't the killer. Wombley had laughed out loud at his response. Then she'd hired him at a ridiculously low wage with the promise of only slightly more money if he performed as she demanded he should. He'd gotten the job. A job that, at the moment, smelled like death.

Linh tried breathing through his mouth to mitigate the growing pungency. It didn't work. A few steps more along the edge of the road, he learned why. There was part of a rotting human leg, a shred of canvas pant still wrapped around the calf. Next to it was a foot. Linh looked away and his eyes caught another chunk of flesh. There was a bone, maybe a rib, spiked through the striated meat. Large flies swarmed the carnage. Linh drew his shirt up over his nose and mouth and swallowed the urge to vomit.

Carefully, he swung his satchel around his waist and unzipped it. He pulled his camera from the bag, aimed the lens at the scraps, and snapped a half dozen pictures.

He was less than a half mile from Hòa Bình. The victim, man or woman, had to be from there. No question. He needed to get there and find out who was missing. Some of the villagers would talk to him even if his Vietnamese wasn't the same dialect. But he had to push forward. he couldn't just stand there. Linh gathered his nerve, tucked the camera back into his bag, and kept trekking toward the town.

He hadn't gotten another hundred meters when a chill ran from his neck down his spine. A familiar howl barked through the air. Linh stopped and closed his eyes to try to figure out the direction of the wail. He listened, trying to ignore the buzz of insects and the rush of the still-swollen river.

A full two minutes passed before there was another howl. This one was different. It was somehow…celebratory. And it was coming from the north, behind him. Linh looked over his shoulder, back from where he'd come. He couldn't be sure until another bloodcurdling call confirmed it. The White Ghost, Ma Trang, was close. Too close.

Uncle Due!

Linh shifted his weight and turned back to the north.

He held his satchel strap tight against his body and began running. His feet slipped in the grass and he almost lost his balance as he made his way onto the road. His feet pounded. His chest heaved. Sweat stung his eyes. He picked up speed, ignoring the tightening cramp in his gut. His uncle was in danger. He knew it.

The road snaked along the edge of the river and Linh kept his pace north. Visions snapped in his mind: the monster attacking his uncle, his uncle fighting back, his uncle losing. Images of the body parts he'd just encountered flashed before his eyes. No matter how much of a judgmental, money-grubbing jerk Uncle Due could be, he was family. Linh didn't want anything bad to happen to him. He prayed to himself as he pushed north, his thighs and calves burning with fatigue. Sweat poured into his eyes and onto his lips.

He rounded a final curve and saw the mudslide up ahead. Beyond the mud was Due's car. Linh winced past the sweat, his eyes blurred. He couldn't be sure what he was seeing, and he dug deep to keep his pace. He bounded from the road, slid down the embankment past the mudslide, and then climbed back up the incline to his uncle's car.

Linh's heart was pounding in his chest. His pulse thumped against his neck. He blinked and wiped the sweat from his face and focused on the scene in front of him. His heart nearly stopped.

The driver's side door was open. From underneath the frame, a man's foot was dangling, blood dripping into a thickening pool on the road. The door's window was shattered, as was the one behind it.

Linh looked back to the mud and then north up the road. He glanced over his shoulder, his pulse racing again.

His fingers tingled as he flexed his hands.

Where is Ma Trang?

Linh swallowed hard and stepped slowly to the car. He approached and leaned over to look inside. His stomach convulsed and Linh vomited onto the road.

Due, or what was left of him, was lying on his back across the front seats. One arm was missing. There was a quartet of parallel wounds that ran from his left shoulder to his right hip. He was shirtless.

He was headless.

Linh bent over at his waist and spit the remnants of the puke from his lips. He leaned on his knees. His breathing sped up and his breaths became deeper and deeper until he couldn't catch his breath.

I've gotten Due killed. My family. It is my fault.

Linh's body shuddered. A cry he didn't recognize as his own voice leaked from his mouth. His knees weakened and he dropped to the road on his backside. One thought consumed him as he struggled to breathe, to move.

Due is dead. Due is dead. Due is dead.

Linh was breathing so heavily, he was so much in his own head, he didn't hear the footsteps behind him. He didn't hear the clicking and popping of joints as they moved closer. He did see his uncle's head fall from the sky and land inches in front of him with a sickening thud.

Due's face was frozen in pain and fear, his mouth agape, his tongue hanging limply to one side. One eye socket was mangled. The other eye was looking blankly at Linh.

Linh screamed and scrambled backward until his hands hit something rough and hot. He rolled over and looked up. The Ma Trang was staring down at him. Its face was soaked in Due's blood. A fresh new adornment that looked like an eyeball hung from the necklace around its neck. It held an arm in one hand and had it draped over its shoulder like a baseball bat. Its lips were smacking and popping. Its eyes narrowed, it lowered its head, and it spoke in a low, guttural growl that almost sounded like an engine purring.

"I know you."

It drew the arm from its shoulder and whipped it forward, slamming it against the side of Linh's head. Linh's neck snapped to the side and his body slumped to the road. His vision blurred again as he lost consciousness.

***

Womack's team had stopped the UAZ when they'd heard the howls. Wolf had to take a leak and had refused to do it into his canteen.

"Give me Wilco's," he'd said. "He drinks his own piss all the time. He likes it."

"Your mother likes it," quipped Wilco.

"Enough, children," Womack said. "We'll stop."

He acquiesced and pulled off to the edge of the highway. He'd told everyone to get out and do their business. He wasn't going to stop again. The first of the three howls sounded unearthly. The next two were worse. Womack wasn't sure if he was glad he'd heard the cries or regretful.

Ferg thumped Womack on the shoulder. "You hear that?"

"I hear it."

"That can't be more than a mile," said Ferg. "Even

with the wind, the mountains to our right, and that valley to the left, I can tell it ain't far."

Wolf was zipping up his pants as he emerged from behind a tree. He motioned with his head toward the south. "That noise coming from the thing we're looking for?"

"It's not a thing," said Shine. He shouldered his way past Wolf. "He's a Marine."

"Whatever," said Wolf. "Thing. Marine. Leatherneck. Grunt. Jarhead. It's our target. He's our target. Get off your high horse, Shine."

Shine had stopped a step in front of Wolf. Without turning around, he said, "Now ain't the time or place, Wolf. I ain't interested in your crap today. Maybe Wilco likes it. Not me."

Wolf mocked Shine behind his back. He mouthed, "Ooooh!" with his lips.

"I see you, Wolf," said Shine, and he kept walking toward the truck. "Quit mocking me."

Wolf's cheeks flushed. He lowered his head and followed the wall of a man back to their ride.

"Men," said Womack, "I think we can agree that noise is coming from our VX-99 Marine. When we load back up, make sure you check your weapons. Lock and load. Understood?"

The team agreed and they piled into the truck. Womack was alone in the front seat. He put the truck into gear and started rolling south again. They'd gone three-quarters of a mile when Womack spotted something crouching in the grass not far from the road. He stopped the truck and turned off the engine.

"We're here," he said. The men climbed from the truck. Each of them had a sidearm strapped to his thigh and a more potent weapon in his hands. Womack was carrying the tranquilizer rifle. "Remember, we keep it alive."

He moved the men in a tight formation into the grass. His eyes stayed on the figure up ahead. He couldn't be sure, but he thought the thing, the so-called White Ghost, had seen him as they dipped off the road into the relative cover of the vegetation. If it had, it didn't react or didn't care.

Womack had split the team. Two men worked on either side of him. One pair had moved faster and deeper into the brush before turning parallel to the road. The other had stayed to Womack's right and kept pace.

They were within fifty meters when he saw a man on the road. The man was bent over and vomiting. He collapsed onto the road and was wailing. Womack saw a leg sticking from beneath the car door. From his position he was able to see half of a body.

Then the thing emerged from the grass. As it leapt onto the road, it tossed a human head over the sitting, crying man. It inched its way closer to the man.

Ferg was next to Womack. "It's playing with him. Taunting him." Ferg raised the China Lake Launcher to his shoulder.

Womack shook his head. "We don't kill it," he whispered. "Wait."

The man scurried backward and bumped into the thing. He turned around and the thing paused before slapping the man across the head with a severed arm. The man's head jerked and he fell onto the road.

"Did he just say something?" asked Ferg. "Did the thing talk?"

"I don't think so," said Womack. He didn't want to

think so. He signaled for both teams to collapse quickly on the ghost.

Wilco and Shine, who'd worked their way deep into the brush, rushed forward toward the road and moved directly behind the beast. Womack, Ferg, and Wolf approached from the north. Ferg and Wolf stayed off the road. Womack stepped onto the concrete and called out to the beast. It was leaning over the man on the road.

"Hey," he called. "You. Are you Trevor Brett, or are you Richard Fern?"

Still holding the severed arm, the beast snapped his head to the right and turned to face Womack. Womack had never seen anything like it. The photograph didn't do it justice.

The beast was thin and muscular. Its skin was so white, it was nearly translucent. Thick, dark veins strained against its chest and neck and arms. Its hands and feet looked like claws or talons. Its body, however, was nothing compared to its bloodstained face.

The mouth looked like a parasitic sucker. The nose was wide, and its nostrils flared. The eyes were bloodshot, but the pupils were vertical and yellow, like an alligator. Stringy long hair hung from the ghost's angular face.

Womack swallowed hard and repeated himself. He was buying time for the others to position themselves and trap the beast. "Are you Trevor Brett, or are you Richard Fern?"

The ghost cocked its head to the right, like a curious dog, and then pulled the arm to its mouth and tore off a bite of fresh meat. It chewed with its tiny razor teeth. Its lips smacked and slurped, but it said nothing. Its eyes blinked, revealing what looked like two layers of eyelids.

Womack stepped closer. He was only ten meters from

the ghost. His tranquilizer rifle was aimed at the ghost's chest. Out of the corner of his eye he saw Wilco and Shine approaching from the east. Ferg and Wolf were at the edge of the road, emerging from the tall grass. Both of them had their weapons in the low ready position.

The team tightened its position as the monster chewed. It seemed unfazed, if not disinterested, by the quintet of armed operators closing in on it.

The man on the ground at the beast's feet moaned, drawing its attention away from Womack and his team. At the moment it dropped its head to look down, Womack squeezed his trigger, unleashing the high-powered drug-injecting dart. It hit the ghost squarely in the chest as Womack applied pressure a second time and sent another tranquilizer into its neck.

The ghost jerked, reacting to the hit, and plucked one of the projectiles from its skin. It tossed the dart to the ground, threw back its head, and unleashed an ear-piercing scream. Its sucker lips pulled back, its tongue lunged forward between its teeth, and it roared.

Before the men could react, the ghost dropped the severed arm, reached down, and grabbed the man by his shirt collar. It yanked the man to his feet and, in one single motion, leapt from the road and into the grass.

Its joints made unnatural clicking noises as it bounded deeper into the brush, dragging the man behind it. The man was coming to and was screaming for help.

Womack raced forward and sent another dart toward the monster, but he missed. It was too quick. Womack signaled his men to give chase.

"Do not kill it," he yelled as he saw Shiner drop to one knee and take aim.

The Stoner 63 unleashed a rapid volley of shots into

the brush. The men advanced another thirty meters but saw nothing. The screaming man was silent. The beast was gone.

Womack slammed the butt of the tranquilizer rifle into the trunk of a tree. "Fig bat futher mucker," he said through his teeth. "He got away."

"He's not gonna get far," said Wilco. "You hit him twice."

"It didn't do anything," said Womack. "Nothing."

"Who was that dude?" asked Wolf. "The one he carried off?"

Womack shook his head and inspected the damage he'd inflicted to the butt of his rifle. "No idea. Could be anybody."

"Should we follow?" asked Ferg. "That guy is going to be dead if we don't."

"He's dead anyhow," said Wolf.

"There's a Navstar tracker embedded in that dart stuck in his chest," said Womack. "If I touch base with that spook Smith, he could probably send us new coordinates to plot on a map."

"That's if he doesn't pull out the dart," said Wilco.

"True," said Womack. "But it's something. Let's get back to the truck. I'll get Smith on a secure frequency. Then we'll find it and bring it home. Next time, open fire with everything but the grenade launcher. You can hurt it without killing it."

***

Brett's vision was fading. His energy was sapped. Still, he pushed forward, deeper into the brush and toward the mountains. He'd reversed his path and was heading northwest along the familiar path he'd traveled for twelve years.

You should have killed them, chided the voice. She wouldn't leave him alone. *One by one, you should have laid waste to them. They could have killed you.*

Brett knew better. The leader was armed with a weapon too small to carry bullets. And the others would have fired from a distance if they'd wanted him dead. Those men, whoever they were, wanted him alive. It was a suspicion that bore true when the leader had zapped him with a pair of darts.

Brett lumbered through the grass, slipping in the occasional puddle as he pushed through the heaviness in his chest and the overwhelming desire to sleep. He resisted the urge, tightened his grip on the man's collar, and put one calloused foot after the other, trying to make sense of what had happened.

He'd heard their truck and smelled its exhaust before he saw them approaching from the north. They were military trained, but Brett doubted they were Marines. They were too casual. They lacked real discipline. And the leader smelled like a distillery. Amidst the sweat and smell of lamb, Brett had inhaled the distinct odor of alcohol. It was old. Maybe a couple of days. But it was there. The men weren't active duty, but they knew him by name. *Trevor Brett.*

He hadn't heard that name outside of his dreams in years.

Trevor Brett. Trevor Brett.

It sent a jolt of electricity coursing through him when he thought about it. Somebody remembered his name. Somebody knew who he was and that he was alive.

Trevor Brett.

Who are they?

Brett had travelled fifteen kilometers before he was too exhausted to continue. There was a thickness in his arms and legs he'd not felt as long as he could remember. He found a thick crop of vetiver and stopped moving. He let go of his captive's hair and dropped him to the ground. The man, thankfully, had been silent since Brett had choked him unconscious in the moments after the five armed men had tried to trap him.

Brett squatted in the brush, working to keep his lids open. His chest heaved in short bursts as he sucked in shallow breaths through his nose. He was on the verge of passing out when the voice kept him awake.

They're not finished with you, she said. *Turning you into this thing you've become, this beautiful, invincible predator, is just the beginning now that they've found you.*

Brett was panting as he dropped on his back and stared up at the thick clouds building in the pale sky above him. He could still smell the latent scent of alcohol on that leader's breath.

If they catch you, the voice said, *they might not kill you. They might lock you up. They might study you. Anyone who could do to you what they did to you is capable of anything. They are the monsters, Trevor. They are the savages.*

Her voice dipped to a whisper. *They are the ones responsible*… Trevor Brett's eyes closed and he drifted to sleep.

***

It was nearly dark when the faint throb in the side of Jimmy Linh's head morphed into a thick pounding that threatened to blind him if he opened his eyes too quickly.

Slowly he adjusted to the dusk, but kept his eyes narrow to avoid the throb that accompanied opening them wide. He was unsure if he was alive or dead until the pain soaked through.

His back ached and there was a sharp current running from his right hip to his ankle. His wounded shoulder thumped with anger at every heartbeat. There were so many sensations it was hard for Linh to distinguish one injury from the next.

Once he'd wrapped his mind around the pain, he started taking in his surroundings. He was on his side, staring at shades of green and brown. An odd-looking beetle with a zebra neck and ladybug wings scurried into and out of his field of vision.

I am on the jungle floor. It is almost nighttime. I am injured.

How did I get here?

Linh pressed his jaw tight, trying to jog his memory. Nothing at first. A blank. He slowly inhaled through his nose. The smell of rot was pungent. It swam deep into his nostrils. It was more than rot, really. It was death.

Linh's eyes sprang open with recognition, and a sharp blast of pain radiated inside his head. He tried moving and couldn't at first. At least he thought he couldn't. Something was on top of him. He tried scrambling, scurrying out from underneath the weight keeping his legs pressed to the ground. He managed to twist his aching body, inducing an electric jolt in his neck that made him bite the side of his tongue in agony.

He swallowed past the newly added pain and saw what had bound him to the earth. It was the White Ghost—a limp, seemingly dead White Ghost.

Linh fought hard against the discomfort in his neck and back and shoulder and managed to free himself from the beast. He scrambled to his feet and leaned his weight against the thick round trunk of a tall jelutong tree. The sun had set, but there was dull ambient light peeking through the canopy above. The chorus of insects was getting louder. Linh smacked his thick tongue against his dry lips. He was suddenly parched, maybe dehydrated.

His eyes darted from tree to tree in search of something familiar. His ears hunted for the wash of the Da River. Nothing. He was lost. His satchel was gone. At least the beast was dead, somehow.

It is dead, isn't it?

Linh slid his hand down the tree for balance as he shrank to a squat at the base of the trunk. The ghost was feet from him. Its white skin seemed iridescent against the low light of the last of the day on the jungle floor. The ghost was on its stomach, its legs and arms splayed and its head turned awkwardly to one side. The tip of its tongue protruded from its swollen sucker lips.

Linh leaned in closer to the beast to look at the veins that strained against its skin. They were thick and dark. They traced a circulatory map across the beast's neck and cheeks and shoulders. By the second, it seemed, it was more difficult for Linh to see. The sun was evaporating more quickly now.

Linh knew he should stand and start running as far away from the ghost as he could. He needed to find a road or a village or the river. But Linh the curious reporter had to know if the beast was dead. He couldn't just go.

So Linh inched closer still, letting go of the tree and crab walking on his feet at first. Still too far away, he lowered himself onto his elbows and extended his aching neck toward the top of the creature's head.

His face was close enough that he could see his breath in the ghost's matted hair. The odor was something between cradle cap and a neglected tube washroom. Linh stretched his nose and fought his gag reflex before moving his face directly above the creature's.

Is it breathing?

Linh turned his head so he could listen for breathing while at the same time keeping his eyes on the ghost's back. If it was breathing, he'd know.

"What happened to you?" he whispered. "Someone *did* something to you."

There were human remnants in the ghost, thought Linh. There were traces of *Homo sapiens*. His ears, his stringy hair, the musculature of his back and legs—all resembled a man's more than a monster's. The shape of his nose, the protruding forehead, the spread of his ribs did not. They were more primal.

Linh focused on the ghost's respiration. Zeroing in on that task in the dark, he didn't see the Ma Trang's left hand twitch or its toes curl and flex. Instead he extended his body over the ghost even farther. He was hovering, almost, above its back. His palms were planted on the ground, his fingers sinking into the wet, fertile soil.

So close to the monster's body, he thought he could see the blood coursing through its veins, the wide spread of its ribs, and the thick knots that traced its spine. By the time he noticed the nearly imperceptible rise and fall of its lungs, it was too late.

First it moaned.

The low, guttural noise was sudden and Linh jerked with surprise. He almost dropped onto the monster. But he pushed himself upward on his arms, away from the ghost's back, as quickly as he could. Before he could put any distance between himself and the monster, though, its yellow eyes popped open. Its lips drew back, revealing its devilish teeth.

With a burst of energy, the beast rolled quickly onto its side and reached out, grabbing for Linh as he fell backward and hit his already aching head on the tree trunk. Dazed, Linh couldn't focus. He instinctively reached for his head as the ghost grasped in the dark for his legs.

A sudden, sharp sting ripped across Linh's shin before he felt a tug at his ankle. The Ma Trang had his foot in its claws. Its groan became more of a growl, and Linh kicked against the tight grip with a series of bicycle kicks that freed him for an instant.

Still disoriented, Linh pressed with his legs and inched his back up the trunk until he was standing. The monster was still on the ground, its arms flailing in the dark. Only its yellow eyes were visible now. Linh felt the blood rush from his head and he almost collapsed, but he leaned against the trunk and kept his balance.

The ghost, while awake and angry, seemed unable to move from the jungle floor. Linh took a deep breath and pushed himself from the trunk. He limped as quickly as he could away from the ghost, leaving it to howl in frustration as he made his way more deeply into the darkness.

He tried to run, but couldn't. Between the ache in his lower back, and the new, stinging weakness in his ankle, a quick limp was the best he could muster. His heart pounded forcefully against his chest, which exacerbated his headache. His breaths were increasingly shallow and ragged as he navigated the black hole of the jungle gym surrounding him.

He repeatedly tripped and fell face-first into the piles of foliage and mud puddles that dotted his path like a minefield. Each time he struggled to regain his footing, it became more difficult. He was bloodied, filthy, and in excruciating pain, but Linh kept moving. After what must have been thirty minutes, he stopped.

He struggled to catch his breath but managed to slow his pulse by inhaling slowly through his nostrils and exhaling through pursed lips. He'd emerged from the jungle into a clearing. The grass was knee high, and the ground under his feet was spongy. He looked over one shoulder and then the other. The clouds had thinned, and the right half of the moon cast a bluish hue across the clearing. There was an intermittent breeze that rode across the top of the grasses like a wave. He spotted nothing. No people. No animals. No monster. Linh was alone.

He was lost. He was badly hurt. But he was alive.

— 26 —

Somewhere between Son La and Hòa Bình, Vietnam
April 24, 1980

Womack finished the last of his C Ration M-2 Meat Unit—Meat Chunks with Beans in Tomato Sauce—and took a swig of warm water from his canteen. He slapped a bug from his neck and flicked the remnants from his fingers. The sound of insects chirping in the jungle around them was almost deafening.

"You know, these new rations are better than the old stuff," said Wolf. He picked spaghetti sauce from his teeth. "Better flavor."

"You mean they *have* flavor." Wilco laughed. "Those old meals, the MCIs, were worse than starving."

"I mean mine almost tasted like actual spaghetti," said Wolf. "What did you have, boss?"

Womack slapped another insect on his cheek. "Pork."

"Nice," said Wolf. "Very nice."

"We need to start moving again," Womack said to nobody in particular. "The longer we sit here, the farther the ghost moves from the last known coordinates."

The men had traveled ten klicks from the truck after getting an updated set of Navstar coordinates from

Smith. The spook confirmed there was satellite intelligence available. It didn't update in real time, but gave a good indication of the ghost's direction of movement. They drove northwest as far as the roads would take them and then hid the vehicle under a thicket of brush and rotting vegetation about fifty meters from the road. Womack marked the location on a map and tucked it in his pocket. They'd be able to find the jeep no problem once they'd accomplished the objective. Some eight hours since they'd first encountered and lost the ghost, they were exhausted and ripe. The humidity was suffocating.

Ferg looked at his watch. "It's oh-three-thirty," he said. "We've got another two hours until sunup. It'll be slow going until then."

Womack nodded. "Agreed," he said. "But any progress is progress. We'll move slow until we can see better. Then we hit it hard. If those darts had any effect, we can gain some ground."

Ferg shrugged. "You're the boss."

Shine was already standing and adjusting his pack on his back. He nodded toward his leader. "Womack's right," he said. "We need to make up the distance now. I don't want to be here any longer than I need to be, and once that drug wears off, that mutant Marine is going to be impossible to find."

"Unless he wants to find us," said Wolf.

Womack stood and slugged his pack onto his back. He checked his rifle to make sure he'd reloaded the two spent darts. "Either way, we need to be moving. We stay here, we're wasting time and we're sitting ducks."

The men followed Womack's lead and the men picked their way through the thick foliage. Each of them had an angled MX-99 with a red filter clipped to the front of their web gear to help guide them. It was slow going and it was familiar.

All of the men had served in-country during the Vietnam conflict. All of them had seen friends die or worse. Womack and Shine had more reason than most to dislike their return engagement. They had spent seven weeks in a prison camp called Portholes. It was along the southern coast of North Vietnam in a town called Bao Cao. It was not a friendly place.

Womack and Shine had occupied adjacent cells that resembled chicken coops. Cramped and barren and exposed to the elements, the cells were three feet wide, six feet high, and six feet long. The men were held in wooden leg stocks and restraints.

The two hadn't known each other prior to their capture, but during the forty-eight days and thirteen hours they spent next to one another, Womack and Shine had become as close as brothers. When one was tortured for lack of cooperation, the other asked for the same treatment. Their captors never broke them, despite their sadistic creativity.

On day forty-nine, their captors transferred them from Portholes to another camp called Skid Row outside Hanoi. It was where unhelpful POWs were sent as punishment. En route, a Cobra gunship rocket attack killed much of their transport convoy. They survived and, over the course of two weeks, found their way back to a forward operating base. C-rats, as prepackaged meals were called during the war, were a luxury for Womack and Shine. They'd eaten far worse as they worked to survive their escape from the Vietcong.

After the war, neither man had found sustained work

outside of clandestine operations. Not that they hadn't tried. Professional baby killer didn't look good on the top of a résumé, and in the months after their return, that was how many civilians chose to see them.

The country wasn't kind, and odd jobs weren't enough to make ends meet. Thirteen days was the longest Shine had held a job. He was a short-order cook without skill. When he lost his cool at the sound of oil popping in a fry basket, he was done.

Womack survived as a day laborer, mowing yards and picking weeds. He was paid in cash, which he quickly converted to alcohol. There was no future for either man until General Reed found Womack half-asleep on the bar of a late night joint in south Philly.

He'd offered them a chance to return to the one thing at which they excelled, where they'd be rewarded for their patriotic heroism and not ridiculed for it. It started with one job and turned into three. Then ten. They'd reluctantly accepted job after job.

Shine coped with his pain by retreating within himself and reading dime-store Westerns. A once gregarious mountain of a man had become a stoic rock who rarely spoke or smiled. None of the other team members knew Shine the way Womack did. They believed he'd always been all business.

Womack maintained his embrace of expensive female company and cheap liquor. He couldn't relate to the post-Vietnam America. It was frivolous and without purpose. Womack was happier in a fog. The only time he didn't drink, or didn't drink too much, was when he was on assignment. He could cope in the surrealism of covert operations, violent engagements, and heroic extractions. Reed had been right about him.

Back in the jungle again, trudging through the muck and grime of a bog, a familiar dread soaked through his body. As much as he hated the desert, southeast Asia was worse.

Phantom bolts of pain tightened around his wrists and ankles as he moved. He could hear the sharp crack of bamboo whipping against his bare back. He could feel the infection-eating maggots working to heal his wounds.

Womack aimed his MX-99 light toward Shine and then crossed a fallen log to march alongside him. Shine glanced at his boss and pursed his lips.

"You okay?" Womack asked.

Shine grunted. "No better than you, boss."

"I feel you," said Womack. "I'd rather be in Iran."

Shine chuckled. "Five words I never thought I'd hear anyone say."

"You and me both," Womack said. "You need anything, you let me know."

Shine nodded and pushed forward, ducking under a low-hanging branch. "You too."

Womack shook his mind free of the distraction and kept his attention on the path ahead. He checked a compass on his wrist. They were headed in the right direction. Soon enough the sun would be up and they could make better time.

He had no clue how far ahead the ghost might be. He didn't know if the dart was still in the ghost's body or if it had ditched it. He sucked in a deep breath of the suffocatingly wet air and stomped through ankle-deep mud.

Twenty minutes later they edged out of the jungle into a wide, circular grassy field. The moon, in its quarter phase, provided little light, but it was enough that the men turned off the MX-99 flashlights. Womack's body shuddered involuntarily. He'd been in too many places like this.

The open fields provided a respite from the dank, bug-laced humidity of the jungle cover. The air was fresher, cleaner smelling somehow. It was also more deadly. The clearings, rice paddies, and grassy flatlands were infected with mines. He'd seen countless men blown into pieces small enough to chew and swallow. They'd also provided an open, easy target for the Vietcong hiding in the trees surrounding the clearings.

He knew the snipers were gone, but those mines were probably still there, dipped into the soft muck that never quite dried out. It was hard enough to traverse in the daylight without tripping an explosive. At night it was nearly impossible.

Womack used a hand signal to move his men forward. He didn't need to warn them. They all knew the dangers of an open field. The men formed a single-file line behind him. He'd work the perimeter of the field, choosing to forego the straight shot through uncertain ground.

The men moved deliberately, slowing their pace, and their boots sucked at the thin layer of mud as they moved. Womack flipped on his light and aimed his weapon at the grass, sweeping it back and forth as he chose his path. They'd crossed halfway from the entry point to the exit on the far side of the clearing when Womack held up a fist. His men stopped.

"Do you hear that?" he whispered and looked over his shoulder at the four shaking heads behind him. None of them had heard it. It was a soft moan or a whimper maybe. Something or someone nearby was wounded. Womack held a finger to his lips. Against the breeze rustling through the grasses in front of them and the tropical canopy behind them, he heard it again. It was a whimper.

Womack turned back to his men again. Shine nodded his head and then motioned toward the middle of the clearing. He'd heard it too. Womack turned his ear toward the clearing and listened until the soft cry warbled a third time. It was human. At least it sounded human. His mind drifted back to the black site in Iran and the bleat of the goats in the pen out back. It was similar. He doubted, however, a goat was in the middle of the clearing.

Womack signaled to his team that he was walking toward the cry alone. Shine protested silently, but the boss insisted. Slowly, illuminating the murky ground ahead of each step, he made his way toward the noise. The slop of his boots in the boggy grassland gave away his position. There was nothing he could do about it, so he moved as ploddingly as he could.

When he was within a few meters of the soft cry, he slung the nonlethal weapon over his back and drew his service weapon. With the pistol in one hand, he canvassed the final few steps until he found what looked like a dying man curled into the fetal position, shivering. His face and legs were bloodied. His bare arms were covered in bruises and welts. There was a leech sucking at his neck.

Womack knelt down, keeping enough distance to defend himself or bolt if needed, and reached out with the pistol and poked the man's foot. He pushed him twice and the man jerked, his head snapping toward Womack before drawing backward in fear. His eyes narrowed against the light. The man drew his hands in front of his face. He whimpered again.

The operator recognized him. He was the man the ghost had carried off into the jungle after getting hit with the tranquilizer darts. He was the man Womack had been sure would have been dead by now.

Womack turned off the light and clipped it back onto his pack. "Hey," he said, gently touching the man's trembling shoulder. The man recoiled and tucked his chin to his chest.

Womack wrapped his fingers around the man's arm and squeezed. "It's okay. We're going to help you."

Having readjusted to the dark, the man's eyes were crazed. They were darting back and forth, back and forth. His breathing was rapid and shallow, like he was panting.

"Can you understand me?" Womack asked, working to maintain eye contact. "Do you speak English?"

The man nodded and swallowed hard. "Y-y-yes."

"Can you walk?" asked Womack. "We need to get you out of here. It's not safe."

The man shook his head. His eyes fixed on some distant spot in the sky. He shook his head again. Womack followed the man's gaze over his shoulder. There was nothing there.

Shine called from the fringe of the grassland, "You okay, boss?"

"Yeah. Be there in a sec."

He reholstered his pistol and helped pull the man to a sitting position. He put his hands on the sides of the man's face. "Can you walk?"

The man shook his head and motioned toward his foot. Womack fished the light from his pack and shone it on the man's leg. The pale light revealed a pair of long deep gashes running along the side and back of the man's leg. His foot was turned unnaturally at the ankle. There was no way he could walk, at least not with any speed.

"What's your name?"

"J-j-j-jimmy. L-l-linh."

Womack knew Jimmy Linh was going to be a liability. He'd compromise the mission, slow them down, and possibly put them at a tactical disadvantage if they did find the ghost again. This wounded man, whoever he was, would put them at extreme risk when they could least afford it. No doubt.

Maybe it was best to put him out of his misery, Womack thought. Chances were an infection would kill him anyhow. He'd been lying in a cesspool with open wounds. Ending it now was probably the best course of action. A quick honorable death beat a lingering disintegration soaked with pain any day. That was a universal truth and it was a split-second rationalization for the seasoned operator. They had a mission.

Womack took a deep breath and turned off the light. "All right," he said. "My name is Nick Womack. I'm going to help you to the edge of the jungle over there. I've got four friends waiting for us."

Linh tried eyeing the others, but they were too far away. He took another ragged breath and looked Womack in the eye. Womack offered a weak smile.

"I'm going to help you up," Womack said. "You're going to walk in front of me."

Linh nodded and reached his arms outward for Womack to pull him to his feet. Instead of facing him, Womack shifted to the side. With one of Linh's arms draped across his shoulder and his own arm wrapped around Linh's chest, the operator hoisted the liability to his feet.

"You good for a sec?" Womack asked Linh. "Can you balance yourself while I adjust my rifle?"

Linh nodded and let go of Womack with a wince and wheezing grunt. He was shaky but managed to stand in the muck with most of his weight on his good foot.

Womack took a single step back and silently drew his service weapon. Standing directly behind the unsuspecting Linh, the soldier of fortune quickly raised the weapon to within an inch of the back of Linh's head. He clicked off the safety, slipped his finger onto the trigger, and—

"I-I-I know w-w-where t-t-to f-f-f-find it," Linh squeaked.

Womack lowered the weapon. "You what?"

"I c-c-can h-help y-y-y-you find it."

Womack holstered the weapon. "The White Ghost?"

Linh nodded.

Womack took a deep breath and exhaled. "All right," he said. "First things first. We need to get you to the others."

He again moved to Linh's side and wrapped his arm around the wounded man while holding his arm over his own shoulder. Slowly they trudged forward. One step at a time. Womack clenched his jaw with every step, not able to light their way back to the edge of the grass and free of the land mine threat.

Linh grunted and whimpered as they slogged in the knee-high grass. Womack glanced over at him and a wave of guilt washed over him. He'd almost killed the guy. He'd nearly put mission ahead of morality.

That last bit, in and of itself, wasn't a new concept. They'd done that before. They'd seen the good of the whole as a justification for violating at least one commandment. This would have been different though. It would have been a cold-blooded assassination of an innocent man. Womack wanted to put the gun to his own head for having considered it.

They reached the edge of the grass, and both Wilco and Ferg reached out to help Womack with the casualty. They bore the brunt of the man's weight and helped him to sit against a tree.

"Who is he?" asked Shine, motioning to Linh with his Stoner 63.

"That's the guy who was with the ghost when we first came across it."

"The one getting dragged off?"

"Yeah," said Womack. "That one."

Ferg looked back at Womack. "This dude's in bad shape. Broken ankle, concussion, bad cuts, maybe even a punctured lung."

"What do we do with him?" asked Wolf. "We can't take him with us."

Shine leaned into Womack and spoke softly. "Do we put him out of his misery?"

Womack shook his head. "I already thought of that. It's no good. Plus he says he can help us find the ghost."

Wolf nudged Womack. "Boss," he said under his breath, "how do we know that he won't turn into one of those things? I mean, if it scratched him or bit him?"

Womack rolled his eyes. "He's not a zombie."

"Yeah," said Wolf, "but what if some creature explodes out of his chest and attacks us."

"He's not an alien either."

Shine rubbed the scruff on his chin and moved over to the injured man. Linh's eyes were squeezed closed. Ferg was burning the leech off his neck. Wilco was fashioning an ankle splint from a branch and palm fronds.

"Hey," said Shine. "How'd you get away?"

Linh opened his eyes and looked up. "I d-d-don't know, really," he said. "I woke up in the middle of the jungle somewhere. The Ma Trang was h-h-h-half on top of me. I thought it was d-d-dead."

Shine had his weapon casually aimed at Linh's chest. "Was it?"

Linh shook his head, wincing as Ferg wrapped gauze from his first aid kit around the gaping wounds in his leg. Tears rolled down his cheeks, streaking the dirt and dried blood that caked his face.

Shine pressed. "How do you know?"

"It woke up," said Linh. "It t-t-tried to grab me. It broke my leg."

"How'd you get away?" Wolf asked, his eyes darting between Linh and Womack. "Did it let you get away?"

Linh shook his head again. "N-n-no," he said. "I just got away from it. It couldn't move much. Like it was w-w-waking up slowly."

"Who are you?" Womack asked. "You're not from here."

"I'm a reporter."

Womack's eyes widened. *Jimmy Linh.* He'd seen the name in the briefing file. "You're *the* reporter," he said. "You're the reason we're here in this jucked-up fungle."

Linh's eyes narrowed with confusion. "I don't understand."

"Your report," said Womack. "That's why we're here."

Linh lowered his head. He put his hands over his face and then grabbed his hair, curling his fingers into fists.

Shine squatted onto his heels. "You have no idea where the ghost is, do you?"

Linh slowly released his grip on his hair and dropped his hands to his sides. He shook his head. "No."

Womack stepped forward. "But you just told me—"

"You were going to shoot me in the back of the head," said Linh. "I had to say something."

Wolf shot his boss a look. "That true?"

Womack nodded. "He's a liability. We can't take him with us if he can't guide us."

Shine popped up on his feet. "I'll stay with him," he said. "Right here."

Womack bristled. "Negative. We need every man. We can't be down one."

"You can't leave him here alone," said Shine. "And you don't want to bring him. Sounds like you have no choice, boss."

Womack bit his lower lip. "Fine," he said. "You stay here with the reporter. We'll get the ghost and meet you back here. If we're not back by sundown, you take him back to the truck. Radio the position. Smith will know where I am unless I've emptied all of the Navstar darts."

"I don't like this," said Wolf.

"Nobody asked you," said Wilco.

"Your mother did—"

"Cut it out," Womack snapped. "Now isn't the time."

Ferg slung his pack onto his back and moved toward Womack. "Boss," he said, "I've got another idea. I think it'll work."

— 27 —

Frederick, Maryland
April 24, 1980

Rick Gibson was watching the television in his office. The volume was off, but he already knew the details of the breaking news airing on the network. An attempt to rescue the fifty-two American hostages in Tehran hadn't worked. Three of eight helicopters failed and the mission was cancelled in the midst of it. During the retreat, one of the helicopters collided with a C-130 transport plane. Eight soldiers died and five more were hurt. It was the latest embarrassment for what Gibson saw as an impotent administration incapable of projecting strength and resolve. It was the same leadership that hedged every time he'd wanted to push the boundaries of modern warfare. Maybe the next president would be different.

Gibson picked up his phone and placed a call. He had questions.

"What?" answered General Anthony Reed.

"I haven't had an update in several hours," said Gibson. "What's the latest?"

"You have got to be kidding me, Major," said General Reed. "I've got a cluster on my hands with eight dead, and you call me for an update on the monster mission?"

"With all due respect, General—"

"Cut the crap, Rick," said Reed. "Whenever you begin with that, you're about to be disrespectful. Just spit it out."

"There's nothing you can do about the failed hostage rescue," Gibson suggested. "It's over. Operation Flame Out is, however, active. I don't think status updates are too much to ask."

Reed huffed. "What's the latest intel you have?"

"I know from your asset Smith the team inserted successfully into North Vietnam. I know they located our subject and then lost it."

"Fine," Reed said. "I'll have Smith get back to you." The line went dead.

Gibson sat there for a moment with the receiver still in his hand. He blankly stared at the television screen. There was no film of the ill-fated operation yet, so the network relied on one reporter standing outside the north side of the White House and another sitting inside some studio in the Pentagon. A ping from his computer drew his attention away from the television.

"That was fast," he mumbled and pressed the space bar on the keyboard. The screen flickered and a new message appeared on the display.

EYES ONLY, CLASSIFIED
SOD, USAMRIID OPERATION FLAME OUT
STATUS QUERY RESPONSE
Navstar-embedded identifier indicates target was immobile but is again moving.
Cluster of Navstar-embedded identifiers indicate team is mobile and moving toward target.

No independent verification. No verbal or visual confirmation available.

"That's it?" Gibson muttered. He was hoping for more. He picked up the phone again and dialed a secure line. "Get me the Air America site outside Hanoi."

There was a series of clicks before the line connected. An impatient man answered the phone.

"Smith here," said the spy. "Who's this?"

"This is Major Gibson. I—"

"I just sent you an update. I don't have time to talk. We're dealing in real time here, Major."

"How close is the team to the target?"

Smith sighed. "It's hard to know exactly," he said. "There's a latency with satellites."

"Then how reliable is your intel?"

"What I can tell you is that each of the tranquilizer darts has a unique satellite signature," said Smith. "We can track them individually. We know that your team discharged two of them. One is still in the target. The cluster of unused darts is still with your team."

"How long is the latency?"

"Ten seconds for the data. Less than a minute to coordinate the data with our mapping."

"Good," said Gibson. The delay was shorter than he'd expected. He hadn't done much studying about global positioning satellites and their reliability. He was encouraged.

"Goodbye, Major." The line went dead.

Gibson hung up the phone and leaned back in his chair. This was the calm before the storm. He could feel it in the bones the way an arthritic senses a drop in barometric pressure.

He trusted the team, who General Reed promised him was among the finest, would bring him the VX-99 Marine. Then the real work would begin again.

Gibson closed his eyes until a knock at his half-open door shook him from his twilight. "Come in," he called and cleared his throat. He opened his eyes to see Dr. Starling moping toward him. The young doctor's hands were buried in his lab coat pockets. His feet shuffled more than they stepped forward. The deep frown lines on his face were the only things more prominent than the bags under his eyes. He dropped into the chair opposite Gibson's desk without pulling his hands from the pockets and without an invitation to sit.

"What is it?" Gibson asked.

"We're ready."

"Everything?"

Starling nodded. "Everything."

"The ballistic coating on the window?"

"Yes."

"The cage?"

"Yes."

"The restraints?"

"It's all ready," said Starling. "Like we're prepping for a state execution."

"What do you mean?"

Starling shrugged. "That's what we're doing, isn't it? Once we have the original VX-99 patient in our custody, we'll end up killing him like the one we killed this week."

A grin slowly spread across Gibson's face. "Is that what has you so defeated?" He chuckled. "Is that why you're so glum? You think we're going to all of this trouble to kill him?"

"I just figured…"

Gibson leaned forward and planted his elbows on the desk. He looked Starling directly in the eyes. "Your hypothesis is all wrong," he said before qualifying himself. "We will use him for tests, but you're wrong."

"How so?"

Gibson's eyes lit up. "When they bring back that beautiful specimen, that VX-99 Marine, we will keep him alive at all costs," he said. "He will be the foundation of all of our work going forward, not just the cocktail. Think what we could accomplish, Dr. Starling. My mind is already spinning with ideas."

— 28 —

Between Son La and Hòa Bình, Vietnam
April 24, 1980

Brett's legs weren't at full strength, but at least he could feel them again. He was moving slowly, but with purpose, as his mobility returned. It was nearly dawn and his vision was sharp, even in the faint yellow light peeking through to the jungle floor. The blurriness was gone. The haze had given way to acuity. He flexed his hands as he moved. It was good feeling the blood course through his veins and into his extremities. The intoxicating sense of invincibility was snaking its way through his body.

He drew in deep breaths through his nostrils. He could smell remnants of the little man who'd escaped him. It was on the leaves of the low-hanging branches and underbrush. It was in the droplets of blood that mixed with the soft jungle floor.

You cannot let him live, crowed the voice. She wouldn't let it go. *If he escapes, he'll tell others. People won't fear you anymore. You'll become vulnerable. You must find him and kill him.*

Brett pushed his way more quickly through the

rainforest. He was getting closer to the man. He could taste it.

He dropped to all fours and tested his legs. They were better. They were strong. He pushed with his thighs and leapt forward, feeling the muscles tense and explode with power. The familiar sound of his joints snapping with each lunge was comforting. He galloped amongst the trees and vines, jumped over a large termite mound that rose three feet tall from a rotting trunk, and sped faster and faster toward his prey. It was as if the little man had left a trail of breadcrumbs for him.

Brett's heart fluttered with a sense of excitement he hadn't felt in so long. He had a purpose beyond the simplicity of killing for food. It was exhilarating and he let out a howl as he moved. The spontaneous call sent a ripple of chills through his body and only served to accelerate his pace. He was racing as fast as he could toward the little man who'd eluded him twice now. As Brett bounded from the cover of the jungle and into an open, grassy field, he knew there wouldn't be a third time.

***

Jimmy Linh shuddered involuntarily. He'd heard the howl tear through the thick jungle air and knew the Ma Trang was close. He couldn't believe he'd let the soldiers leave him alone, wounded and unable to fend for himself.

He sat there at the edge of the field, his back against a tree, cursing his predicament and lamenting his ambition. If he'd not pushed to do a story on the Ma Trang, he wouldn't be about to face it for the third time. If he somehow survived round three, he had other problems.

He'd missed Gertrude Wombley's deadline for a

follow-up story. She wouldn't be forgiving of any excuse short of death. Add to that his having essentially stood up Molly for their first date. He should have called her the second his flight was changed. He should have done a lot of things. Linh calculated he'd lost more than he'd gained by choosing Ma Trang as his first big assignment.

Linh adjusted his back against the tree. The pain wasn't as intense as it had been since one of the soldiers had slipped him some morphine. The trade-off was that his senses were dulled. He'd probably be unable to put up much of a fight this time.

Linh shifted his weight again and, from the corner of his eye, caught a glimpse of the Ma Trang. It was standing on the far end of the field at the edge of the dense vegetation marking the jungle's entrance. He swore he could see its lips popping as they puckered in and out, in and out. Its yellow eyes were red with blood and it was staring directly at him.

He dug his fingers into the soft ground and grabbed at the earth. Linh swallowed hard and closed his eyes as the monster leaned forward and leapt into the grass. He couldn't see it, but he could hear the clicking of its joints as it beat an invisible path through the grass.

The sound of its body moving grew louder and louder. Linh tensed, which caused his back to seize, and he cried out in pain. He opened his eyes in time to see two of the soldiers appear above the waist-high grass directly in the ghost's path. One of them, the leader called Womack, jerked repeatedly with the pop of his tranquilizer rifle.

The other one raised his weapon and maybe got off a shot or two, but the Ma Trang dove at the soldier and tackled him into the grass. There were screams, a short volley of rapid gunfire, more screams, and the growling of a rabid animal with its teeth bared.

***

Womack was sure he'd lodged at least three more darts into the ghost. It hadn't done anything to stop it, and it leapt onto Wolf, driving him beneath the sea of grass. Wolf had maybe been able to hit the beast with his sidearm. Maybe.

"Wilco, Shine, Ferg," yelled Womack. "I need you now."

Wilco emerged from the jungle behind the reporter. He had the Grease Gun in his hands. He leveled it waist high and, without thinking, bolted into the grass. He pulled his weapon to his shoulder and drew his finger to the trigger. His feet beat a quick path through the grass, gliding across the spongy turf, when he hit something hard and a percussive blast ended his advance.

A land mine blew Wilco and his Grease Gun into the air. Unrecognizable pieces of both slapped the wet earth in a syncopated chorus of sickening thuds. Womack watched his friend explode and froze for an instant, staring at the hint of blood and dirt that hung in the early morning mist. He only snapped from the paralysis when Shine called to him from across the field.

"Boss," he said, "it's on the move."

Womack turned and found the beast bolting for the jungle and their bait, the reporter. "Blast it, Ferg!" he yelled, panic dripping from his voice. "Cut it off!"

Ferg, who was camped not far from Linh, pumped the China Lake Launcher and unloaded a pair of grenade shot shells in the path between the ghost and the reporter. The ground erupted with a spray of grass and dirt and rock and forced the ghost to change its course. It headed straight for Ferg.

Shine had his weapon ready and he tracked the beast as it rose and fell with each leap. He pressed the trigger of his Stoner 63 and released a quick burst at the ghost. It was too fast. He'd missed. He scanned to his right and found the target again. A quick pull. A short burst.

"I got it!" Shine called. "It's down."

***

Brett felt the bullets tear through the meat of his thigh. They were hot and burned the inside of his leg as he tumbled to the spongy ground and skidded to a stop.

Get up! growled the voice. *Attack them. Make them pay.*

Brett rolled onto his stomach and lay still, breathing slowly through his nose. He was hidden in the grass a few feet from the soldier with the grenades. He could make a leap for it and maybe tear into him as he had the other one just seconds earlier. The wound to his leg was painful, but not debilitating. Instead he closed his eyes and listened.

"Where did he go?" asked the one with the grenades. "Where is he?"

"I know I got him," called another. "I saw a hit in his leg. At least one. Maybe more."

"Did you kill it?" asked the leader. "Shine? Did you kill it?"

"Negative," said Shine.

"Then where is it?"

"I don't know," said Shine. "In the grass somewhere."

Brett inhaled deeply. His body tingled and a familiar warmth began to radiate from his neck. He reached to the source of the heat and felt a pair of darts. He plucked both of them from his body and held them between his claws. The darts were barbed with hypodermic needles at one end and mechanical or electronic devices on the other. He tried to focus on the marking on the dart's housing but couldn't. His vision blurred. Suddenly he couldn't control his breathing.

What's happening? asked the voice angrily. *What is going on with you? Attack them now.*

Brett listened to the voice one more time. From his prone position on the ground, he jumped forward and hit the soldier with the grenade launcher, knocking the weapon from his hands. The soldier fell onto his back and grasped for his sidearm. Brett was too fast. He straddled the soldier, wrapped his hands around his neck, and squeezed before he twisted.

The soldier's neck cracked and went limp before Brett took out his frustration on the rest of the man's body. He was blind with rage.

***

Womack couldn't believe what he was seeing. In a matter of seconds their plan disintegrated. The beast was too fast. He stepped quickly but carefully through the grass toward the snarling and slurping noises coming from where he'd seen the ghost attack Ferg.

Shine was moving too, stepping toward the awful noises of their friend and compatriot being devoured by a mongrel Marine. Womack held the tranquilizer rifle and pressed it tight against his shoulder. He was within a few feet and aimed the rifle downward at a forty-five-degree angle.

Shine mirrored Womack but with his Stoner 63. They tightened the noose one step at a time until Womack could see hints of the thrashing and tearing through the thick tufts of grass.

He checked with Shine and nodded before taking aim and pumping two more ballistic darts into the ghost. It slapped at the sting of the hits and stopped its feral attack on Ferg.

The ghost stood on its hind legs, wobbling, and bared its teeth. Its round sucker lips were dripping with blood, and there was a long, thin piece of flesh stuck to its chin. It rolled its shoulders forward and stared Womack in the eyes. It opened its mouth wide and howled.

At that moment, Womack applied pressure to the trigger and thumped another dart right into the ghost's mouth, hitting the back of its throat. The beast snapped its jaw shut and grabbed at its own neck. Its eyes were wide with panic. It swayed back and forth, seemingly searching for balance, before it convulsed and collapsed to the ground.

Shine approached the downed ghost quickly. Standing over it, his eyes found Womack's. "It's down. Ferg is too."

Womack approached Shine, his eyes drifting downward as he did. The beast was unconscious. Its breathing was rapid and shallow. Its tongue hung from between its nasty, swollen lips.

Ferg wasn't Ferg anymore.

Womack swallowed the thick knot pressing against his throat. He blinked away the tears welling in his eyes. His friend, the man he'd thought should have long ago had his own team, lay dead, an unrecognizable heap of flesh and bone, of blood and hair. Womack tightened his grip on the rifle. He reared back with one of his boots and kicked the toe solidly into the ghost's spine. The beast's body was limp. There was no reaction.

"Are they dead?" called a voice from the edge of the jungle. It was the reporter. "Are all of them dead?"

"The Ma Trang is alive," said Womack. "You're alive. I'm alive. Shine's alive. Everyone else is—"

"Help!" The raspy, weak call came from the middle of the field. "Help me."

Wolf?

Womack looked over at Shine. "Watch the beast," he said. "I got this." With the rising sun, it was an easier trip through the grass. Womack sidestepped two mines on his way to Wolf. He found the young man lying on his back. He was as pale as the ghost and missing the lower half of his left arm. He'd somehow managed his own tourniquet to ebb the bleeding.

"You okay?" Womack knew it was a stupid question, but he wasn't sure what else to say.

Wolf lifted his head from the muck and nodded. "I'll be okay," he whispered. "I think I lost a few pounds though."

Womack smiled weakly. "You'll be easier to carry, then."

Wolf laughed. "Get me outta here."

"You bet." Womack lifted Wolf to his feet and acted like a crutch to help him weakly hobble back to the edge of the jungle. He found the reporter still leaning against the tree. Shine had dragged the ghost from the grass and had him bound with cord around his ankles and wrists.

"Can you walk?" Womack asked the reporter.

Linh nodded. "Slowly."

"Wolf?"

"Yeah," said the injured operator. "I can make it."

"All right then," Womack said. "You both walk, then. Shine, you and me carry the ghost."

Wolf looked around, his eyes searching from right to left and back again. "What about Wilco? Where's Ferg?"

Womack shook his head, unable to look Wolf in the eyes.

Wolf cursed and bit his lower lip. "Both of them?"

Shine nodded.

Womack pulled his shoulders back. "Let's go, men," he said. "No time to pout about what we can't change. We've got a hike."

— 29 —

Hanoi, Vietnam
April 25, 1980

Linh watched from the corner of the large warehouse as the surviving trio of mercenaries talked privately with another man he'd not yet met. He sensed they were talking about him. The one called Wolf kept looking back at him as the others whispered and gesticulated.

They'd managed to find their way back to the truck, into the tunnel, and to the secret government site before the Ma Trang awoke from its sleep. They had it caged and bound with floor-bolted chains. The beast paced back and forth but didn't howl or wail as it had in the jungle. The only noise coming from the cage was the sound of the chain links scraping across the metal floor of the barred enclosure. Linh almost felt sorry for the Ma Trang. Almost. He looked at the beast as if it were a deadly cobra or rabid dog. It couldn't help what it was. It wasn't the Ma Trang's fault for obeying its instincts.

Linh shifted in his seat and carefully lifted his injured leg as he did. His ankle was set in a proper cast, and a doctor had given him drugs to ease the pain that attacked various parts of his body. He was in a haze, but somehow cognizant of the predicament in which he found himself.

These men who'd saved him weren't supposed to exist. The mission to trap and transport the Ma Trang wasn't supposed to exist. The hi-tech warehouse in which he sat wasn't supposed to exist. Linh knew about all three. It would have been bad enough had he been some random villager who'd stumbled into the middle of this conspiracy, but he was a reporter.

He looked over again at the Ma Trang in the cage and wondered if he'd be safer inside the bars than sitting in a chair outside them. He stiffened when a slick-looking man he didn't recognize walked purposefully toward him.

"Hello," said the man, extending his hand with a wink. "I'm Smith. And aside from my name, I'm not going to lie to you."

Linh looked at the extended hand and took it. "I'm Jimmy Linh."

"I know who you are," said Smith, squatting into a baseball catcher's position. "You're the reporter who started this whole ball of wax. You're a hero in a way."

Linh pressed his back against the seat. "Who are you with?"

"Special Operations Group. Part of the American government that nobody talks about. Understand what I mean?"

Linh nodded.

"So here's the rub, Jimmy Linh," said Smith. He planted his elbows on his knees and clasped his hands together in prayer beneath his chin. "I'm going to need your help. You help me and I help you."

"What if I don't help you?"

"Then I can't help you," said Smith. "You don't want to be in a place where I can't help you."

"I'm not an American," said Linh. "I'm British. You can't—"

Smith held up a finger while his hands remained clasped. "You're not anyone right now," he said. "You have no passport. You have no identifying documentation. You haven't checked in with your boss for days. Your uncle is dead. Who's going to vouch for you?"

Linh searched Smith's face. Any hint of a smile was gone. His eyes looked straight through him. Linh shrugged.

"So are you going—"

"Molly," Linh blurted. "Molly can help me. She works for the Home Office. She knows me."

Smith smirked. "Molly."

"Yes."

"Okay," said Smith. "Let's go with that. Let's say Molly can help you. Who's going to help Molly?"

The words hung there. Both men knew exactly what they meant without either having to clarify. Smith winked again.

"Before you go concocting some plan on your own, which won't work, let me play out a scenario that helps both of us."

"Okay."

"You're going to quit your job at the paper. You're going to work for your father's business. You're—"

Linh clenched his jaw and snarled through his teeth. "How do you know about my father?"

"Linh," said Smith calmly, "I know things. That's all you need to know. Please let me finish. May I finish?"

Linh nodded.

"You will not report what you saw here. Ever. If you

do, we will send these three men to find you. They'll do whatever they have to do. That's part one. No report, new job. Stay quiet. Got it so far?"

Linh nodded.

"Part two. To make your silence a little more palatable, we will deposit a healthy sum of money into an account on a monthly basis. That money is yours. We will also provide your parents with an alternative reality for how your uncle died. We will take care of the paperwork, photographs, everything that makes his death kosher and not a result of the VX-99 Marine. Still with me?"

Linh's eyes narrowed. "VX-99? What's that?"

"That's our code name, nothing more. I should have said Ma Trang. Got it?"

Linh nodded.

"Part three, and this is new because you just brought her to my attention, you call Molly and enlist her help in getting you back into the country. That keeps our fingerprints off it. We might be able to grease the skids a little bit with MI5."

Linh glanced past Smith's shoulder and saw the mercenary's leader looking at him. The man named Womack. His hands were on his hips. He was frowning. Linh didn't know the man any more than the few hours he'd spent with him, but he could tell Womack had left something of himself in that jungle. He wasn't the same man he'd been before the hunt for the Ma Trang. His eyes shifted back to Smith. He sighed.

"I don't have a choice, do I?"

Smith winked. "Not really. Let's be honest, though, Jimmy Linh, none of us really have choices, do we? You think that thing over there, pacing back and forth in that cage, had a choice?"

Linh shook his head without looking. He couldn't look at the Ma Trang anymore. He wanted to go home. He wanted to live as normal a life as possible. If that was possible.

"Okay," he said. "I'll do what you ask."

"Good," said Smith. "Let's get started. I'll find you a phone and you can make your calls. I've already got a script written for what you need to tell that boss of yours, Gertrude Wombley. It's some of my best work. And if Molly gives you a hard time, we'll make it right. She'll be putty."

— 30 —

Frederick, Maryland
April 30, 1980

Rick Gibson could hardly contain himself. He'd not slept for three days. Now, after a dozen years, one of the original VX-99 Marines was coming home.

Gibson ran his fingers along the front page of Lieutenant Trevor Brett's personnel file. He knew the Ma Trang was Brett. The transmissions Smith had sent him over the last forty-eight hours had confirmed it.

He took a bottle of Liquid Paper and shook it before uncapping the internal brush. He ran the brush across three letters in Brett's file. Gibson pulled the piece of paper close to his lips and blew gently on the liquid, drying it as he did. He then slipped the document into his IBM Selectric typewriter and typed KIA over the letters that had previously occupied the space. He then cranked the paper to the bottom of the page and began typing.

AWARD OF THE BRONZE STAR MEDAL—By direction of the President under the provisions of Executive Order 9419 4 February 1944 (sec. II WD Bul. 3, 1944), and pursuant to authority in AR 600-45, the

Bronze Star Medal with Letter "V" device for heroic achievement in connection with military operations against an enemy of the United States is awarded posthumously.

Gibson had already forwarded the recommendation to General Reed. Reed had made sure the award was approved and Brett's remaining family made aware of the honor. He was pulling the page from the typewriter when Starling bounced into the room.

The scientist had more energy than he'd shown in days. Maybe it was the raise Gibson had given him, the promotion to senior research fellow, or the idea that *this* time they would get it right. There was promising parallel research about the concurrent use of viruses that interested both the scientist and the major.

"They're here, Major Gibson."

"Good."

Gibson stood from his desk and followed Starling through the maze of hallways. Gibson walked with a renewed purpose. They'd been so close to losing his life's work that now it was as if he'd been reborn.

They reached a secure lab in the middle of the facility. Inside was General Reed, a scruffy-looking man in fatigues, and a cage containing Trevor Brett. Gibson adjusted his uniform jacket and keyed himself into the room with Starling.

"Gibson," said General Reed. He was pointing at the scruffy man. "This is Nick Womack. He's responsible for retrieving your…lost property."

Gibson offered a hand to Womack. "Thank you for your help," he said with a strong, genuine grip. "How was the flight back?"

Womack smirked. He shrugged. "Long," he said, exhaling as he spoke. "You've probably been briefed on it, but I lost two men and a third is bad off."

Gibson eyed Reed before acknowledging Womack. "I'm sorry for your loss. I can assure you, however, the recovery of this asset is… It's world changing."

Womack tucked his tongue in his cheek and raised an eyebrow. "World changing, huh?" he said, the words dripping with suspicion.

"Without a doubt," said Gibson. "Without. A. Doubt."

Womack thanked the major for the opportunity and excused himself.

"Thanks again for your service," said Gibson. "I'm sure we'll call on you again."

Womack nodded. The major smiled, bowed slightly, and then turned his body to the cage as Womack exited the room.

This was Gibson's first look at the new and improved Trevor Brett. He gasped with wonder and exhaled to a quickened pulse. His palms were sweaty. This was like seeing a present unwrapped and under the tree on Christmas morning. The corners of his mouth twitched into an uncontrollable grin.

Lieutenant Brett didn't look human. Not really. Yet, in some way, in those yellow eyes streaked with blood, Gibson saw the man he'd met so many years ago in that tent.

He stepped to the cage and wrapped his fingers around the bars. Brett was strapped tightly enough he wasn't a threat, so Gibson pressed his face to the cage.

"Hello, Lieutenant Brett," he whispered. "Welcome home."

Brett's eyes blinked, both sets of lids sliding forward and back. He cocked his head to one side and smacked his sucker lips.

Pop. Pop. Pop.

Gibson wondered if Brett recognized him, if there was some part of the young soldier still inside the beast of a warrior they'd created, he'd created. Of course, VX-99 hadn't done exactly what they'd anticipated. It had created for them all sorts of problems, sleepless nights, questions without answers. But looking into their creation's eyes, Gibson considered it all worth it. The sacrifices would be worth the price of blood. In the end, Brett and the other men in his lost platoon would help Gibson continue and perfect the VX-99 program. It needed perfecting. It had to be perfect, and Gibson believed, especially now that he once again had its origin in his grasp, he could mold the project into what he'd envisioned.

The major studied Brett's features, his eyes lingering on the mutations that were most prominent. There was a beauty to the creature's hideous features. Something majestic about him. The lips and teeth, the extremities, the sinew of the muscles, and of course the eyes. Oh, those eyes. They were reptilian in their coldness, but Gibson saw something human in them. Brett was still in there. The longer he stood there, his gaze locked with the Ma Trang, the more convinced of it he became. As feral as Brett appeared, there was something calculating inside him.

The monster leaned forward, muscles straining against virtually translucent skin and the binds straining against his muscles. Gibson held his spot at the bars to watch Brett strain harder against the binds and iron shackles.

Brett leaned his face as close to Gibson as he could get. His eyes blinked again. His lips popped and then they stretched into what looked like a grin.

"You," snarled Brett. "You did this to me."

The words hung in the air between them, sticking to Brett's fetid breath. The dank, rotten odor filled Gibson's nostrils. He winced at the strong scent, his lips quivering. He tried not to react, imagining that Brett could sense fear or apprehension or shock.

Brett's eyes blinked, but his gaze was fixed. His lips popped. His talons curled into fists.

Gibson felt the thick, hard beat of his heart in his chest, neck, and temples. He tried not to look away from the beast. He knew from his studies of predators that he could not show any weakness.

"What you did to me is nothing…" Brett hissed, his voice full of gravel.

The beast's body relaxed, the chains clinking as they rattled and twisted between the cuffs. Brett flexed his hands and the joints cracked. He tilted his head to one side and then the other, the air pockets in his neck snapping like popcorn. He slurped back the thick saliva that threatened to drop from his lower lip. He rolled his shoulders and exhaled through his nose. His broad nostrils flared and his eyes never left Gibson's. He was playing a game. He was teasing Gibson and Gibson knew it.

Lieutenant Brett was the one restrained, but he was also the one in control. Gibson couldn't deny the aura surrounding the beast. It was more than monstrous. It was ethereal. There was something palpable about the creation's ascension to something more than a normal man could ever be.

Gibson went to speak when Brett's jaw popped wide, the hinges cracking like a frog. His tongue ran the rim of his lips, and then the beast spoke again.

"What you did to me is nothing…compared to what I will do to *you*."

A chill ran through Gibson's body, but he steeled himself and offered what he hoped was a defiant grin. He kept his face pressed to the bars, not willing to give an inch to the monster and his threat.

"I admire your spirit," he said, hoping the condescension wasn't lost on the monster. He let go of the bars and stepped back. He waved his hand around the room but never lost eye contact with Brett.

"It would have been a pity for all of this," he said, "that is to say everything that's happened, to have dampened your enthusiasm for the job."

Brett didn't react. He didn't blink. He didn't snarl. Nothing flared or popped or smacked. He just stared unblinkingly at Gibson. It was almost as if he'd melted into the shadows of the cell like a chameleon.

Gibson rapped on the bars with his knuckles. The bars clanged and echoed.

"We'll be moving you," said Gibson, certain now that nothing was lost on Brett. "You'll be in a secure facility, where we can more properly assist your…transition."

The reptilian eyes flitted as Gibson moved toward the door, reminding him of eyes on a Dalí-esque baroque painting on which a warped central figure followed the observer no matter where he or she moved in a room.

Gibson spun on a boot heel and took a purposeful step toward the guarded door. General Reed stood there, blocking the exit. The major had forgotten the general was still in the room.

Reed cleared his throat as Gibson approached. He glanced past the major at the cage and then narrowed his focus on his subordinate officer.

"So what's your plan?" asked the general. "You're moving him?"

"Yes, sir," said Gibson. "We've got a facility not far from here. I think it's better suited for the type of testing we want to pursue."

"This is as secure a location as you'll find, Major," said Reed. "Are you sure it's worth taking the risk?"

It wasn't a question despite the interrogative. Gibson knew it. He also knew there were too many prying eyes and ears at this facility. He wanted privacy.

"With all due respect…" Gibson started, but let his words trail off, knowing the general's feelings about that phrase.

"I hope you know what you're doing," said the general. His tone indicated he didn't believe the major had a clue. "While I'm a believer that past performance isn't an infallible indicator of future wins and losses, it's pretty damn close. And your past performance—"

"I've got a plan, General," interrupted Gibson at the same moment his eyes widened with the realization he shouldn't have cut off his superior. He almost swallowed the end of the word *general.*

Reed bristled. "Do you, then?" he asked flatly. The expressionless look on the general's face turned upward, as if he'd smelled something rotten. Without saying another word, Reed scratched his chin, nodded, and turned his back on Major Gibson.

The two guards at the door followed the general, leaving the major alone in the room with his creation. Gibson listened to Brett's raspy breaths.

"You've got this, Major Gibson," Brett mocked.

The sound of the *S* in his last name was like a snake flicking its tongue. He stood there for a moment, his back to the cage, until a bloodcurdling shriek pierced the air.

The major shuddered. His throat tightened. His muscles tensed. He said nothing and marched from the room, leaving Ma Trang alone in his chains, cackling and crying out in defiance.

— 31 —

Odenton, Maryland
May 1, 1980

The shrill alarm woke Major Rick Gibson from his brief and uneasy sleep inside his underground quarters at the edge of a secure, registered facility adjacent to Fort Meade. His immediate disorientation gave way to the measured panic of a seasoned officer. The first thing he did was go for his gun, a Beretta 1911 that rested on the nightstand. Then he glanced at the analog clock on the wall across from his bunk.

It was four thirty in the morning. He'd been out for thirteen minutes at most, but he didn't remember dozing off. He'd been thinking about the day's events and how seamlessly it had gone.

The transfer from one facility to the next had been accomplished without any notable problems. They'd sedated Lieutenant Brett with nitrous oxide pumped into his holding room before the move had begun. Brett had remained conscious, his breathing rapid and shallow, but the gas had done the trick and kept him calm.

A constant flow of N2O into the sealed rear of the military transport truck provided a backup measure of security, as had the air support and the orders to destroy every vehicle in the convoy via remote detonation if necessary.

Gibson had, of course, not been in the convoy. He'd traveled ahead to make certain the preparations near Fort Meade were to his specifications.

The facility itself was off-book and top secret. It had been the only set of permanent structures when Fort Meade opened as Camp Annapolis Junction in 1917. Two years later, when the Army officially opened the camp with larger, more modern facilities, the original buildings were modified and buried as a subterranean complex. The military renamed the secret complex ESEF, Experimental Security Enhancement Facility, and it had housed a secretive national security apparatus during World War II. ESEF had laid the groundwork for the National Security Agency's move to the region in the 1950s. The underground complex was again modified to house experimental laboratories of varying types and sizes.

It was the perfect place, Gibson believed, for what he had in store for his prized recruit. At least, he'd thought it was the perfect place until the damned alarm slapped him awake.

Groggily, he sat up and spun his feet to the floor. The terrazzo under his feet was as the same as the air in his room, the entire facility kept at a constant twenty-three degrees Celsius with a humidity between forty-eight and fifty percent.

He sniffed and rubbed his nose with the back of his index finger, freeing crumbles of dried snot from the edges of his nostrils. The taste in his mouth was thick with sleep despite the lack of it.

"Great," he mumbled to himself, feeling more

exhausted than he had fourteen minutes earlier. But the anxiety and adrenaline of the moment pushed him to his feet, and he shuffled the short distance to his desk. The alarm, seconds old, was giving him a headache, but more importantly it gave him pause. What had happened? The truth was, deep in his churning gut, he knew it involved Brett. He glanced at the clock again.

Four thirty-two.

He cursed to himself. He shouldn't have left the lab. He couldn't trust the guards. They didn't fully grasp what was at stake. They didn't know what he'd sacrificed to make this moment possible, to make VX-99 the program it was intended to be.

He was on the verge of changing the course of human history, or just history as it were. And he should have known better than to leave the lab. Even for a moment.

Brett was more than intelligent. He was evolved. He was one, three, ten steps ahead of anything some guard could anticipate. Tightening the grip on the 1911, he moved toward the door to his room. Time to stop thinking and take action.

His hand was on the door lever when the black rotary phone on his desk rang. The orange light near the handset flashed with the warbling ring that was nearly inaudible under the buzzing alarm.

Gibson set the gun on the table and plucked the handset from the phone. He was ready to ask about the alarm when the sounds on the other end of the line gave him his answer. There was the rapid-fire percussion of a semiautomatic rifle.

"Sir?" came the tremulous voice in the receiver. "Major Gibson, are you there?"

"What's happened?" asked Gibson. He already knew

the answer. And this was, after all, May Day. It couldn't pass without a call for help.

"He's—it's—the—it's loose," he said. "That *thing* is loose. It's already killed four men. We've got it—"

"I'm on my way," he said and slapped the handset back into the cradle and grabbed his gun.

Gibson slid back into his fatigues, and as he hiked on his boots, he could hear Lieutenant Brett's voice in his head. It was louder than the alarm.

You've got this, Major Gibson.

Gibson laced his boots and eyed the phone again. Should he alert General Reed?

No. The decision was instantaneous. There was absolutely no cause to tell the general or anyone else outside the facility what was happening until he had it back under control.

He grabbed his magnetic card key from the desk and set off through the complex catacomb of hallways and laboratories that made up the clandestine facility, his handgun raised.

Red swirling lights gave the hallways a hellish glow as he jogged down them. The buzzing alarm grated at his eardrums on his route to the control center, better known as the MCC. It separated the two primary areas of ESEF—the labs on one side of the facility, barracks and offices on the other. One couldn't get to the other side without moving past the MCC.

It was the perfect place from which to have eyes on the unfolding situation. From the security of that room, he could task those under his command to stop the threat. He swallowed, thinking about the threat, and considered for a brief second that he should pray. He reconsidered, remembering that he'd long ago forsaken such things when he decided he should play the creator and destroyer of man.

Gibson pushed through another doorway, which hummed and clicked as he waved his magnetic pass across its locking mechanism, and wound his way closer to the MCC. Each time he went through a door, he brought his gun up and scanned the hallway. He leveled the weapon, sweeping it as a first line of defense. It found no targets.

Where were the sentries? None of them were at their posts. Every door, protected by coded card keys, should have had two guards. Not now. Not as the alarm droned deafeningly through the facility.

He stopped and spun around, taking note of the desolation along the path he'd already traveled and the distance ahead. He was nearly there. He sucked in a breath of the cold, dry air and marched toward his destination. He waved his card across the magnetic lock at the MCC entry. It buzzed and turned green. He then punched in a six-digit passcode and shouldered the heavy metal door inward, weapon up. He was barely into the dark space, awash with the bluish gray glow of television monitors, when the door nudged past him and slammed shut.

The mind-numbing buzz of the alarm was muted beyond the thick metal door that protected the MCC from the rest of the complex. Now it was part of the chorus he'd heard over the phone: the sounds of battle.

Gibson's eyes adjusted to the dark room and focused first on the bank of monitors that lined a wall across from him. There were seven monitors, their screens split into quads. Four images graced each of the boxy displays. It was state-of-the-art equipment, technology not available to the rest of the world yet, but it was far from perfect.

The grainy images of the darkened spaces were only somewhat visible because of the flashing red lights and the automatic gain in the wall- and ceiling-mounted cameras. They compensated for the low light by adding pixels of white into the moving images. The cameras were not outfitted with infrared. Auto gain, then, was better than nothing. Though in this case, as Gibson saw the horror unfolding on some of those displays, nothing would have been better.

Of the twenty-eight camera monitors available to the MCC, eight were black. They weren't functioning, or there was no light at all to feed the cameras. He knew four of them were cameras dedicated to the lab where they'd secured Lieutenant Brett. Two of them were inside the lab and two more were in the hallway immediately outside the lab's lone, secure entrance.

In some way, Gibson was relieved to see nothing on those square imageless screens. It would have been irrefutable proof of his own incompetence. As if the rest of the displays weren't proof enough of that.

Ten displays revealed empty hallways. An armed guard limped from the bottom of one screen and through the top. The injured man repeatedly glanced over his shoulder, his lame left foot leaving a dark smear along the middle of the corridor.

Flashes of the red line drawn on the map of Vietnam snapped in his head. It was a deep, dark, indelible red line that traced the power and violence of the thing he'd created. Gibson blinked at the image after the man was gone. He waited for something to follow, to give chase, but nothing did. His eyes moved along the wall, stomach lurching at the gore.

Eight cameras on two screens revealed the carnage left behind by Lieutenant Brett.

There was blood. Pooled and splattered.

There was flesh. Shredded and splayed.

There was bone. Sharp and broken.

Gibson's eyes flitted from one working display to the next, searching for his creation that had left behind another red line. The last two didn't reveal anything new.

As he moved down the monitors, he still couldn't see Brett, but he could hear his handiwork. The screams, the futile cries for mercy, the exclamations of fear and resignation all crackled across the communications system and clung to the walls of the MCC with a resonance that wormed its way into Gibson's ears and into his core.

"Major," said one of two men in the room, sitting at a bank of phones and computer terminals on the broad desk beneath the displays. "Major, I didn't see you there."

Gibson's heart thumped as he instinctively leveled his 1911 at the men. He'd not seen them either, having been fixated by the grainy, blood-soaked images on the monitors above them. His wide eyes darted between them, and he lowered the weapon.

He exhaled, happy to see live soldiers. "Turn off the alarm," he said. "It's not doing anyone any good. We all know what's happening."

The guard nodded, returned to his keyboard, and punched out several commands. The flashing lights went solid. The two-tone blare silenced.

Gibson swallowed, suppressing the burn of bile in his throat, and acknowledged the young man, whose name was Lawson. He was more of a boy, Gibson thought. What was he? Nineteen? Twenty? The average age of the men who'd died in Vietnam was nineteen. How old had

Lieutenant Brett been when he'd shipped off, when he'd been ordered to take the dose of VX-99?

Gibson didn't have time to talk. They needed action. They needed to soothe the beast.

"Where is he?" he asked.

Lawson opened his mouth to speak but closed it again and glanced over his shoulder at the other guard. The young man, pimple-faced and wide-eyed, shrugged and shook his head. He mouthed the words "I don't know" and glanced past his comrade to Major Gibson.

Gibson grunted his disapproval, stepped forward, and shouldered his way past Lawson. He motioned for the pimple-faced recruit to move aside, which the man did. He found a lever at the base of a gooseneck microphone and, yanking the mic closer to his mouth, he pressed the lever down. Stenciled above it were the words ALL CALL. When he held the lever, the incoming communication ceased. It was muted. The silence inside the MCC was deafening. He could hear the hiss of clean air filtering through the vents in the ceiling and floor. "Lieutenant Brett," he said, "I know you hear me. This is Major Rick Gibson. I am ordering you to stand down."

Gibson let go of the lever and leaned back in the chair to eye the monitors. Four more were recently dark, and none of the others showed any movement. The cries that echoed through the halls and bored into his bones had stopped.

Was that a good thing? Likely not.

Gibson pressed the lever again. "I know what you are, *who* you are, Trevor," he said. "I know you served your country and your country did not serve you. Semper fidelis was a one-way street for you, Trevor."

Gibson's eyes darted from one working monitor to the

next. He kept his finger pressed down on the lever. He licked his lips, hoping for a connection.

"I know about Stacey Arbuckle," he said, hesitating after saying the woman's name aloud. "I know she hurt you, Trevor. I know she was the love of your life and you sacrificed it for your love of country."

Gibson's eyes found his own long, extended finger straining against the lever. He craned his neck to one side, releasing the tension to the sound of a crack in the vertebrae. Then he searched the monitors again. Nothing.

"I know where…" He considered his next words for an agonizing three seconds before he continued. "I know where Stacey is right now. I know where she lives. She's in Richmond. It's not too far from here. We could make arrangements."

He didn't specify the sort of arrangements he was offering. The truth was he had no idea where he could find Stacey Arbuckle. He didn't know for sure the woman was even alive. And if he did, it wasn't as if he'd ever arrange for anything involving her.

He let go of the lever and exhaled, just now realizing he was holding his breath.

Lawson, the young guard, whispered behind Gibson's shoulder. "Who is Stacey Arbuckle?" he asked. "Do I need to—"

Gibson held up a hand to silence the young guard. He didn't answer the question. His attention was on the monitors and the sounds coming from the spaces outside the MCC.

Nothing at first. No movement. No sounds other than the silence between pops of static. Gibson searched the desk in front of him and found a volume control. He spun it to the right, elevating the audio inside the protected space. The speakers built into the walls hissed. And then Gibson saw movement in the corner of his eye. He glanced up to see the beast, his beast, standing front and center before a ceiling-mounted camera.

"Where is he?" Gibson asked. "What part of the building is that?"

Brett's puckered, dark red lips made popping sounds. His face was spattered with blood, as if he'd dipped his face into a fruit pie and moved it back and forth to slurp up the filling. The gore stained his uniform and exposed flesh.

Gibson moved his finger back to the mic lever and held it there, hovering above it and waiting for Lawson to confirm. The young man leaned in for a better view.

"Where?" snapped Gibson.

"Corridor four," said Lawson. "It's corridor four."

"That means nothing to me," said Gibson. "Where in relation to—"

"Major Rick Gibson," the voice hissed through the speakers, filling the MCC, "you know…nothing."

Gibson turned down the volume and touched the standing hair on his neck. The adrenaline that coursed through his body was a strange mixture of excitement and fear. His finger, the one hovering above the mic lever, was trembling uncontrollably.

The monster looked to the left and then to the right. He eyed the camera lens again, glaring straight through Gibson. He spread his sucker lips as wide as they would open, revealing inhuman teeth stained with bright red at the pale gums. His thick tongue waggled in and out of the hole, scraping along the jagged edges of his teeth. His knees cracked beneath the fleshy muscles that framed his thighs.

Gibson lowered his finger, pressing the mic lever. "I know you have a soul, Trevor. I know you're still inside there. And I know you don't *want* to do this. I can make it so you don't *have* to do it."

Of course, Gibson was as likely to find and reconnect Stacey Arbuckle with Trevor Brett as he was to figure out how to stop the electrical impulses that he knew VX-99 pulsed through Brett's morphed body, but he was out of options. He was grasping. He was playing politics, as he'd done for a dozen years.

"I want to help you, Trevor," he said. "That's why you're here. We want to help you, not hurt you. We will make you whole again."

As Gibson spoke, Lawson displayed a map of the complex on the desk. He pointed to the spot where he believed Brett was holding court. Lawson traced a finger toward the MCC. It was close. Gibson released the lever.

"How soon before the reinforcements are here?"

"I called for them immediately," said Lawson. "Any second now."

Brett popped his lips again and then flexed his talons at his sides. "You can't make me whole," he said through the fog in his voice. "But I can tear you apart, Major Rick Gibson." He licked his lips again. "I can't wait to find out how you taste."

Before Gibson could respond, before his heart could beat or his eyes could blink, the Ma Trang exploded from the floor toward the camera. The display filled with static and then went black. White noise filled the MCC.

— 32 —

Odenton, Maryland
May 1, 1980

The alarm ceased and the lights flickered off, shrouding the hallway in darkness. Brett took a moment to wipe warm blood from his eyes and blinked into the shadows. They could kill the lights, but that didn't affect his sight. His vision had adapted for conditions just like this. Hunting in the jungles of Vietnam and avoiding enemy patrols had made him an apex predator. Transformed him into something most soldiers only dreamed of becoming.

The soldiers pursuing him through the corridors had no idea what they were hunting, and had made a very fatal choice to pursue him, thinking they were the hunters.

Fools.

Brett had already shown a dozen of the men what the face of the devil looked like, and now dozens more had shown up to learn firsthand. It was the last face they would see on this Earth.

Kill them all and take new trophies! The crackly female voice tempted Brett to continue his killing spree, but he had grown stronger over the years and ignored her when he knew it wasn't in their best interest.

Memories of battles that should have left him dead played in his mind, sending spurts of adrenaline coursing through his modified blood. The time when he was being pursued by ten hardened Vietcong soldiers through the jungle. Men that had hunted in the deadly terrain for their entire lives.

She had screamed at Brett then, urging him to skin the men alive and hang their bodies from trees. But Brett had hidden in a cave and waited for them to pass. His patience had countered her hunger. That night, he'd entered their camp and killed them one by one after taking out the guards.

He had feasted well. When the sun came up, his full belly slowed him on his way back to his underground lair. She'd reluctantly congratulated him on his victory but urged him to do more.

You are invincible. You are perfection. You can have whatever you want. Take it with the gift given to you!

Over their time together, her voice had become almost soothing. The familiar rocky tone was, in a way, the closest thing he had to a friend. She was always there, the only person he hadn't killed, always encouraging him to keep fighting.

Turn around and kill them! she shouted now. Her voice dripped with vitriolic impatience.

Brett ignored her again. There was only one person he cared about dispatching right now. The others were obstacles to that end and nothing more.

He ran harder through the passage, away from the shouts following him. A muzzle flash followed by the chatter of automatic gunfire came from the next intersection, and he dove under the spray. The rounds peppered the wall and ceiling, taking out a bank of lights. The shower of glass rained down on his body as he scrambled away and bolted in the opposite direction.

Another guard charged around the next corner and went to bring up his rifle, when Brett launched his body into the air. He wrapped his legs around the man's chest. Before his prey could scream, Brett sank his sharp teeth into his neck, pulling away a strand of gristle.

The satisfying gurgle that followed filled Brett with joy. They landed on the ground in a heap, and he wasted no time going to work on tearing the man's face off with his talons. Brett had done this a hundred times before, and like any person with a skill, his was sharp tuned.

But this time he didn't have a chance to finish the job.

More gunfire cracked behind him. Brett quickly reached down and grabbed the soldier, rotating his body to use as a human shield. The rounds peppered the dead man's back, jerking his body in the grotesque, weightless dance of a tangled puppet.

Brett dropped the warm corpse, bolted away, and made a run down the next corridor. At the intersection, he slid on a trail of blood that had pooled out of the two dead guards he had previously gutted. He tried to steady himself by reaching out with both arms, but his naked feet skidded and he crashed to his back.

Gunfire lanced through the air where he had stood a moment earlier. In the glow from the muzzle flashes, he identified three more shooters, all wearing full body armor and night-vision goggles.

He pushed himself back up and made a run for cover, but when he reached the next pile of crumpled bodies, he saw there was nowhere else to run. He had mapped out the corridors in his mind, and if the map was correct, then the reinforcements were closing in from all directions.

There was only one way past the guards.

Looking up, he saw a broken camera lens. He jumped up and grabbed the metal limb of the video camera, using it to hang from the ceiling with his back to the wall. Pushing up with his head, he tried to move the vent cover, but it was secured with several bolts.

Kill them! the old female voice shouted. *The only way out is to kill them!*

Brett knew better. Killing these men would result in his death. And while he hadn't feared the reaper in more than a decade, he didn't want to die without completing his new mission—destroying the man who had turned him into the monster he'd become.

Gritting his teeth, he slammed the metal vent cover with his skull over and over until the cover popped up. He slid it into the passage and climbed through the opening. Then he carefully sealed the vent and looked through the grate at the floor below. Voices sounded in the passage, and several helmets moved underneath the grated vent. He waited until they had passed before moving on all fours in the opposite direction.

The narrow passage made movement difficult, but he wasn't like most men. He could squirm and squeeze his popping joints through places much smaller than these.

Another memory surfaced of the tunnels in which he had hidden during the war that seemed like a lifetime ago. The dirt caves crawled with all sorts of tasty creatures, from nutritious bugs and snakes to plump rats. He had lived in one of the abandoned tunnels for several months. It was the same tunnel in which he had killed a dozen soldiers during the war.

He felt safe underground.

Brett continued crawling through the dark passage, blood dripping from his prison uniform and his arm. He stopped to feel the injury where a bullet had grazed his flesh.

Bringing up his wrist, he sucked on the metallic-tasting fluid. The flesh wound was deep, but it would heal in days. The chemicals had made him a supersoldier, but he knew even superheroes could die. It didn't matter how impressive their power, every hero had a mortal flaw.

Moving like his favorite childhood hero, Spiderman, he continued through the vent. Something about the memory of his childhood comic-book hero made him faster and filled him with strength.

He had no idea where he was going, but instinct told him to keep moving away from the voices. Several shouted in the corridor below and he froze.

"Where the fuck did he go?" someone yelled.

"He couldn't have gone far. Check every room, every space, dammit!" yelled another man.

"Get Major Gibson and everyone else topside," replied a third voice.

"Working on it, Sarge," said a fourth.

Brett's eyes widened, and his blood warmed. He knew where he was going now. As soon as the voices drifted away, he continued crawling through the passage until he was out of breath and his muscles burned.

Even *his* body had a breaking point.

He squirmed, moving on his elbows to keep the momentum. At the next intersection, he checked through the vent opening. Instead of a hallway below, he saw a room. Some sort of office.

Listening, he checked for voices, and hearing none, he broke the vent cover and grabbed it before it could fall to the floor. He quietly dropped down, his blood-soaked feet hardly making a noise on impact.

He was in a different area of the facility now. He looked out into a hallway and saw signage. Brett stepped out to read the map, stopping on an arrow pointing to an exit. Somewhere in the distance a door opened.

Ambush them, said the female voice. *Take their eyes!*

Hushed voices followed the metallic thunk of the closing door, and the click of boots on the tile floor. He counted six of them. Too many to fight in such a confined space given the waves of exhaustion that threatened to end his primal quest.

Instead of confronting them, Brett made a run for the exit and strained to see through the darkness. The door was just at the end of the hallway. This one had no keypad. He had dropped into a non-secure area of the facility. Superheroes also needed luck, and Brett had just hit the lottery.

It opened when he was five feet away, and a woman in a lab coat walked into the hallway, a flashlight in hand. She directed it at him, the beam hitting him in the face.

Brett shielded his eyes from the bright light and darted away, watching her as he melted into the shadows.

She remained standing there, mouth agape, trembling, searching for him with the beam. For a second, he glared at her from a crouched position, a memory of a woman from his past surfacing in his mind. There was something about her youthful features and short brown hair. And her brown eyes that were wide with unmitigated fear.

"Please stop," she said, lips quivering. "Major Gibson sent me to bring you in peacefully."

He thought I would go with a woman who looks like Stacey…Brett realized. That explained why she was all by herself. He had a feeling there were more women sent out in other parts of the facility.

The soldiers behind him entered the hallway and, shouting, called out, "Stop him!"

"Get out of the way!"

Gunfire cracked, and Brett ducked down and scrambled over the floor on all fours. Rounds peppered the woman, blood blossoming away from the entry wounds and punching through her fragile flesh.

She crumpled on the ground, gasping for air as her life source drained from her. He again stared at her, trying to understand why he was feeling this…

The word escaped him.

He hadn't felt like this for as long as he could remember.

It was empathy, he realized as he moved through the open doorway and slammed it behind him. A pointless emotion that he had long since forgotten. So why remember it now?

The woman wasn't Stacey. Stacey was gone forever.

Brett crushed his emotions like a bug and loped up the stairwell, away from the men hunting him, so he could continue his own hunt for the true villain—Gibson.

He listened as he moved onto the first landing and looked around the corner. The area was lit by overhead lights, and he could see it was clear. So were the next stairs and the next landing. He made it to the sixth sub-ground floor before he heard voices again.

"Go, go, go!" someone shouted.

A male. Definitely a soldier. Probably guiding civilians out of the facility or more sheep to the culling. Below, voices sounded where the soldiers who had gunned down the scientist were running up the stairs.

Again, enemies were closing in from all directions.

Brett grabbed the door handle at the next landing and twisted it slowly with his sharp talons. They should have cut them, he thought. The hardened nails were almost as good as knives.

He entered a room of desks and wall-mounted chalkboards. Bolting across the space, he made his way to the next door. That one opened into another room. Several soldiers in uniforms were crouched on the floor, hunkered down. One of them, a bald man with glasses, screamed.

Brett almost laughed at the coward. He jumped onto a desk and then leapt into the air, bringing the guy down as he went to run for the door. He traced a line across the man's throat with a talon, opening up a gushing gash.

Hot blood squirted Brett in the face.

He was moving again before the dying officer hit the ground. Two others rushed to his aid, and Brett left them to deal with the distraction.

Stop! came the voice in his mind. *Don't let any of them take another breath!*

Brett kept moving; he had to be getting close to the surface now. That was where Gibson was going, and time was running out to cut him off.

At the next hallway he darted for the next door that was marked *Floor 1*. It swung out and into a hallway that opened to two glass doors. Sheets of rain hit the pavement outside. Beyond that, a wet lawn and barbed-wire fences blocked his escape.

Brett had scaled fences taller than these before, but that was under the cover of darkness. He stopped to think, realizing he couldn't go out the front entrance. There were several guards posted outside in the rain, facing away from him. He went back into the building and found another room, abandoned and dark. Moving to the windows, he forced one open and stepped out into a flower bed.

Keeping low, he moved against the whipping wind. Rain pattered his body, rinsing away the fresh blood. He scanned his surroundings, trying to get his bearings.

A *chop*, *chop* sound caught his ear. Faint, but recognizable. He scanned the skyline to his right, where a black dot was crossing below the storm clouds. That son of a bitch was trying to escape!

Brett took off across the lawn, trying to keep low, but having a difficult time restraining himself. Shouting came over the howl of the wind, and a gunshot cracked.

The round hit the dirt by his feet.

A sniper.

If he could just get around the next…

Brett dove into the dirt as another crack sounded. This time the round whizzed by his body, so close he could see the streak pass on his left. He pushed himself up and bolted around the corner before the sniper could get off another shot.

Around the bend he saw the helo pad, and a group of four soldiers surrounding two officers in uniform. His senses all seemed to snap alert in that moment: his hearing, sight, smell, taste… everything was even more potent and intense.

He could hear the voices of the two officers and smell the adrenaline coursing through their veins, like a wild animal.

They were afraid.

And they had good reason.

Lieutenant Trevor Brett, the super soldier, the *White Ghost*, was coming for them.

He went down on all fours and skittered over the grass like the beast into which they had molded him. By the time anyone saw him, he had closed the gap by half. Gunshots cracked, and rounds zipped into the grass. He kept low and zigzagged, as he had done in Vietnam when four soldiers on a hill had him in their sights.

The Black Hawk helicopter lowered over the pad, its blades thumping and the rotor gusts slamming into the soldiers firing at Brett. The two officers ducked down, and one of them made his way to the open door of the chopper, but the other man stopped.

"Don't kill him!" the man yelled.

Through the rain Brett saw him. It was his creator.

Gibson grabbed one of the soldiers and forced his barrel toward the ground. The other three men kept their guns aimed at Brett as he continued his approach.

"Sir, he isn't stopping!" yelled one of the soldiers.

Gibson pulled out a handgun and aimed it at Brett, closing one eye.

Brett stood on all fours and ran as fast as he could, muscles straining, veins bulging, heart thumping like an automatic weapon. He was ten feet away when the crack came. Something hit him from behind and exploded out his upper chest, snapping his collarbone. Blood, bone, and grit blew out the exit wound. He flailed with his left arm, but his right went limp as he crashed to the ground in a heap.

"Hold your fire!" Gibson screamed.

Brett lay in the dirt, looking up at the officer as he approached with his handgun angled down. The other four soldiers fanned out, their barrels pointed at his head.

Brett tried to get up, but his right arm wouldn't work, and his body was numb from the high-caliber round that had blown through his back and out his chest.

Get up! Kill them! Rip their lungs out like wings! screeched the voice in his mind. She sounded mad, panicked almost. He had never heard her like this.

This was the worst injury Brett had ever suffered.

But he wasn't about to give up.

Brett pushed at the ground with his left hand. It wobbled, and gnashing his teeth, he let out a scream of agony as his strength gave out and he crumpled back to the ground. Blood pooled in the thin grass, and his wispy wet hair hung like a curtain in front of his eyes, but he could still see his creator.

Gibson crouched down, his uniform soaked from the rain. He used a sleeve to wipe his face clean and then stared at Brett for several seconds.

"Nothing..." Brett muttered. "This is nothing compared to what I will do to you."

Gibson laughed and then shook his head. "You don't give up, do you? That's good, son. That's why you're so important."

More soldiers ran across the grass. Brett couldn't see them, but could hear their boots sloshing in the mud over the chop of the rotor blades.

"Don't worry, we'll get you all fixed up," Gibson said. "You're too valuable an asset to let bleed out in the dirt. I still have grand plans for you."

He looked up at the soldiers and jerked his chin. The men surrounded Brett, their weapons still angled down, all of them appearing terrified of the beast laying in the pooling blood.

"Get him up!" Gibson shouted.

The other soldiers joined the group, at least ten now.

Get up! the woman screeched in his mind. *You have to kill them!*

Brett let out a shriek of his own as two men grabbed him under the armpits and yanked him to his feet. The pain was worse than anything he could remember enduring, despite all of the torture over the years. His head slumped against his chest, the jagged end of his collarbone slicing his veiny cheek.

He didn't bother moving his face, his view of the man he was going to kill was perfect at this angle. Gibson walked away from the chopper and pointed toward the buildings.

Brett blinked as his vision darkened. He wasn't sure if he would survive this wound, but if he did, he was certain he would have his revenge either in this living nightmare, or in the hell that awaited them.

About the Authors

Nicholas Sansbury Smith is the *USA Today* bestselling author of the Hell Divers series, the Orbs series, the Trackers series, and the Extinction Cycle series. He worked for Iowa Homeland Security and Emergency Management in disaster mitigation before switching careers to focus on his one true passion—writing. When he isn't writing or daydreaming about the apocalypse, he enjoys running, biking, spending time with his family, and traveling the world. He is an Ironman triathlete and lives in Iowa with his wife, their dogs, and a house full of books.

Learn more at NicholasSansburySmith.com

Tom Abrahams is a member of International Thriller Writers and a veteran television journalist. He is the author of more than twenty novels, including the Traveler Series, A Dark World: The Complete SpaceMan Chronicles, the Alt Apocalypse, and the Jackson Quick Action Adventure Trilogy. He lives in the Houston Suburbs with his wife, his children, his dogs, and a mind that never shuts down.

Learn more at TomAbrahamsBooks.com

Continue the adventure with

EXTINCTION HORIZON

book 1 of the Extinction Cycle saga

Available wherever books are sold.

Made in the USA
Monee, IL
06 September 2020

41471814R00164